NO TIME FOR LOVE

Hugo Meenan

BRANDON

NO TIME FOR LOVE

They call it the law; we call it apartheid, internment, conscription, partition and
 silence.
It's the law that they make to keep you and me where they think we belong.
They hide behind steel and bullet-proof glass, machine guns and spies,
And they tell us who suffer the tear gas and the torture that we're in the wrong.

No time for love if they come in the morning,
No time to show tears or for fears in the morning,
No time for goodbye, no time to ask why,
And the sound of the siren's the cry of the morning.

(from 'No Time For Love' by Jack Warshaw)

First published in 1987
Brandon Book Publishers Ltd
Dingle, Co Derry, Ireland
and 27 South Main Street, Wolfboro,
New Hampshire, 03894-2069, USA

© Hugo Meenan 1987

British Library Cataloguing in Publication Data
Meenan, Hugo
  No time for love.
  I. Title
  823' .914 [F]   PR6063.E3/

  ISBN 0-86322-092-4

This book is published with the assistance of
The Arts Council/An Chomhairle Ealaíon, Ireland

Cover design: Paula Nolan
Cover photograph: Pacemaker
Typesetting: Koinonia Ltd, Manchester
Printed by Richard Clay Ltd, Bungay, Suffolk

One

THERE WAS NOTHING out of the ordinary about the van. It belonged to a local butcher and there was every reason for it to park in the Derry Diamond at two-thirty on a Friday afternoon.

The driver was appropriately dressed in a butcher's white hat and coat. His companion in the back wore the same, and alongside his right leg lay a .308 hunting rifle. Cool and hard against his thigh it made him feel secure, even more so than the .357 Magnum pistols both he and his partner had concealed beneath their coats.

Two policemen strolled leisurely up Carlisle Road, hands hooked casually behind their backs. They were at peace with the world and its pedestrians as they passed through the ancient walls of the city and entered Ferryquay Street, one hundred yards from the Diamond.

The van had been hijacked an hour earlier in the Creggan. The driver had been sitting at his dinner when two gunmen had walked into his kitchen and asked for the keys of his van. He had not thought about arguing, hardly even pausing in the rhythm of his eating as he handed the keys over and finished his dinner.

The man behind the wheel broke the silence. 'Here they come: two of them, just outside John Collier's.' Like a waking cat, his companion shrugged himself out of his slouched position and braced his back against the rear of the driver's seat. He was already facing the two small windows at the rear of

7

the van.

'Drive round the corner and park with the engine running.'

The van snaked slowly out of the Diamond and parked with its rear facing into the mouth of Ferryquay Street on the opposite side of the open square. All that was visible from where the policemen approached was the silhouette of a man on the driver's side of a butcher's van. What way he was facing and whether he had anything in his hands was impossible to tell.

Constable Sammy Henderson, the younger of the two, was thinking of the five-twenty train to Belfast and a long weekend with his girlfriend.

Constable Willie Gray was thinking of his wife in the Waterside and wondering whether she had told their three children that they were going to the seaside the next day.

The man in the back of the van pulled the sacking from the .308 and flicked off the safety catch. He squinted at the two policemen, to their left and right and behind them. The rifle flowed naturally to his shoulder as he spoke to the driver.

'Don't move until I tell you.'

The authority of the voice made an answer unnecessary, even undesirable. He decided to hit the older man first in the hope that inexperience would delay the younger one's reactions. He aimed for Willie Gray's chest just below the throat, squeezed the trigger, held his breath fractionally, and fired.

The rifle roared a deafening explosion in the confines of the van. The armour-piercing round smashed the rear window into the roadside in a thousand, splintering fragments. Pedestrians stopped, crouched, screamed and ran in all directions.

Willie Gray's feet kicked into the air as he landed heavily on his back. The front of his flak jacket was dragged grotesquely into his chest by the velocity of the bullet. A pool of blood spread rapidly from beneath his body.

Constable Henderson made the mistake predicted of him: he turned and stared in confused horror at the body of his fallen comrade. The next shot hit him in the left ear, ricocheting off his skull to exit at his right jaw-bone. He was dead before he hit the ground.

'Let's go home,' said the sniper. The voice was calm and determined, like that of a serious workman who had just completed a satisfactory task.

Ten minutes later the legal driver was given the keys to his van and told to report to the police that he had been hijacked by two masked men.

Superintendent Len Haslitt pulled a cigarette from the open packet on his desk and lit it. He stared at an open file in front of him, but his mind was not on his work. It was one of those days when a power greater than himself forced his mind to drift aimlessly. He soaked up the sunshine, listened to imaginary waves breaking on a distant shore and contemplated the pleasures of unknown horizons. His thoughts were interrupted as Chief Inspector Wall burst into the office.

'We just lost two men in Ferryquay Street.' He made it sound like twenty-five per cent of the force.

'Oh Christ,' moaned Haslitt, his mind thumping onto dry land. 'What happened?'

'Apparently a sniper opened up from somewhere in Butcher Street. I sent Inspector Miller out to investigate. We're just waiting for someone to claim it.'

'Who was shot?'

'Willie Gray and a young chap from Belfast by the name of Sammy Henderson. He only joined us a month ago.'

'God, poor Willie,' said Haslitt.

Three hours later Inspector Tony Miller had made his report and was concluding his questioning of the van driver when he was informed by a young detective that he was wanted upstairs. He hurried up two flights to his superior's office to be greeted by sombre faces. Haslitt posed the inevitable question.

'Did you get anything from him?'

'Nothing,' returned Miller. 'Two masked men, average size, average build, average clothes. He's either well briefed or he kept his eyes closed the whole time.'

'In other words, he's too scared to talk,' interrupted Chief Inspector Wall.

'That's about the size of it: he lives in Creggan and he doesn't want a hole in the head.'

The Chief Inspector looked at the Superintendent who nodded his head, saying, 'Okay, let him go.'

Miller did not protest as Wall dialled an extension and said, 'Take a statement from the butcher and release him after he sees a doctor.' He replaced the phone as the Superintendent spoke to Miller.

'The Samaritans just got a statement, Tony: Saor Eire have claimed it.'

'Hugh O'Donnell,' said Miller confidently.

Chief Inspector Wall intervened: 'I just left his file with you this afternoon, sir. We wanted to pull him in for seven days as we felt that. . .'

'I know,' interrupted the Superintendent, 'I was just reading it when you brought me the news.' He turned to Miller. 'How significant is Saor Eire, Tony?'

'They're damned significant now that they've killed two policemen. Their main strength lies in this maniac O'Donnell: he seems to be a one-man organisation.'

The Superintendent turned to Wall with a questioning look. 'That's true, sir,' he responded, 'O'Donnell seems to be a phenomenal organiser. Saor Eire didn't exist in this town a year ago, now it's on a par with the Provos and Officials. He spent six years in the paras, of course; I'm still waiting for a copy of his army record.'

'Where does he stand, Mervin, is he a communist or a nationalist or just a simple yobbo? What's he after?'

'I don't think there's any doubt about his communist instincts, sir. He professes to be a Trotskyist, and he seems determined to turn Saor Eire into a nation-wide organisation. We suspect he's on their GHQ Staff as he makes a lot of trips to Belfast and Dublin.'

It crossed the Superintendent's mind that all this was probably in the report which he had not read. 'He's certainly a

10

very dangerous kettle of fish,' he said quickly. 'I gathered that from the report. Why didn't you pull him in before now?'

'We didn't know enough about him until last month. Two months ago we didn't even know his name.'

'Do we have any informers in their organisation?'

'That's how we got onto him. Sergeant Taylor has persuaded one of them to co-operate.'

Bill Taylor had not spoken yet. He was a short, powerfully built man. He knew his place; fifteen years in the force had taught him when to speak and when to hold his tongue. What knowledge he had was limited, but extremely valuable. He spoke with a slow, deliberate, County Derry drawl: 'I have quite a bit of gen on the outfit, sir. I know some of their safe houses and there's a strong possibility of one of their dumps. The man giving information is on the Command Staff.'

'How dependable is he?' queried the Superintendent.

'He's been reliable up to now, but even if he wasn't I can usually check his information through some other source.'

'I see,' said the Superintendent, glancing at his watch.

The meeting was important but he could not keep his mind on it. At one time he had enjoyed being wrapped up in the thrilling escapism of a case: a grown-up child's game of sorting out the pieces and putting them together. He had always looked on it as a game, and if he won he received the unrestrained praise of his superiors. But his enthusiasm had waned since he had reached the ranks of Chief Inspector and Superintendent. These promotions had widened his social life, and in throwing himself fully and conscientiously into this new life he had acquired what was called 'a drink problem'. Now as Sergeant Taylor was talking, he felt an urgent thirst. Behind the dryness the memory of Willie Gray surfaced for a fraction of a second but, 'What the hell,' he thought, 'the man's gone now and I can't ignore my own problems.' He made a snap decision.

'Right Mervin, I'm putting you in charge of this case. Take any steps you feel necessary tonight and report to me first thing in the morning. Okay, any questions?'

'I take it Inspector Miller and Sergeant Taylor will be working solely on this as well, sir?'

'Mervin, the whole damn RUC in Londonderry will be working on nothing else but this for the next fortnight at least. Now get yourselves out of here and get that madman before tomorrow morning.'

The three detectives left the room. When their Superintendent took that attitude there was nothing to do but retreat.

Chief Inspector Wall, the leader of the departing group, was a university graduate who had chosen the Northern Ireland police force as a career. He was always conscious of impressing his superiors, making sure they noticed. And he was good at it. After only ten years in the force he had risen to his present rank faster than anyone else, and he had no intention of stopping there. He knew that with the right sort of application he could push himself to the rank of Superintendent before his fortieth birthday. The knowledge drove him like a man with a mission. Every enquiry he pursued was handled with painstaking precision. He set to work on his present task immediately. By eight-thirty that night he had organised a plan of action.

His first task was to phone Ebrington Barracks which housed the British Army's headquarters for all counter-intelligence operations; he asked for extension 124. A cultured English accent answered. Wall was brief.

'This is Crowsnest, can I see you?'

The answer was just as brief: 'On my way, old chap.'

The code word was a signal to his opposite number in Ebrington, Major Barry Down, to signify that an important operation was imminent and that he was required to put his men on standby.

While waiting for Major Down, Wall discussed the plan with his two colleagues, Miller and Taylor. He authorised them to second twenty-four constables from other duties for the operation. The Major arrived twenty minutes later. Wall took him to his tiny but modern office and came straight to the point.

'It's in connection with the double killing today, Major.'

'I thought it might be.' The accent was clipped but not strained. 'Do you know who the bastards are?'

'Yes,' said Wall confidently without offering further explanation. 'How many men can you give us for tonight?'

'Well,' said the Major, settling back in his chair, 'we have ten Special Air Service troopers on standby. After that "A" Company of the Third Battalion Greenjackets are on one-hour standby. That's about one hundred men. Then. . .'

'That should be enough,' interrupted Wall. 'We will probably want to hit about thirty houses as well as covering all the exit routes out of Creggan. The only one we will be leaving open is the New Road. We can watch that from the observation post on the walls so that if anything happens to interest us we can act on it immediately.'

The ancient walls surrounding the city looked across the entire area of the Bogside to the hill of Creggan. It was an ideal vantage point for observing the activities of the area. Built on top of the formidable ramparts was another fifteen-foot wall surrounding the grounds of the Masonic Hall – the headquarters of the Freemasons in the city. On top of this wall stood the army's most important observation post in the city. It was equipped with sophisticated radio equipment, including a Barkgunst telemike mk IV which could pick up any conversation the operator observed in the area. It also had a Japanese camera which could photograph an object no larger than an orange in perfect detail on the last street in Creggan, almost two miles away.

Chief Inspector Wall and Major Barry Down crouched in the cramped confines of this well-equipped and camouflaged post. They had three radio channels to monitor: one to Ebrington Barracks in case they needed reinforcements, a second to the Strand Road RUC Barracks to keep them informed on all activities and a third to all units involved in the operation. The Major spoke into this third channel. It was exactly seven minutes past eleven.

'Hello, all stations, this is Earlybird. Over.'

The answers crackled back over the B13 high-frequency radio set. 'Earlybird, Out.'

The operation to apprehend Hugh O'Donnell had begun. It involved eight Saracen armoured cars, sixteen army and four RUC landrovers. In addition ten Special Air Service troopers in civilian clothes and carrying a variety of weapons from sawn-off automatic shotguns to silenced machine-pistols patrolled the Creggan and Bogside areas in five unmarked cars. Only these troopers, along with the RUC and seven army officers, had been shown photographs of O'Donnell and told to get him at all costs, even if they had to kill. The bulk of the soldiers on the operation knew about as much as the population at large – precisely nothing. To them it was a simple, straightforward raid.

Each vehicle had two houses and a certain area to cover. That made almost fifty houses, some known to be Saor Eire houses, others simply republican houses, and yet others with no political history whatsoever. Each squad was ordered to scrutinize civilians in its area and arrest any who resembled O'Donnell. Any house where the occupants appeared suspicious was to be searched and the occupants arrested.

Chief Inspector Wall had done a thorough job in a short time. If he did not catch O'Donnell in one of the 'known houses' his plan was to flush him out to where he would be spotted by one of the patrols or else panic him into leaving the area, in which case he would be apprehended by the RUC who had all the exits solidly blocked.

At ten minutes past eleven O'Donnell left his mother's home in Creggan. He was on his way to a Saor Eire Command Staff meeting scheduled for eleven-thirty in the lower part of Creggan. Just before the bottom of Inniscarn Road he saw the convoy approaching the estate. Fear leapt violently inside him: they were coming for him! He walked quickly across the road and into the garden of the first house. The side of the road he had just left was an open green with no cover; he cursed himself for the mistake and hurried to the back of the house. Three Saracens and five landrovers passed along Inniscarn Road. He walked casually back to the front garden to view their progress. One of the landrovers stopped and four soldiers and a policeman tumbled out.

'That's a Provo house,' he thought. 'So they don't believe our statement. Or are they just throwing a wide net?' He felt an acute sense of satisfaction as he continued his journey. He passed one more landrover, but this raid was already in progress as the screams and insults blasting from the house told him. Both the constable and army officer were inside. The two soldiers on guard were so occupied with the commotion that they hardly spared him a glance.

The meeting was held in Frank McGuire's council house in the middle of Leenan Gardens. Frank was a pensioner of sixty-six whose wife had been dead for two years. His family had grown up and left home years earlier: three sons worked in England and the other two along with two daughters were dispersed through America. Since his wife died he had lived alone and took every opportunity to assist the IRA and its support groups. From the inception of the Northern Ireland state in 1921 Frank had been aware of the indifference, bigotry, hatred and conniving brutality of the various institutions of government towards the Catholic minority. He had been on the dole for over thirty years and blamed the English, Irish and Northern Ireland governments for his plight. His feelings about America were ambiguous: he loved that country for its opportunities and he hated it bitterly for attracting his children away from home.

'Come in, come in,' he greeted O'Donnell, the enthusiasm showing in his voice. The Command Staff were in the living-room, with the exception of Con McDaid the training officer.

'Are you going to wait for Con?' queried Frank, standing at the open door.

'No, we'll go ahead without him,' said O'Donnell, glancing

15

round the room.

'Right, I'll leave you to it, then. If I bang the floor, you'll know a patrol is in the street, okay?' This was what he enjoyed most about the meetings: the feeling of taking part in an important operation. He sat at his upstairs window with the dedication of a religious fanatic watching High Mass.

The assembled Staff consisted of an adjutant, quartermaster, operations officer and explosives officer.

'Do you know the Brits are raiding?' asked O'Donnell, addressing the group.

Mick Mulhern, the adjutant, nodded. 'We were just talking about it before you came in. It looks like someone upset the RUC today.'

'How do you know?' asked O'Donnell.

'Saw the convoy coming up the New Road; and they were raiding on Broadway when I passed.'

'I saw them raiding Broadway too,' said O'Donnell, 'and it sounded as if they were wrecking the place.'

'Think there's a chance of them raiding here?' said the quartermaster, Dermot Donnelly.

'There's a possibility,' said O'Donnell. 'This house must have held guns for every organisation in the town at one time or another. Are any of you carrying?'

'I've got a thirty-eight,' said Dermot.

'Well if they do raid, you get off-side with Mick and myself. Sean, you and Seamus stall them until we get clear. Right?'

'Right,' said the operations officer with jovial sarcasm. 'I'll chew up their SLRs and spit them back at them.'

'Don't go that far,' said O'Donnell in the middle of general laughter, 'just pick an argument with whoever's in charge and keep them occupied until we get out the back. I think they've only got one landrover to each house so you shouldn't have too much bother.'

Sean Donnelly, the explosives officer, and Seamus McLaughlin nodded their heads in agreement as O'Donnell continued. 'We'll keep the meeting as short as we can. The first thing is the job today. There can be no complaints about that, it was a good job. What we have to ensure now is that it wasn't a once-off effort. And the best way to do that is to make another hit tomorrow.'

'You're joking, O'D?' said Seamus McLaughlin, using the common abbreviation.

O'D was far from joking. He gave an outline of what he had in mind, without naming a target. There was a general discussion on operations before the agenda switched to the state of preparedness of the battalion area. No one was happy, least of all O'D, but it was felt that things were going to change radically in the immediate future. O'D spoke of pressures about to be put on the national leadership in Dublin. No one had much faith in Dublin; they only followed its directives when they had to; but whatever O'D said was believed with a reverence befitting the highest authority.

'Next item,' said O'D. 'Mick, I want you to see all Battalion OCs at twelve o'clock tomorrow.'

'In here?' replied the adjutant.

'Sort that out yourself. I don't care where it is as long as it's secure.'

O'D flew through the agenda. 'Next item. Dermot, give me a list of all the stuff we have.'

The quartermaster rhymed it off without a thought. 'Twenty-eight rifles, twelve of which are obsolete .303s. Forty-six handguns, five of which are .22s. We also have a rake of shotguns and .22 rifles – one of them is a pump-action. Altogether there's seventy-two pounds of jelly, plenty of dets, cordite and fuse, and, of course, we can make all the mix we want. We also have ten thousand assorted rounds of ammo.'

O'Donnell was about to speak when two loud thumps pounded on the ceiling. He rose quickly and moved to the window. A landrover was crawling slowly along the street, almost a hundred yards from the house.

'I think we're going to be raided,' he said, more to himself than anyone else. Then, without taking his eyes from the street, he called: 'Mick, open the back door in case they raid. Dermot, you go with him and be ready to take off.'

The landrover drove slowly, inching its way along the street until it reached the bottom of Frank's front garden. Then it stopped. 'That's it,' said O'D. 'Take off!' he shouted at the men poised at the back door.

'What about the plan?' asked Sean Doherty as O'D moved away from the window.

'Scrap it,' said O'D. 'We've time to get out the back.' Frank McGuire was excitedly descending the stairs. 'Thanks, Frank,' O'D said without stopping. 'Go easy on the Brits.'

'I'll close the door behind ye,' was all Frank had time to answer before the last man disappeared through the kitchen, leaving the curtains flapping on the windows as if a wind had just blown through the house. Two men were already over the high hedge surrounding the garden and the other three were scrambling their way through in a flurry of flying leaves as Frank reluctantly closed the door. 'Head for the shops,' were the last words he heard O'D calling to the others as the front door-bell rang and the men in his back garden scattered in five different directions.

No one even looked at the back of the house. The officer searched all the rooms, closets and potential hiding places along with the RUC man, and two soldiers remained in the front garden while a third leaned carelessly against the land-rover.

'Do you know a Hugh O'Donnell?' asked the RUC man after the house had been searched.

'Never heard of him,' replied Frank sharply, making it plain that it was nobody's business if he had.

'What about Michael Mulhern?'

'Never heard of him.' The tone remained the same.

'Dermot Donnelly?'

'Never heard of him.'

'What about the Prime Minister, Edward Heath?'

'Never heard of him.' His voice was a drone of monotonous boredom. The constable looked hopelessly at the army officer and shrugged his shoulders. They turned to leave but the officer said over his shoulder: 'We'll be seeing you, Mister

McGuire, a little later.'

The implied threat only served to stimulate Frank. 'The problem is,' he said, as both backs negotiated the garden path, 'I don't take an interest in these foreign politics, ye see. The only thing that interests me is Irishmen in Irish politics.' Neither of the men turned, fearing it would only throw fuel on a fluttering old fire.

As O'Donnell approached the Creggan shopping centre he saw two of the Staff were already there: Sean Doherty and Seamus McLaughlin. He did not waste time.

'Sean, I'll see you here at twelve-thirty tomorrow to work out this operation I have in mind. Seamus, I want ten pounds of explosives with a ten-second fuse in a duffle bag at exactly five o'clock tomorrow. Now, if I don't see you before those times, these orders will stand. Okay?'

Both men acknowledged.

'Right, I'm off. Don't be hanging about – the Brits are everywhere and they might just pick you up on spec. Pass the word to the others.'

'Where are you staying tonight?' asked McLaughlin.

'I don't know yet, but I'll be around somewhere. Take your problems to Mick if you have any immediate ones. You know where he is, don't you?'

'Yeah.'

'Right, take it easy. Slán.'

'Slán,' both men replied.

O'Donnell made it a rule never to tell anyone other than his adjutant where he was sleeping. He was prepared to bet his life on his men not informing on him, but he would not bet a breath on them not telling their girlfriends, mothers, mates or brothers. With that his whereabouts would become private gossip and public knowledge before he could get out of bed in the morning.

In the blood-red dusk he made his way to the cul-de-sac of Culmore Gardens and rang the bell of a small upstairs flat. The door was opened by a young woman with brown hair and piercing blue eyes. Her face beamed a broad smile as she

19

greeted him.

'Where the hell have you been?'

'Working,' he said, reaching forward and gently touching her left nipple with his right thumb and forefinger.

'Jesus!' she exclaimed in alarm. 'Do you want to have the bishop down on top of me?'

'Is that an attempt to blacken the bishop's name?'

'Get inside before I throw you out.'

He collapsed onto a large sofa in a display of exhaustion.

'Have you anything to eat, Brenda? I'm starving.'

'The chef's gone for the night, but I'll get the slave to make you something.'

He ate the meal with the appetite of a starving man. It was only when he had finished that he noticed the silence. He grew concerned as the atmosphere soaked into his consciousness.

'What's up?'

'I got that job with the BBC.' She sounded upset, as if the news had been a great disappointment.

'Oh shit! When did you find out?'

'Just this morning – got a letter. I start Monday week.'

'Monday week? For Christ's sake! That's only an hour away. Don't they believe in giving you time?'

She looked at him with an expression of ancient honesty but did not answer. The aggression which had flared in him for an instant subsided. 'When will you go?'

'I'll have to go next week to organise a flat and things. It's not all that easy to get a place in London with a five-year-old under your arm. But I'll leave it as late as possible.'

'You don't have to go at all, you know.'

'Hugh, you might not care what sort of future your son grows up to, but I do. I'm going.'

'Why didn't you marry me six years ago, before he was born?' he said, feeling the recurring hopelessness of this long-standing argument between them.

'I wasn't ready,' she fired back at him. 'Why don't you marry me now?'

'Will it stop you going?'

'No.'

After an uncomfortable silence he muttered, 'How the Christ do we get out of this?'

'We don't until you get out of the situation you're in,' she said a little too quickly.

'Brenda, I'm not prepared to think about that yet. My mind is made up on the situation here and I have to live out the idea.'

'Yeah, I know,' she said sadly, sinking back into her chair with a sigh, 'and we've been over it a thousand times. . .' She paused, looking at him more tenderly. 'Will we change the subject?'

'Yeah, for now anyway. I think I'm too exhausted. We'll take it up later when I'm thinking straight.'

'I didn't mean to catch you off balance, but we have to have it out,' she said by way of apology.

'I know,' he said and fell silent, staring moodily at the glowing bars of the antique electric fire.

Brenda rose from the chair and moved across the room. 'Is there anything I can do to take your mind off it?'

He played the game. 'Well, I don't know.' A concentrated frown wrinkled his forehead. 'Come here beside me for a minute and let me think about it.'

She stretched along the sofa until they were lying full-length facing each other. Then her hand explored his body until she looked down and, with just the barest hint of surprise in her voice, said: 'It's well seen you haven't been with another woman in the past week.' She had an impish smile on her face now.

'What would you have done if I had?' he asked with spurious indignation.

'Killed you,' she answered, still smiling.

'Good God! Get off your clothes and into bed you vicious woman.'

'Yes sir,' she said rising and taking his hand.

He touched her shoulder in the hallway saying, 'Let's have

21

a look at the kid first.'

She lowered her voice as she opened the bedroom door. 'Don't waken him,' she warned, 'he has to be up for school in the morning.'

He didn't answer as he tiptoed to the side of the bed and gazed down at the angelically peaceful figure of his son. She had no way of knowing what was passing through his mind but, as he stared intently, she hoped. After a few minutes they went to her bedroom where they undressed in silence. In bed she slid her naked body across until it touched his.

'What are you thinking?' she asked softly.

'Nothing,' he returned mechanically.

'Bullshit,' she answered. 'Tell me.'

'I was wondering how he will grow up.'

'I wonder about it all the time,' she answered.

Major Barry Down entered the observation post balancing two plastic cups of scalding tea and two sandwiches.

'Well, what do you think, Chief Inspector?'

'It looks like we missed him, Major,' said Wall, taking the tea and sandwich. 'We'll not get him now.'

The patrols had searched their designated houses and come up with nothing. They had arrested six people, all of whom were still detained, but none of them was the man they sought. They still patrolled the area stopping people, searching them on the street, before sending them on their way like chastised schoolchildren. By twelve-thirty the personnel involved in the operation were becoming frustrated and angry. At first it had been an adventure to leap from a moving landrover and confront passing pedestrians at gunpoint. There was always the danger, however remote, of encountering an IRA man with a concealed weapon. The fantasy of a suburban gunfight added to the excitement. As long as it remained a fantasy.

After three hours of routine harrassment of civilians the soldiers had become thoroughly resentful of the thankless task and their actions grew increasingly irrational. Civilians stopped now were beaten to the ground if they did not quickly comply with commands and most ended up with bloody heads. Discontent crept into the radio messages – and it began to worry the Major.

'Everyone seems to be getting edgy out there,' he said.

'Think they'll last another half-an-hour?'

There was a dull humour on the surface of Wall's question. But the situation did not merit humour in the Major's opinion. His nerves were a little ragged as he answered tensely, 'They will stay all night if they have to, but do you think it will achieve anything?'

Wall thought for a minute before answering. 'No, you're right, we've missed the bastard tonight. We'll call it off and try again in the morning. What do you think?'

'The same houses?' the Major asked doubtfully.

'Maybe. I'll spend tonight working out a complete dossier on every house he has lived in and every house he is likely to stay in and we'll hit them all.'

'What time do you want to start at?'

'Are you using the same men?'

'Probably.'

'Well, we'll leave it until eight o'clock then, that'll give them time to get some rest.'

The Major pressed the switch on his microphone. 'Hello all stations Earlybird, this is Sunray calling; Nightcap, over.'

All stations acknowledged their return to base. Wall went straight to the Strand RUC Barracks

The Strand Barracks was a brand new building which had been constructed to replace the delapidated Victoria Barracks, which festered in ruins two hundred yards away along the Strand Road. It had white single cells with artificially marbled walls and wooden benches. There were interview rooms and offices which ranged from the drabbly functional for working-class terrorist suspects to the brightly aesthetic, reserved for VIPs. It also held a small unit of military police and soldiers, who guarded it like a front-line fortress with heavily armed men in turrets on every corner. Electrically operated doors and a series of mirrors enabled anyone inside to observe who was approaching.

Wall entered his office on the top floor and lowered himself thoughtfully into a swivel chair. After a moment's contemplation he rang for Inspector Tony Miller. Miller looked haggard when he appeared a minute later. Wall pointed to a seat.

'Is Bill Taylor still here, Tony?'

'Yes, he's questioning one of the prisoners who looks promising.'

'In what way?'

'He's on the Saor Eire Command Staff. . . Con McDaid – I think he's the training officer.'

'Let me know how he gets on. In the meantime, the same op's on tomorrow morning at eight o'clock. Give the men the usual pep talk and make sure they're all here. As soon as you do that, see Bill and tell him I want the complete dossier on O'Donnell immediately. This McDaid character might be able to supplement it. I want to know everything he's done since he was fifteen – everything! And that includes every house he lived in and every job he had; every girlfriend he ever had and every mate. All their addresses and their parents' addresses. This bastard is still in the city and he's staying with someone he has known for years – he'll feel safer that way. Got it?'

'Yeah,' said Miller. 'Just one thing: do you want us to lean on McDaid?'

'Yes,' said Wall without hesitation. 'Put as much pressure as you can on him, but don't mark him.'

'Right. How long have we got to get all this?'

Wall glanced at his watch. 'Four o'clock at the latest, or before it if possible. If I'm asleep when you're finished, wake me gently.'

'Okay,' said Miller departing.

At four-thirty he returned and gently shook his chief awake as ordered. Wall untangled himself from the two chairs he had been sprawled across.

'Anything good?' he croaked hopefully.

'Afraid not,' said the disappointed Inspector. 'It's all routine and McDaid won't come across. I sent Bill home for a couple of hours kip, by the way,' he added, handing over the folder.

Wall waved his hand casually, 'That's okay.'

He had no way of knowing what was important and what was irrelevant in the report in front of him, but he somehow had to work out a massive raiding operation on the strength of it. He had almost finished reading it when a name caught his eye.

'What do you think of this Brenda McGlinchey?'

'She's a dim possibility. O'Donnell gave her a kid about five years ago and has seen her a few times since according to our information. But it seems for the sake of the kid more than anything else. McDaid says he has never heard of her.'

'Do you believe him?'

'Yes. . . I think so.'

Wall bowed his head thoughtfully for a moment, then said, 'We'll give her a try anyway. What's her address?'

'The last address was Creggan Heights with her mother, but that was five years ago.'

'Put her on the end of the list and we'll do her last.'

'You know, I was thinking,' said Miller, a little agitated. 'This operation is going to take at least two hours if we include even half of these addresses. It's going to be ten o'clock by the time we get round to doing the last houses on the list. Isn't that a little late?'

'I don't think it will matter in this case. For a start, I would say that this particular yobbo will stay in bed until dinner time, and even if he doesn't there is still no way he can get out of the area; we have all exits blocked.'

'Whatever you say,' said Miller.

The search began at exactly eight o'clock. Brenda McGlinchey's mother's house was entered as the nine o'clock news on RTE radio was just ending. The search lasted ten minutes: it was a mild affair but when it finished the officer in charge confronted a shaken and bewildered Mrs McGlinchey as she

25

sat hunched on her living room sofa.

'Sorry to have caused you any inconvenience.' His voice was kind and his accent beautifully polished. 'Would you like to check and make sure nothing is damaged?'

Mrs McGlinchey shook her head, blushing with embarrassment. The last thing she expected from these intruders was consideration. 'Naw, son. I'm sure ye left everything just as ye found it.'

'I hope so,' said the officer, smiling. He pointed to a photograph on top of the television. 'That is a beautiful girl, is it your daughter?'

'Aye, that's our Brenda.'

'I thought I recognised a resemblance,' said the smiling face. 'Does she still live with you?'

'Naw, sure she got a wee flat of her own down in Culmore Gardens.' Mrs McGlinchey responded to the officer's pleasant manner, suspecting nothing.

'Do you know the number?'

'Aye,' said Mrs McGlinchey, and told him.

Hugh O'Donnell was woken out of a pleasant sleep by a forty-five pound weight dropping on his chest in the person of his son, Philip. 'Yes Mucker,' he grunted affectionately, lifting the child to ease the pressure on his ribs.

'Yes Daddy,' replied the eager little voice. 'Mammy told me to come in and waken you before I went to school.'

'And quite right too. We couldn't have you going out to do a hard day's work without saying hello, could we?'

'I go to school myself now, you know,' said Philip, swelling with pride.

'Do you indeed? Well, aren't you the great man yourself? Do you learn anything there?'

'I do,' said the boy and he launched into a litany of achievements. He stopped reluctantly when his mother entered the room with the news of breakfast. O'Donnell followed both of them into the small kitchen and listened to Philip talk ceaselessly until he departed for school.

'Do you think it's safe to let him go to school by himself at this age?' he asked when Brenda returned from seeing the boy on his way.

'He doesn't go himself at all,' she answered. 'He walks fifty yards along the footpath to Donaghey's house and then goes on with Mrs Donaghey and wee Brian.'

'The little bugger,' said O'Donnell admiringly. 'He told me he went by himself.'

'He thinks he goes by himself. And, just like his father, if he thinks he is doing something, then no one will tell him he isn't doing it.'

He assumed she was hinting and asked, 'Are we about to start talking revolution again?'

'Now's as good a time as any,' she said, shaping up for the contest.

'Well, for a start, you're not opposed to the struggle yourself, are you?'

'You know I'm not. I just don't think it can be successful.'

'Well, you're wrong: it can be successful and we can have victory within a year.'

'You know that for a fact, do you?' She was self-consciously sarcastic as she stood facing him, her arms folded across her breasts.

'Don't be so sarcastic. I spend most of my waking hours thinking and working to make it come about. Before now it was only a dream of wrecking the state and attempting to create some worthwhile kind of life. But the movement has grown so much in the past year I can hardly believe it. We have the means now – or will have soon – to create a situation that can't help but lead us to victory. All we have to do is get the factors together in the right way. That will happen this year. If it doesn't I will hang up my hat because it's now or never.'

'Does that mean we'll be able to start living our lives together next year?'

He was instantly evasive. 'Brenda, that's unfair. I want to

27

get married just as much as you do, but it would be the height of stupidity to do it now. I'm not on the run yet, but the chances are that I very soon will be – and once that happens I will be hunted day and night. I won't be able to stop in one place, can't have a social life, can't go to a dance or have a drink outside the area. Anyone who shared my life would be so harrassed by the Brits that they would be totally neurotic inside a month.'

Brenda threw up her hands in exasperation. 'I can't argue with you on this level. You have the whole bloody thing worked out like some gigantic formula which only you know the answer to. If we could talk about jobs or houses or weans or our future I might be able to communicate, but this shit! What keeps blocking out my mind is the fact that you don't have to do it. All you are doing is sacrificing yourself for a bunch of shitheads who are only in the thing for profit or prestige or worse.'

'Do you think I'm an idiot?' he said, raising his voice.

The argument raged for half an hour with neither of them yielding ground, and it came to an abrupt and unsatisfactory end when he told her he had to go.

'Will you come again tonight?' she asked, changing her tone with more than a little effort.

'Yes,' he said, still smarting from the bruises of the argument.

'Don't forget.'

'I won't,' he said, taking her in his arms and kissing her softly. Both lingered in the soft, electric moment and then he pushed her gently away, looking into her eyes. 'I love you.'

'And I love you,' she answered.

'Now go and wash your dishes.' He smiled.

'Piss off,' she mocked. She returned to the kitchen as he went down the stairs and out the front door.

He actually saw the soldier coming up the path. It was just a moving image in the side of his eye as he closed the door. He thought it was a neighbour. Then he turned and saw it was not.

Two

THE SEARCH OPERATION was called off the instant it was confirmed that O'Donnell was in custody. Chief Inspector Wall rushed to the barracks to report and entered the Superintendent's office with Miller and Taylor.

'Well, Mervin,' began the Superintendent stoutly as they entered, 'you are to be congratulated on an excellent job.'

'Thank you, sir,' said Wall. 'I had a good team. And these two in particular done a wonderful job.' He waved his hand at the well-spread Inspector and the small Sergeant. 'Sergeant Taylor's information on Saor Eire was invaluable.'

'Did it turn up any guns?' Haslitt asked hopefully.

'Unfortunately not, but it was very comprehensive in many other respects.' Wall hoped the Superintendent would not ask him to be more specific as he was not entirely sure of what he meant.

'Right, take a seat the three of you,' Superintendent Haslitt passed on, 'and let's decide what we are going to do with comrade O'Donnell.' His subordinates laughed at the joke. Adopting a serious expression, he continued, 'You know this trouble has gone too far with the killing of policemen. It must be stopped. As for this organisation Saor Eire, it seems to be the most dangerous new development. And this character O'Donnell seems to be the brain behind it. Is that right Mervin?'

'That's correct.'

'And some of you are of the opinion that he is the man who pulled the trigger on Sam Henderson and Willie Gray,

29

is that also correct?'

'That's correct, sir,' repeated Wall dutifully, 'we think so: in fact I don't have any doubt about it. He certainly set up the operation himself, and if he didn't actually pull the trigger – which I'm sure he did – you can bet your pension that he was right on the scene when it happened.'

'Have you any proof of this?' Haslitt had no intention of betting his pension on anything.

'None, unfortunately.'

'So the only thing you can depend on for a conviction is a statement from O'Donnell himself?'

'At the moment, sir, yes.'

'Are you likely to get one?'

'Very unlikely, he looks like a hard nut to me.'

'That's what I thought,' said the Superintendent with what seemed like satisfaction. 'But I can tell you right now that I want a statement, and I don't care how the three of you get it. If you can't get any other evidence on this killer then I want a statement. Do I make myself clear?'

'Yes, sir,' said Wall uncomfortably.

'Yes, sir,' said Miller decisively.

'Yes, sir,' said Taylor eagerly. 'I'll get a statement out of the bastard.'

'That's what I want to hear, Sergeant,' said Superintendent Haslitt encouragingly.

'Don't worry, sir,' said the Sergeant. 'God Almighty couldn't intimidate me from getting the truth out of this bastard.'

'That's good, Bill.' Then he turned back to Wall. 'Mervin, that's all I have to say, you have seven days to get a statement out of this man, or whatever it takes to put him behind bars, for that's where he belongs and that's where he is going. And hopefully it will put an end to this Saor Eire gang. Any questions?'

'No, sir,' the three men answered almost in unison before filing out of the office.

The interrogation of Hugh O'Donnell began at precisely eleven o'clock on the morning of his arrest. A record in the jailer's journal stated that at that time Inspector Miller and Sergeant Taylor removed the prisoner from cell four in the basement. The jailer did not know where he had been moved to but, in fact, he had been escorted silently to a functional interview room on the second floor of the building. Inspector Miller began the questioning across a conventional office desk, while Sergeant Taylor sat hunched on a hard-backed chair in the corner.

'What's your address, Hugh?' asked Miller in a friendly manner, with a pen poised above what looked like a report sheet or questionnaire.

'Inniscarn Road, Creggan,' answered O'Donnell.

'How long have you lived there?' continued Miller, scribbling on the pad as he spoke.

'All my life.'

'Have you ever lived outside Londonderry?'

'I spent a few years in England and I was in the British army for six years.'

'In the Brits, eh? What mob?' His mood was almost jovial.

'Listen, let's cut out all this crap, what did you lift me for?'

'Oh, we just wanted a chat with you. What did you work at in England?'

'I was a prostitute. What's your name?'

'Sorry, Hugh, I should have told you that. I'm Inspector Tony Miller and this is Sergeant Bill Taylor. Have you heard of us before?'

'Never. Now are you going to tell me why I've been lifted?'

'We are just carrying out routine enquiries. Don't get excited about it. If you have nothing to hide then you have nothing to worry about. Now, when did you come out of the army?'

'I don't believe this! You characters have all that information on record, so why are we going through this routine?'

'This is for my benefit. I don't have access to any information concerning you at the moment.'

'Well why don't you go and get it?'

'Because it's not my job. I have been ordered to get your background so I must get your background. Now, for the third time, when did you leave the army?'

'I want to see a solicitor.'

With startling speed Taylor sprang out of his chair in the corner and brought his fist crashing down on the table. O'D jumped involuntarily at the suddenness of the movement. He closed his eyes as Taylor roared into his face, spraying him with spittle. 'You're not entitled to a fuckin' solicitor!' he screamed. 'So start answering the fuckin' questions!'

'I thought for a minute you were sleeping.'

The Sergeant's face bulged as he held a bunched fist in front of O'D. 'Don't get cheeky with me, cunt, or I'll box your fuckin' head off.'

Miller intervened as if he were doing O'D a favour. 'Hugh, you're not making this easy on yourself. Don't get me wrong now, personally I don't care whether you make a statement or not. . .'

O'D interrupted him quickly. 'Oh, so it's a statement now, is it? A statement about what? I thought a minute ago that I was just here for a nice friendly chat with your good self and bulldog friend here?'

Miller continued in his pleading tone of voice. 'Look, there's no call for all the sarcasm, I'm trying to do a job of work here. That's all it is to me: a job. And, as I said, I couldn't care less if you walked out of here in an hour's time, but I'm not the boss. There are people above who want an account of your movements – which they are quite entitled to – and I can tell you that they intend to get it one way or the other.'

'Since when did the law say that I had to give an account of my movements?'

'The law has always said that, Hugh,' said Miller with a smug grin.

'You see, Tony, the problem is that I don't think I am

32

obliged to give an account.'

'You can think what you like, but the fact is that you are – and will.'

'I'll tell you what: you let me see my solicitor and I'll take his advice on the matter.'

'You are entitled to see a solicitor, but only when we say so.'

'Tell you what: let me have some dinner and I'll think about it.'

'All I'm looking for is a simple account of your movements. Give me that and you can have a dinner.'

'Right, let's see, where will I start? Oh yes. I was born in Derry, lived all my life in Creggan until I was fifteen. Then I went to England and worked for three years before joining the BA. After that I came back home and here I have been ever since. How's that?'

'Not good enough, I need more detail.'

'Now wait a minute, Tony, the deal was that I give an account, not that I fill it with all the intimate details of my private life.'

'I'm beginning to get tired of this,' Miller declared. 'We're going to leave you for five minutes to think about it, and then Sergeant Taylor is going to come back and talk to you by himself, and he's not as easy to spar with as I am.'

'He looks like a bit of a wrestler all right. See you in five minutes, Sarge.'

As the two detectives closed the door behind them O'D rose and began exploring the room minutely, beginning with the window. He was softly whistling the 'Red Flag' without being fully aware of it. At the back of his mind was a nebulous idea that a gateway to freedom might be concealed in some corner. But he did not hold much store by it, it was simply a motivation to keep him thinking.

Outside, Miller and Taylor walked the full length of the building. 'What do you think, Bill?' asked the Inspector.

'He's a bastard,' the Sergeant answered. 'We're going to have to come the heavy with him straight away.'

'It might be a bit early for that.' He stopped, undecided,

for a few seconds and then said, 'Stay outside the door and let him sweat for a while until I see the boss.'

Miller entered Wall's office to find him swamped with a pile of paperwork. 'How's it going?' Wall queried, glad of the interruption.

'It's not. I think we have to start putting pressure on him straight away or he will go on like this for days.'

Wall was hesitant. 'I don't think we should start pushing him yet, Tony. It's too soon. Let's wear him down gradually. After he spends a night or two without sleep he'll change his tune. And, after all, it will only take an hour to get what we want out of him.'

'I doubt that,' said Miller with a touch of sarcasm. 'If this client can hold out for five or six days, you can bet your wife's housekeeping money he won't say another word after that.'

'Well, we'll see,' said Wall. 'In the meantime, no heavy stuff. Put three teams of two on him until tomorrow morning. Keep him going all night and you and Bill take a break.'

Six detective constables were chosen to question O'D continuously about anything they considered relevant. They were not to give him a break, other than for meals. If he wanted to go to the toilet he could only do so during these breaks.

When Miller and Taylor reported for duty at nine-thirty the following morning their first stop was Wall's office. From the constable in charge of the interrogation team they learned that O'D was still refusing to answer any relevant questions. At ten-thirty Miller and Taylor entered cell number four and found him asleep on the wooden board that served as a bed. He was shaken awake.

'All right, sleeping beauty,' growled Taylor, 'let's go.'

O'D, coming slowly out of a dead sleep, assumed the same attitude of flamboyant irony as the day before. 'By God,' he said, stretching himself, 'is it morning already?'

He preceeded the two men to the interview room on the floor above and as he entered the cubicle he was pushed by the Sergeant.

Miller opened the conversation in a serious tone of

34

voice. 'Well, Hugh, have you changed your mind any since yesterday?'

'Indeed I have, Terry. After giving the matter serious consideration in the solitude of my cell, I have come to the conclusion that your request is entirely reasonable and that no matter what I personally might feel on the matter regarding the legal aspect, I should. . . I should. . . I should. . .' The two policemen looked at him as if he were mad. 'Fuck it! Where was I?'

'You were about to tell us what you were doing before you came back to Londonderry.'

'Was I? Would you believe that I can't remember a thing right now? Strange isn't it?'

'Think about it for a minute,' said Miller. 'It will come back to you.'

O'D sat in silence for as long as he thought the Sergeant's nerves would hold, and then said brightly, 'It's no good, Terry, it's not coming back. Maybe if I had a rest for a couple of hours it might help. See, all I can think of at the minute is this grand, big, fluffy bed with a mattress – I'm sorry – with a pillow. Well, it has a mattress as well, of course, but the pillow is the important thing: it keeps sucking my head in like a vacuum and shutting out all the noise. Now don't interrupt now, let me finish as this is very important. I think I'll buy a bed like that when I get out of here because it's very. . .'

Sergeant Taylor leapt out of his chair. O'D tried to put his hands up, but he was too slow. He had half-turned his head when the punch caught him on the side of the eye, knocking him off the chair. Taylor kicked the chair violently out of the way and aimed a foot at O'D's kidneys. 'Bastard! You're going to start answering the questions or I'm going to start beating them out of you! Do you hear?'

O'D was on his back in the corner with his knees bent in the best defensive position he could adopt. He made the mistake of thinking that the position was secure enough for another act of defiance. 'I didn't catch it all, Sarge, could you repeat it?'

The burly Sergeant came in kicking. O'D kicked back from his horizontal position but he came off the worst. Beaten, he was yanked from the floor and held by the throat.

'Steady on there, corporal, you're fuckin' chokin' me,' he croaked.

Taylor butted him in the face, encouraging Miller to interrupt. 'That's enough, Bill, I think he's got the message now.'

Taylor stared with a look of insane rage into O'D's eyes, then pushed him into the chair before returning to the corner. Miller had a deliberate chill in his voice when he spoke.

'Well, we're waiting.'

'Can I take it from this, Tommy, that our honeymoon period is over?'

Taylor leaped from his chair, roaring. O'D had his hands up this time.

'Now hold on there, brigadier, before you come leaping round the table with your fists flying again, I have made a decision here. Are you listening, Tommy? Course you are, I can see that. Well, here's the decision: I'll talk to you on the condition. . .'

'What's that?' said Miller sharply.

'That the monster here is put back in his cage, that is if you have one in the building to hold him.'

Miller could not resist a sadistic smile. 'You're asking for another thumping.'

'I know, I'm a masochist, but that's the condition.'

Miller glanced at the Sergeant, who shrugged. 'Okay, if that's the way you want it.' He paused at the door, drawing himself up and speaking in his slow drawl. 'Just let me tell you this before I go: you better sing like a blackbird while I am out or I will insist on coming back and talking to you personally.' He closed the door slowly, quietly, peeking through the last crack with all the threatening significance he could muster.

O'D gave a short, spontaneous laugh. 'Very strange company you keep there, Tommy. You can't feel too safe driving round the Bog with him at your side at night.'

'This is your last chance to cut out the sarcasm, O'Donnell, so let's get on with it.'

'Okay, Adolf, fire away.'

'What did you do when you came out of the army?'

O'D was satisfied that he had at least stalled them for a day. 'I came back to Derry and signed on the dole,' he said quietly.

'What did you work at?'

'Nothing much, I sold a bit of scrap here and there and did a few labouring jobs.'

'Had you a steady job?'

'In this town? You must be joking.'

'What about politics, did you take an interest there?'

'I went on a few Civil Rights demonstrations, but that's about all.'

'You didn't get involved with any organisations?' Miller was a man standing in the middle of his own minefield trying to entice his enemy to approach.

O'D started skirting the perimeter. 'Like what?'

'The Provos or Officials?'

'I'm not interested in anything they are trying to do.'

'The Communist Party?'

'No way!'

'What about Saor Eire?'

'I hear they're pretty active in town at the minute.'

'You should know whether they are or not.'

'How do you mean?' O'D felt it was time to start digging his trench.

'Do you take me for an idiot? Aren't you on the Command Staff of Saor Eire?'

'I am not!'

'Come off it, O'Donnell, we know all about you.'

'If that's the case, why was I battered into answering all these questions?'

'You weren't battered into answering anything. You got a few clips for being cheeky and you'll get a few more if you're not careful. Now, what about Saor Eire?'

'I know nothing about it.'

37

'What about Mick Mulhern and Dermot Donnelly, do you know them?'

'I know them. . . slightly.'

'What do you mean slightly? Aren't you on the Saor Eire Command Staff with them?'

'You're out of your mind. I didn't even know Saor Eire had a Command Staff.'

'O'Donnell, you must think everyone in this force is an idiot. We know everyone on the Saor Eire Command Staff and we know what positions they hold. And we know exactly what they've done and who done it for them, so don't be trying to come the smart alec.'

'I'm not in Saor Eire,' said O'D, deciding it was time he dropped into his trench.

'When did you join it?' Miller was angry now.

'I tell you I'm not in it. I thought you were going to talk about my past.'

'We are talking about your past – your recent past. Like, for instance, last Friday morning: where were you then?'

'I can't even remember when Friday was never mind Friday morning.'

'What day do you sign the dole? You lift your money on Friday?'

'Hey. . . very good there, Sarge. That's good thinking there and it's beginning to bring it all back to me now: I collected my money in the Creggan Post Office around dinner time. Then I bought a few groceries for the mother. Then I went home.'

'What about that night?'

'I stayed at home, I think.'

'You think wrong. You weren't there when we raided the house.'

'Wait a minute. . . That's right I wasn't in the house. In fact, I had just left it, for I was walking down Inniscarn Road when the raiding party was coming up.'

'Let's go back a bit. Now that you realise that you weren't in the house all day Friday, what about the afternoon?'

'Oh I was in the house then, in fact I was in it from dinner time.'

'You're telling lies again.'

'Now why would I tell lies?'

'We have four people telling us that you were in the Diamond that afternoon.'

'They would be gravely mistaken, and so would you for believing them. It's months since I've been in the Diamond.'

'I don't think so. One person: this person knows you better than I do and he certainly isn't mistaken.'

'Well. . . think what you like, but I wasn't there.'

'What about this character Michael Mulhern, how long have you known him?'

'I'm not sure, maybe a year or so.'

'Where did you meet him?'

'Can't remember.'

'When was the last time you saw him?'

'Can't remember.'

'Was it him recruited you into Saor Eire?' The question slipped into the conversation so smoothly that O'D was almost snatched out of his trench.

'I'm not in Saor Eire,' he said loudly.

'How long has he been in it?'

'I don't know that he is.'

'I know he is – and I know that you are too. Were both of you on this job on Friday?'

'What job?'

'Don't give me "what job". The killing of two policemen, that's what job!'

'Good God! Is that what all this is about? You think I killed two policemen?'

'I can tell you this, O'Donnell; every policeman in the town knows you killed them, and there are some who are determined to get you to admit it by hook or by crook.'

'Does that mean you're going to turn the bulldog loose on me again?'

'It means that every able-bodied man in the place is going

39

to be turned loose on you. And some of them are going to succeed, so why don't you make it easy on yourself and make a statement?'

For the first time O'D dropped his defensive, patronising tone and with all the sincerity he could muster, said, 'Wise up, Inspector.' At this stage, the course of the game became clear to O'D. He knew what the inspector said was true. The police were not speculating about his activities, they had his scent and they intended to get him. There could be no more stalling, no more bluffing, no more deflections or flamboyant indignation. He had either to own up or shut up right now.

'In that case, Inspector, you can politely go and fuck yourself.' They would have to come in and dig him out.

The interrogation continued for the rest of the day. He received some personal attention from Sergeant Bill Taylor who attacked him three times, beating him about the head and kicking him. No one else assaulted him; their abuse they expressed only verbally. Meal breaks were minimal, the longest lasting half-an-hour. After that it was continuous interrogation at a high or low intensity. He was beginning to hallucinate mildly by the time they left him.

As soon as his head hit the wooden pillow he fell into a black, macabre nightmare. Brenda and Philip were screaming. At first he couldn't see them and began to panic at the sound, then his mind focused. A troop of pyjama-clad soldiers dragged the mother and child from the flat and beat them mercilessly with batons. Mick Mulhern came charging into the dream from the vast darkness surrounding it. He scooped the two figures into his strong, sinewy arms and charged again, this time through the cordon of police and soldiers. He leapt through, leaving the attackers in disarray, but his strides were in slow motion, tearing every nerve-end loose in O'D's body as he watched their untouchable progress.

He knew what was coming before it happened. In a slow-moving, half-conscious world he willed it to come quickly so

40

that it would be over with. A Ferret scout-car appeared in front of the escaping trio, its heavy .30 Browning spitting flames. The three were cut into pieces in a mangled mess of blood, skin and shattered bones. O'D saw it in such detail that he found himself staring at the torn pieces of flesh, wondering which belonged to whom. With enormous effort he turned his head away. The commander of the scout-car was himself. He was destroying the three people he most loved.

He felt something close to relief when he was rudely wakened by two strange policemen. Once on his feet he was shoved the short distance to the jailor's office.

'Sign here,' said the jailor, handing him a pen and pointing to a space in a large ledger.

'What for?' said O'D, more than a little confused.

'Your property.'

'Where is it?'

'The detective has it.'

'Then let him sign for it.'

'He can't, it's your property.'

'Then give it to me and I'll sign for it.'

'Are you refusing to sign?'

There was no answer to that unless he wanted to be beaten again. He stood silently and absorbed the insults until the constable signed the book himself. Then he was taken to a police landrover which immediately left the barracks under army escort.

His spirits had soared for an instant on leaving the cell. He thought he was being released. But the elation quickly died: he was going to Ballykelly Army Camp for further interrogation. No one spoke during the journey. O'D thought it was not a healthy sign. He forced himself to think of a few standard jokes about Ballykelly. They stuck in his throat like cotton wool. By the time they had reached Ballykelly his mind had recoiled, had shut off all hope of escape.

At five o'clock on a half-dark Monday morning the small convoy of vehicles drove through the gates of the army camp and made its way to the police interrogation centre on an isolated part of a disused RAF airstrip. O'D was pulled roughly from the landrover and half-pushed half-pulled through a confusion of corridors. He arrived finally at an empty room measuring twelve feet by twelve. A single light bulb hung from the ceiling, filling the room with a sickly yellow glow. It appeared to throw shadows where there were no obstacles. The room was windowless. He thought that the bulb might allow him to slash his wrists. A policeman opened the door.

'Let's go, me old son,' he said.

He was taken to another room containing a table and four chairs. This was also lit by a pale yellow light and had no windows. Suddenly the door flew open and three policemen he had not seen before came charging in. The first grabbed the lapels of his jacket and shook him, shouting, 'So you're the fucking cop-killer, are you? You're the bastard who thinks he can kill policemen and get away with it. Answer me, you fucking fenian bastard!'

'Go and fuck yourself,' was all O'D got out before he was butted in the face and thrown against the wall. He crumpled to the floor and lay motionless. He heard one of them say, 'Get the fucker on the table.' He tried to struggle but their combined strength was far too great. They lifted him off the floor in one swoop and bounced him on the table. Two of them sat on his legs, almost breaking his shins, and the third held his arms behind his head.

'What,' screamed one, hitting him a blow in the groin, 'have you got to say about killing policemen now? Come on, speak up!' Another blow. 'Willie Gray's widow wants to hear what you have to say! Do you hear me, eh? Speak up! Give me a message for her!'

'Come on, bastard,' said the one holding his arms, 'answer the questions.' He leaned forward and spat in O'D's face. 'You're not talking.' He hit O'D another blow. 'Have you lost your tongue or something?'. He reached and grabbed O'D's testicles, squeezing them hard.

For the first time O'D screamed. He opened his mouth and screamed as loud as his lungs would force the noise from his

42

throat. Distantly he heard the three of them laughing.

When he regained consciousness he was drenched with water and only one of them was sprawled across his legs. The second was still holding his arms, but the third was now standing by his side. His voice had the cold, calm assurance of someone who was an expert at his trade, who knew exactly what he was doing and who had been doing it for a long time.

'Don't think you're getting out of it that easily,' he said with a hint of a smile on his face. 'There's only one escape from what we have in store for you.'

'What's that?' croaked O'D, almost curious.

'Talk,' was the answer.

'I'll kill myself first, you fucking sectarian bastard.'

'You've got it wrong,' he said, smiling with the confidence of someone who couldn't be contradicted, 'we're the ones who's going to kill you.' He struck O'D a sharp punch to the solar plexus which made him vomit in uncontrollable spasms. As they held him impaled on the table the puke spilled over his face, neck and upper chest before spattering onto the floor.

'What the hell are you at?' said the one behind, hitting O'D a glancing blow on the side of the head. 'You just sparked my fucking shoes!' The three of them scattered from the table as O'D continued retching his stomach empty.

'Would you look at that?' said one in a bout of sarcastic banter. 'The stupid bastard has gone and messed up his clothes.'

'Not to mention our floor,' returned one of his companions.

'Well, he'll clean that up, of course,' said the first one starched with confidence, 'but we'll have to take his clothes and get them cleaned for him. We can't very well leave him in dirty clothes, can we? Give him a hand to get them off.'

His clothes were removed amid a hail of blows; after this the beatings intensified. The treatment continued for hours. Then someone opened the door and said something he could not comprehend. After a final rain of blows and curses he was dragged from the table and forced to limp to the original cell where they dropped him on a rubber mattress.

O'D lay staring at the bulb, the only object in the cell to stare at apart from the mattress, and thought about the first idea which had come into his head on entering the place; the ultimate escape. A tight smile sat on his lips as the idea lurched across his brutalised mind. 'Maybe later,' he murmured to himself, 'they haven't broken me yet.'

The door opened and a military policeman entered with a mug of tea and a single slice of bread. He placed them on the floor inside the door and disappeared. The thought of food nauseated O'D, but he knew he had to eat to keep his strength up. They were giving him little enough, and he would have to force himself to eat it. He noticed the mug had no handle and grabbed at it with his hand. He drew away with a cry of pain. It was scalding hot. For the first time he noticed a furry chemical dryness in his mouth which tasted of vomit. He crouched over the tea and dipped his bread in it, blew it cool, and then sucked the moisture from it until it dissolved in his mouth. When the bread was finished he had to wait for the tea to cool.

He lay back on the mattress while he waited, slipping into the lurking nightmare. But it did not last long. Another pair of Special Branch officers roughly shook him awake. He struggled to get his eyes open. His body was cramped with pain; his stomach muscles so bruised that they refused to lift his back from the mattress.

'Get up,' one of the policemen said coldly.

'I can't, you'll have to give me a hand.'

The other one leaned over, grabbed him by the hair and yanked him awkwardly to his feet. O'D thought of the unfinished tea and his sandpaper thirst. 'Let me just get a drop of tea before I go,' he pointed, moving towards the mug.

'You're too late for that', said one of them kicking the mug across the dirty floor.

He was pushed into the corridor and forced to flop along on his bare feet to the room. He was told to sit in one of the chairs, which he did, noticing that the contents of his stomach had been removed from the floor. A few minutes later the

44

door opened and a well-dressed middle-aged man entered.

For some inexplicable reason O'D assumed that he was a civil servant and not a branchman. The two detectives were about to leave, but the stranger stopped them. The tone of his voice was harsh.

'Where are this man's clothes?'

'Don't know, sir. Someone else took them.'

'Get them immediately.'

'Yes, sir.'

O'D was cautious as a cornered animal. The new arrival sat across the table and looked concerned, though in an un-emotional sort of way.

'Have you been badly treated?' His voice was mild-mannered.

'Are you fuckin' joking?'

'No.'

'Can't you tell by looking at me whether I have been badly treated or not?' O'D tried to sound incredulous.

'Well, I can't see any marks, but you look badly shaken.' The mild manner did not falter.

O'D exploded. 'Don't come that soft-hearted crap with me, you slimy fuckin' bastard! I know what you're at and you're getting nothing out of me! Do you hear? Nothing!' He realised that he was screaming and fell silent. He was on the verge of hysteria.

'Calm down,' said the man. 'No one is going to harm you while I am here.'

O'D thought instantly, 'Use the bastard!' and the thought snapped another charge of energy into his exhausted brain. 'Why was I not allowed a drink?' he asked.

'When were you refused?'

'Just before I came in here, your two mates wouldn't let me drink my tea.'

'Who wouldn't?' It was a reference to the term rather than a point of identification.

'The two characters you sent to get my clothes. They brought me from the dungeon and kicked my tea over the

45

floor.' He knew he sounded like a whinger.

'I see,' said the man, thoughtfully. 'I don't know whether I can get you any tea now, but I will certainly try. Will you take a glass of water if I can't?'

'I will.'

He walked slowly to the door and opened it slightly, speaking to someone on the other side. The thought grew in O'D's mind; this would be the easiest session he would have.

For ten minutes the soft-spoken man tried to debate the futility of an armed struggle to gain independence for a country which did not want it. But O'D was in no state to argue – and knew it – and he refused to come out of the mental trench he had so carefully constructed. The tea arrived in a canteen cup and saucer; the conversation veered towards crime. O'D dodged the questions and stretched the answers as best he could in an attempt to prolong the session. About half way through the conversation one of the branchmen returned with a blanket. His clothes had gone to be cleaned and it was the best they could do. He had to accept.

Huddled in his blanket and trying hard – but failing – to regain his dignity, he once again concentrated on stretching his answers. But the interview ended as if at a pre-arranged time, the branchmen returning to bring him back to his cell where he was given his dinner on a plastic plate with no cutlery. He gave a few token bangs on the door, but was not disappointed when no one answered. He ate everything – cabbage, meat, potato, gravy – with his fingers.

As soon as he had finished he felt an urge to go to the toilet. This time his assault on the door was more insistent. He spent five minutes banging with one degree of loudness or another. After that he had to give up as he could wait no longer. He reluctantly went to the corner farthest from his mattress and with an ingrained sense of loathing thankfully emptied his bowels.

The first three branchmen he had met at Ballykelly entered his cell at one o'clock and found him sleeping fitfully.

'What the fuck's that smell?' said the first one instinctively pinching his nose.

'The cunt shit in the corner,' said the one behind him.

The three of them seemed insulted; they dragged O'D from the mattress and beat him into the corridor before he was properly awake. The next session lasted until seven o'clock with no variation in the treatment of the previous day. He was beaten until his body became numb to the blows and his mind slipped exhaustedly into a removed acceptance of the torture.

When it was finished he was dragged back to the cell, bare feet trailing limply along the floor, and flung onto the mattress. His meal consisted of beans and sausages, one slice of dry bread and a mug of tea; he forced himself to eat. The tea scalded him again. He lay back on the bed and collapsed into nightmare while the foul smell still fermented in the corner.

He was dragged from his bed and it was three strange men who took charge of him, but not before giving him the usual beating for offending their nostrils. Now, instead of beating him in the static position, they chose to knock him about from one to the other as if he were their favourite rugby ball. A particular trick was to push him towards the wall just as a branchman, who was positioned to catch him, stepped out of the way. By morning he was unable to walk. The most he could do was to stagger drunkenly against the nearest wall when he was left to support himself. There was no rest and no escape. Continuous movement and constant beating left his mind in a half-crazed condition. All he could do to communicate his unwillingness to talk was to scream and roar, roar like an animal: it was a shield through which his weakness could not escape.

Eventually he was returned to his cell and his first thought was for something to eat, but this time there was no food and he knew it was futile to ask for anything.

He lay on the mattress staring at the bulb and his mind slowly reversed its decision to desert him. 'At least I'm winning the battle against you,' he thought. Sleep did not come automatically this time. He took stock of his position. He knew for certain that he had been arrested on Saturday morn-

ing and that the order detaining him lasted seven days. He
felt fairly sure that he had been moved to Ballykelly in the
early hours of Monday morning. All he had to do now was to
figure out how long he had been there. But he could not
remember how many meal-breaks he had had, and night and
day were as one. After a lot of guesswork he came to the conclusion that he had been there for at least two and at the most
four days. It is either Wednesday or Friday, he thought. In
the end he opted for Thursday. Then he drifted into a stupified
and troubled sleep under the comfortable impression that he
had only another twenty-four hours to do in Ballykelly. He
did not care where he went after that.

Sleep brought spasmodic nightmares interspersed with
periods of waking hallucinations, but it was the longest break
he had had since his arrest. It was eight o'clock before his
breakfast came and an hour later before he was taken for the
next session. He felt almost revived though his body ached
and he shook uncontrollably.

Another trio of strange branchmen took over. He did not even
think about it. This time a black hood was placed over his
head and tied at the neck as he entered the interrogation
room. He was forced to lean at a forty-five degree angle against
the wall and support himself with only his fingertips and toes.
He was greeted with silence for the first five minutes, then a
voice said, 'We won't be asking you any questions this time,
cop killer, but just let us know when you want to say something. I'll be standing right behind you.'

O'D tolerated the pain in his fingers and arms until it
became unbearable, then he collapsed in a heap on the floor.
He was quickly yanked up again; an electric fire was placed
in front of where he stood to discourage him from falling a
second time. His naked body, vulnerable to the heat, blistered
in torment for the rest of the day and he fell frequently, sometimes hitting the red-hot fire, but he did not say a word.

He was returned to his cell where he got dinner and tea

48

together, and was then left for the night.

The next day saw another variation. He was marched naked from the cell to be greeted by two lines of silent, staring, hating soldiers all the way along the corridor to the interrogation room. It gave him a feeling bordering on the macabre; they looked like zombies. A branchman pushed him along the corridor, but as he stepped level with the first two soldiers they started beating him about the head with their fists. He tried to pull back but the branchman pushed him on. He had no option but to stagger through the gauntlet of blows.

When he finally reached the interrogation room he collapsed. After a few seconds he was hauled to his feet again. But on the way up it was as if some mechanism in his mind activated itself, a mechanism to protect him from the horrors surrounding him. All he could think of after that was, 'Something very important happened to me today, but I can't remember what it was.'

For the rest of the day his brain, like a faithful servant defending a dying master, refused to register what was happening. He was beaten systematically, but he did not comprehend the significance of the blows. Whereas before he would have tried to avoid a blow by crawling under the table or rolling into a ball in the corner, this time he merely sat or lay with his arms down and let his captors beat him until they tired. Questions were meaningless to him now. Even if he had understood them, he would have been incapable of formulating an answer in his mind.

It was when he was in this condition that his captors presented him with a typed statement admitting to the double murder. He felt like signing, for an instant almost did. The single sheet of paper lying on the table did not look in the least dangerous. It was his passage to a comfortable bed and a normal atmosphere. He tasted these ideas and was tempted by them. But some deeper reasoning came charging forward like a bull snorting in anger and scattered all illusions of comfort. Only one illusion remained – escape! And its foundation was anger, which was the greatest strength he had. He tore

49

the statement to shreds.

That day also passed without food until he was returned to his cell. He felt certain by now that his time for release was imminent. He was, in fact, beginning to wonder whether he had not been detained over his time, illegally. Of only one thing was he absolutely positive; that he had beaten the naked bulb. His morale rose slightly. He no longer contemplated suicide. He almost felt cheerful. Almost smiled. Almost.

He was permitted a long rest that night, but was brought again to the interrogation room in the morning where another sheet of typed paper containing the same statement was placed in front of him. He was coaxed, cajoled, bribed and tempted to sign. He refused. Interrogation continued with only one break for a meal. By then he felt certain he was being detained illegally. The bare bulb threw its palid yellow light onto his doubting, battered face. If he was held illegally then no one would know where he was. The police could always say they released him after seven days – which they were probably saying already – and then do what they liked with him. His head pounded with a pain that seemed eternal.

The next day began in the usual way but many hours later and, after a particularly heavy beating which he felt he could not survive, the room suddenly emptied and he was left alone with a solitary branchman, who helped him into a chair and then said calmly: 'You know you are not going to be released from here?'

O'D was numbed by the statement even though he had expected it for some time. 'I don't give a fuck,' he croaked.

'You have two choices,' continued the branchman as if he had not heard him. 'Either you sign that statement or you will get a bullet in the back of the head.'

'Fuck off!'

'Right, you asked for it. . . Bill!'

One of his companions came quietly and soberly, as if he were at a funeral, into the room.

'He won't sign.'

'Okay, nut the cunt,' said Bill drawing a revolver from his

50

hip holster and handing it to his mate.

The man took the weapon, displayed it to O'D and said, 'Now, just to show you we are not bluffing. . .' He pointed the gun between O'D's bare feet and fired.

The noise was deafening in the small room. O'D felt the floor vibrate as the bullet smashed through the wood; then the gunman walked behind him and pressed the gun against the back of his ear. The barrel was still hot.

'Now you fenian bastard,' he said. 'This is your last chance. Are you going to sign?'

O'D shivered and sweated simultaneously. He stared at the pen and paper silhouetted sharply on the scarred table and thought, 'Oh, Jesus, this is how they do it.'

'Sign, fuck ye!' the gunman screamed into his ear.

'No,' said O'D, trembling, ready to pass out.

He heard the shot – actually felt it burn the back of his head – but he was still sitting upright in the chair.

'The next one splits your skull,' said the man behind him.

It was then that O'D noticed the wetness in his mouth. He tasted it and realised, with complete unconcern, that he had been slowly sinking his teeth into his lower lip. Then he fainted.

He regained consciousness in his cell, staring at the wall. His head turned reluctantly towards the smiling bulb. 'You bastard,' he thought, 'So you've beaten me. But how do I do it?' He would have to jump to smash the bulb with his fists, and if he did that the noise would alarm the guard. He thought furiously, attacking his mind as if it was the cause of the trouble and had to be punished. And his mind came up with the solution. He would smash the bulb in the blanket. He would outwit the bastards yet – he would deprive them of their statement. He had just begun to drag himself from the filthy mattress when two vaguely familiar branchmen came for him.

An overwhelming wave of self-pity flowed through him as his naked feet dragged along the rough hall; they had even taken from him his final act of dignity. But the movement jerked his mind into thought. He was going to sign the statement! The torture had become too much. He reasoned firmly that signing the statement was a better option than being shot or committing suicide. He had been out of his mind to contemplate suicide, and even more stupid to let the police come so close to shooting him. His feet flopped heavily along the hollow hall. He was resigned: it wasn't such a bad option after all. They would sentence him to life, probably be out in fifteen or twenty years. Plenty of people had done that much time before and survived. A weird sense of relief surged through him at the thought that it was all over.

But this time they did not stop at the interrogation room. Instead they made a left turn at the bottom of the hall and took him to a different room. As soon as he entered he saw his clothes lying on a chair beside a hand-basin.

'Wash yourself and get dressed,' said one of the branchmen. O'D obeyed without answering. He knew a new decision had been taken, but he dared not let himself hope as to what it might be. The branchmen watched in cold silence as he slowly pulled the clothes over his complaining limbs. O'D wanted to shout, 'Don't shoot me. Please don't shoot me. Give me the statement and I will sign it now.' But he could say nothing.

He was led through a confusing series of corridors to emerge through a final door into bright, crisp morning sunlight. His spirits soared instantly and he almost moaned with pleasure. He had not tasted fresh air, let alone seen daylight, for almost a week. Now he could feel the new sun warming his face and forcing hope and life into every pore of his body. He drew the air into his lungs in long, slow, nasal breaths.

A branchman took his elbow and led him to a solitary car in front of the building. The flat, wide expanse of Ballykelly airport was spread all around. He could see the main Belfast-Derry railway line running along its edge, and the brilliant blue sea of Lough Foyle and beyond that the mountains of Donegal. His heart strained against his chest. How had he ignored these sights? How could he? There could be nothing more beautiful in the world.

The idea of escape flashed across his mind, but he could not contemplate it seriously. There was too much flat ground to cover and he would have been shot before he had travelled fifty yards. He wondered if that was what they were hoping for. He sat dumbly in the back of the waiting car. It left the camp and turned right for Derry. He sweated all the way to the city.

On his arrival at the Strand Road RUC Barracks he was lodged in a cell, but there was no further interrogation. When his first meal arrived he asked the jailer for the time. 'Twelve-thirty,' said the uniformed man, who had just come on duty.

'What date's today, by the way?' said O'D as casually as he could manage.

'Twenty-fourth, today.'

'Twenty-fourth,' echoed O'D. 'That means it must be Friday?'

'That's right,' said the constable, stalling on the last syllable with the thought that he had done something wrong. He left the cell quickly, closing the door.

O'D was able to work out a clearer picture of his position after the snatched conversation. He had been lifted on Saturday the 18th, now it was Friday the 24th – so they had held him for seven days after all.

He felt as if he had been held for two weeks, if not three or four; but that was unimportant now: he was going to be released – he knew it. He realised that they had brought him back to rest before he saw a doctor. They didn't want him exhausted and brutalised when he was examined. He checked his body for bruises but there were precious few, and those he did have would certainly not substantiate the treatment he had received.

Superintendent Haslitt stared sullenly across his desk at Inspector Miller and Chief Inspector Wall.

'Well, you didn't get a statement?' he asked with a patronising sneer.

'I'm afraid not, sir,' said Wall, wincing. 'We had some of our best men on him in Ballykelly, but he just wouldn't crack.'

The Superintendent was still unconvinced. 'Is there anything we can charge him with?' He immediately qualified the question: 'Anything we can hold him on?'

'Afraid not, sir; not that I can see, unless Inspector Miller here has something.'

'Nothing,' volunteered Miller, 'that the Director of Public Prosecutions would accept.'

The Superintendent caught the connotation, but he was inclined to be cautious. The statement he had made a week earlier meant nothing now. He had wanted to see the streets of Derry rid of what he considered psychopathic killers whose main pastime was intimidating the population; but that was, after all, only one part of an overall problem. There were many factors to be considered – not the least of which was his relationship with the DPP.

'We'll have to release him in that case,' he said reluctantly.

At eight-thirty the following morning O'D was examined by the police doctor. He made a formal complaint about his treatment and all the bruises remaining on his body were noted. Fifteen minutes later he was released.

As he left the barracks all the old familiar landmarks appeared the same as before. No better, no worse, they had not transformed themselves into the glittering domes of freedom he had imagined them to be over the past seven days. They stood silent and grey under an overcast sky. They did not radiate happiness or reach out to embrace him as he had imagined they might. Rigid, inanimate objects, they were not even aware of his existence.

Three

AFTER MAKING SURE he was not being followed O'D
went directly to Mick Mulhern's house, knowing it
would be the centre of activity in his absence.

'How's the form?' Mulhern greeted. 'We were worried about
you.'

'Bloody awful,' said O'D, dismissing the subject impatiently.
'What's been happening for the past week?'

'Nothing,' said Mick sheepishly. 'Dublin's been on the
phone every day telling us to stay quiet until you were
released.'

'Have there been any problems?'

'You were the only problem we had, we didn't know where
they were keeping you.'

'Ballykelly, but I don't want to talk about it until I get my
head straight.'

Mick took a letter out of a jewellery box on top of the television set and handed it to O'D, saying, 'Brenda left this.'

'Where is she?'

'She went to England on Wednesday.'

He put the letter in his pocket as if it had been an expected
bill. Mick continued: 'Dublin wants you to phone them as
soon as you can.'

O'D rose immediately, asking only that a Staff meeting be
organised for nine o'clock. He rang a Dublin number and the
phone was answered by a familiar voice. 'Yes, John,' he said
in the usual Derry form of greeting, 'this is Hugh here.'

55

'Glad to hear you, kid. How's the form?'

'Terrible. Have you got a problem?'

'I'm afraid so. There's a meeting tonight.'

'I can't make it.' He had no hesitation.

'You have to, we cancelled the thing last Wednesday waiting on your release.'

'That was very confident of you.'

'What?'

'John, I am incapable of thinking tonight.'

'The thing won't start until tomorrow – and you have to be there whether you can think or not.'

'Okay,' he said reluctantly. He knew nothing could be stated as both phones were tapped. 'What time is the pick-up?'

'Same as last time.'

'Has my transport been told?'

'Yes, they all know.'

'Right, slán,' said O'D.

'Slán.'

'I have to go to Dublin tonight,' he said to Mick Mulhern wearily, 'but I want that Staff meeting to go ahead anyway. You take charge of it yourself.'

'Have you something in mind?' asked Mick, his eyebrows lifting slightly with interest.

'Yeah, remember that operation we looked at on the back hill?'

'The one at the piggery?'

'That's it. I want you to set it up.'

'How much explosive?' asked Mick, and O'D smiled in appreciation of his adjutant's characteristic practicality.

'Use two hundredweight of fertiliser and prime it with five pounds of jelly,' said O'D.

Later he left to make arrangements for his trip, and in a quiet moment he opened the letter Mick Mulhern had handed him.

Dear Hugh,

You were arrested outside my own front door and I didn't

even know about it until Philip came home from school and told me his father had been taken away by the army. I don't know whether that's a reflection on the street, the State or society at large. All I know is that I can't take any more of it.

I haven't slept since I heard the news and I think I am now beginning to take it out on Philip. He only has to look at me sideways and I am screaming at him. He brought a stray dog into the flat yesterday and I actually kicked the poor brute out again (I mean literally kicked it!). It was the expression on Philip's face that made me realise for the first time that I am turning neurotic.

That's what decided me to go to London as quickly as possible without waiting to see you again. You make me forget about my neurosis. And whenever I listen to you overflowing with ideas the thought of being anywhere else but beside you is unbearable.

But now in the cold soberness of solitude I can see that I just can't stay. This society is so fucked up that it is going to take a lot of tears and blood to rectify it – that is if it can be straightened out at all. I don't want my children growing up to become part of that lake. I don't want to watch you becoming part of it! And I don't want to end up at the bottom of it myself.

I'm sorry, Hugh, it's just too hard for me. A few years either way in the history of this sad country and we would have been beautiful together. But it can't happen at the moment. Maybe in another couple of years – if your head can stand the bashing – we will be able to get it together. In the meantime. . . ??? I will leave you until then.

I will send you on my address in London as soon as I get one. Don't judge me too harshly, Hugh: you are stronger than I am.

Philip sends his love and kisses.

My deepest love, my darling.

Brenda.

The journey to Saor Eire's GHQ Staff meeting began at nine o'clock that night. Saor Eire, like all wings of the IRA, treated these meetings with the utmost secrecy and employed the tightest security. The Special Branch police on both sides of the border kept constant surveillance on all people thought to be in positions of leadership in republican organisations. For this reason the meeting place was known only to the drivers on the last leg of the journey, who were almost always themselves members of the GHQ Staff.

O'D left Derry on foot and crossed the few fields separating Creggan Heights from the border in a matter of minutes. Once in Donegal he made his way to a hillside farm about a mile from the border. The owner of the farm drove him, in a delapidated Morris Minor that looked as if it was used for ploughing, to Letterkenny. The twenty-mile journey took almost an hour and it was ten-thirty before he walked into his next pick-up point: a quiet country pub on the outskirts of the town. This contact was sprawled in front of a blazing turf fire reading a copy of *The Irish Times*.

'Well, Paddy-Joe,' said O'D warmly, 'how's the fishing this weather?'

'By God, it's yourself Hugh,' said Paddy-Joe, forcing the paper into unnatural folds. 'What'll ye have to drink?'

'Nothin' thanks, Paddy-Joe. I'm just looking for a lift into town.'

'Well there's no better man to give ye one,' said Paddy-Joe, dropping the bruised paper on the floor and rising.

They set off initially in the direction of Letterkenny, but once satisfied they were not being followed they took the first road to the south. Neither of them spoke once they had related the situations in their respective areas. O'D gave a brief outline of his detention, to a chorus of curses from Paddy-Joe, and they both settled to a quiet concentration on the journey.

It was the early hours of the following morning before they drove into a small village in the corner of County Leitrim. O'D transferred to the pillion seat of a motorbike and Paddy-Joe went to lodge at a nearby farmhouse. The motorbike ride lasted ten miles, at the end of which he was left at a small village post office. Two members of the GHQ Staff were already there. Fifteen minutes later a landrover arrived to take them to their final destination, a large, isolated farmhouse on the shores of the Shannon.

The place was deserted, but the driver knew the routine. He collected the front door key from an outhouse and they entered to explore the premises. It was a typical farmhouse with flagstone floors and an open range. It had seven rooms and looked as if the owners had only recently departed. The kitchen was fully stocked with food and after a meal the four men settled down to talk. Later, when the others had headed off to bed, O'D found that he was incapable of sleeping. He was still agitated after Ballykelly and he feared that sleep would bring the same recurring nightmares.

The night air was warm but a cool breeze blew gently across a wide stretch of the Shannon in front of the house. He walked beside the river, allowing the gentle waves lapping against the grassy bank to soothe the frayed nerves of his mind. He lay with his back against a broad tree and contemplated the scene. A full moon swam brightly in the sky throwing hypnotic patterns of light on the water. He stared unthinking, allowing the magic to sweep through him. Then, quite suddenly, he fell into a deep, untroubled sleep.

He awoke shivering with daylight dew and felt he had slept through death. He walked back to the house with a spring in his step; his depression was gone.

After breakfast the lookouts were changed and the GHQ representatives, whose numbers had grown now to twelve, assembled. The Chief of Staff briefed them on the procedure to be followed in the event of a raid. After the usual greetings, grumbles, banter and commiserations the meeting finally got under way at ten o'clock. No notes were allowed but each man was given a typed sheet of paper with an outline of the agenda:

1. Finance
2. New OCs
3. Unit operations
4. Recruitment
5. Weapons lost
6. Distribution of weapons
7. Strategy

Anyone could scribble on these sheets, but they had to be handed back at the end of the meeting for burning. In the event of a raid each person was responsible for destroying his own notes.

O'D did not play a very active part in the proceedings. The last item was his main interest, where all his ideas were concentrated. As for everything else, he was either reasonably satisfied or prepared to put up with the decisions for the sake of harmony.

'Last item,' said the Chief of Staff, '"Strategy". I don't think we need any discussion on that. Our aim is to create havoc in the North, to bring about the maximum political instability. I just wish we could be creating a little more havoc.'

'We could be,' said O'D.

'What's that, O'D?' said the Chief of Staff.

'I think we're going about this campaign the wrong way.'

'How do you mean?'

O'D outlined the plan which had been fermenting in his head for months. It represented a change of tactics rather than strategy, but such niceties did not require definition at Saor Eire meetings. He proposed that rather than spread themselves out in a full frontal campaign against the British army they should instead concentrate their resources in one area and try to control it.

'What have you got in mind?' asked the Chief of Staff, 'another South Armagh situation?'

'Something like that,' answered O'D, 'only I was thinking more in terms of a city this time. The Brits aren't worried about the country areas — we control plenty of them as it is.

But if we take over and control a built-up area it will give them an entirely different type of problem. An election under those circumstances would be an ideal situation for us to step into the political arena. We would become the main election issue, not to mention an international issue. And Christ knows that could bring the Brits to their knees permanently. Under the right circumstances we could see it becoming a United Nations issue. And that, of course, would be ideal.'

An abrupt silence followed his speech, which was eventually broken by a Belfast representative. 'It sounds good, but haven't we got that sort of situation already in the Falls and the Bogside?'

'Those areas are ghettos,' replied O'D. 'What I was thinking of was an entire city: banks, shops, factories – the lot. We would run it like an independent state and set up a revolutionary council to control it, like the Soviet in Limerick in the Twenties.'

'Wise up, O'D,' said another Belfast man, 'we can't even knock out a fuckin' foot-patrol never mind take over an entire city. We couldn't even take over Ballycastle, for Christ's sake!'

'We could take over Derry,' O'D said calmly.

There was a chorus of laughter and jeers from the Northern men, incredulous grunts from most of the rest.

'Are you serious?' asked the Chief of Staff.

'What do you think?' said O'D. 'Don't think I haven't thought about this. I know every observation post in Derry and the number of Brits in each one. I know the strength of all their barracks, and their main strength lies in the Waterside – that means the opposite side of the river from us. I know all their movements, how they operate, how they think – and I know we can take over the city side of Derry and hold it if we concentrate our energies. In fact, taking it over is a relatively simple operation. The problems really begin when we try to hold it. But even then there is only one bridge and we can control that with little difficulty. Our main problem will be the commandos they send across the river and the paratroopers they drop into the area afterwards. But I think we

61

can still handle it.'

'You've certainly got me interested,' said the Chief of Staff. 'What sort of equipment would it take?'

'More than we have at the minute, but we can always work at that,' said O'D, launching into an inventory of items. 'This is an obsolute minimum, remember: two hundred automatic rifles, two bazookas, twelve GPMGs, twenty sub-machine guns, one hundred shorts, about one hundred grenades. And the rest we can do with molotov cocktails.'

The debate on the proposal swayed to and fro for six hours without a break. In the end it was finally agreed that the plan might just have a chance of success. The go-ahead for initial planning was given and the quartermaster was instructed to go to the continent and set all his contacts working on the collection of arms.

The meeting was just breaking up as the guard-commander came into the room. He went to the Chief of Staff and whispered something in his ear. No one heard, but they all saw and waited expectantly; silence settled swiftly on the room. The Chief of Staff lifted his head and looked straight at O'D.

'Three men have just been shot in Derry.'

'Did it say Heather Lane?' asked O'D.

'I don't think so, but there was something about a piggery.'

'That's it,' said O'D, his face distorted. 'Do you know what happened?'

'It didn't give much in the headline, just said that three men had been shot from a helicopter while setting up a Saor Eire ambush.'

'A helicopter?' uttered O'D in astonishment, 'sure, they don't carry armaments in Derry.'

'Well this one did.'

As soon as the meeting broke up he headed straight for home, arriving at midnight on Tuesday night, and went immediately to Mick Mulhern's house.

Mulhern and Seamus McLaughlin had planted two hundred

pounds of explosives for the ambush the previous Saturday night. Backed up by three snipers they had lain in hiding all day Sunday. But when no soldiers appeared they had broken off, returning to their positions before daybreak on Monday morning. The scouts were posted and the snipers took up their previous positions about fifteen yards apart from each other. Mulhern and McLaughlin were just two hundred yards in front of them and about the same distance from the explosives. McLaughlin had not brought enough cortex to stretch as far as the snipers. He had not extended it after Sunday in case it interfered with the current: too many bombs had failed to go off because of a break in the cortex.

Nothing happened until ten-thirty when a helicopter came from behind them, very low and very fast, and opened fire without warning. Despite the fact that the snipers had been well camouflaged and should not have been spotted from the air, the army flew straight to their positions and opened up. Mulhern and McLaughlin, who had been openly exposed from behind, had nevertheless not been fired on and had escaped. Stories, rumours and half-truths trickled in until finally the picture was complete. The three snipers had been cut to pieces by a .30 calibre machine gun and the two scouts had been caught in the follow-up operation and were being interrogated.

'So you definitely think you were set up?' O'D said to Mulhern when he had heard the story.

'No doubt about it, the chopper knew exactly where to go.'

'How many people knew the exact position of the snipers?'

'The only ones left living outside of the scouts are Seamus, Sean and myself.'

'That's worth a thought or two,' mused O'D in a flat under-statement.

He appeared to forget about the problem as the next fortnight passed in a bustle of activity. O'D was fully occupied organising his OCs into effective area commanders. There were meetings, training sessions and lectures. Their main activities until now had been recruiting manpower and passing it on to the Command Staff for further training and operations. But suddenly they found themselves upgraded to the position where they had to plan, explain and execute their own operations, at least in theory. Rapidly the movement began to take the shape of an organised army. At the end of the first week OCs began sending patrols into the streets to act on their own initiative. In the second week the entire Creggan and Bogside areas were patrolled twenty-four hours a day by Active Service Units. A few shots were fired and an odd skirmish took place, but there were no serious injuries.

At the end of two weeks O'D was summoned to Dublin. From a pre-arranged pick-up point he was taken to a suburban house on a tree-lined terrace where he met the Chief of Staff. In a comfortable Victorian living room John came straight to the point.

'Well, O'D, we have good news. We have everything we need with the exception of the rifles.'

'Have you any ideas for getting them?'

'Yes, we have information on a Brit camp in Germany where we can pick up a hundred SLRs. What we need now is someone to go over and look at it.'

'I'll go,' said O'D, flatly.

'What about your training programme in Derry?'

'That can take care of itself for a few weeks. Where's the camp?'

Four

THREE DAYS LATER he was in Germany with an ex-soldier who had been stationed at the particular camp for two years. It was an open-plan camp about fifty kilometers from Hamburg and lay at the end of a quiet country road near three other camps – one of which housed elements of the German army. It was surrounded on three sides by trees. Inside, it was laid out in four three-storey blocks with various surrounding buildings which were used as garages and stores. The nearest autobahn was only three kilometres away, which would leave a getaway car in Hamburg within minutes. It seemed ideal for a raid.

He made only one reconnaissance trip: the night he arrived both he and the ex-soldier approached through the woods on foot. That was all he needed: as far as he was concerned the job was a relative walkover.

After the reconnaissance they drove straight back to Hamburg. O'D parted with the ex-soldier and then went to look up an old contact. It was the early hours of the morning but he had no fear of being turned away. Jim Murray had emigrated from Ireland two years previously but still had close ties with home. O'D knew him well as they had operated together in what everyone liked to call 'the old days'. He had a flat in a dark, dimly lit street near the docks in Hamburg. O'D approached it with some elation; it was just the quiet, out-of-the-way sort of place he wanted. He rang the bell aggressively as if to communicate his excitement and, as the door opened some minutes later, declared to the squinting face: 'Give us a kiss!'

'What the Jesus!' growled the man in faded jeans. Then recognition dawned and he leapt into the street barefoot and bare-chested, lifting O'D in a crushing bear-hug and exclaiming, 'Jesus Christ, kid, it's great to see you!' Returning O'D to the ground he continued in the same state of excitement, 'What the fuck are you doing in Hamburg?'

'Looking for a job,' answered O'D.

'Doing a fucking job more likely,' said Murray slapping him on the back and repeating over and over how good it was to see him.

They talked until dawn. Mostly they reminisced in alternating moods of nostalgia and joy, but occasionally the talk drifted into more serious consideration of the future. By noon they were approaching the serious business of robbing an army barracks, and they talked as two men versed in similar conversations since childhood.

'I hope there's something I can do?' said Murray, sounding worried in case there wasn't.

'There's a lot you can do. For a start, we need a garage to hold two lorries.'

'No problem there,' interceded Jim quickly.

'You're joking? You mean you know a place?'

'Just at the bottom of the street – about fifty yards from the front door. There's an old warehouse there. I know how to get into it and I also know the caretaker. He never comes near the place. In fact, I usually keep him informed as to what condition it's in.'

'That's incredible.'

'And if it's no good, we can find a hundred more just like it. The place is full of them.'

'I think it'll do,' said O'D smiling. 'That just leaves one problem: a billet for about six men.'

'You can put them up in the flat here.'

'That's out of the question, you could be raided after the hit. Are there any locals you know who might put them up?'

'No problem, kid, there's dozens of 'em.'

'You're making it sound almost too easy. I wish all my operations were like this.'

'How about men for the operation?' said Murray, becoming more animated. 'I wouldn't mind another tickle myself.'

'That's something I hadn't thought of,' said O'D. After a minute's pause, he said, 'Do you know any locals who would be interested in hitting a Brit barracks for a hundred SLRs?'

'Are you jokin'? Half the fuckin' dockers in Hamburg would be interested.'

'I'll tell you what: if you can get three good men along with yourself, we might be able to do it without bringing a crew over from Ireland.'

'You've got a deal.'

'I'll have to confirm it with Dublin first though.'

The following morning he flew from Hamburg airport promising to ring Murray that night. The formalities in Ireland were straightforward. GHQ sanctioned the operation and arrangements were made for the operational materials to be collected in Germany.

O'D only had time for a short overnight trip to Derry. The situation was the same, as he had expected. No full scale operations had taken place, but the streets were being patrolled by Active Service Units which intimidated the Brits. An odd shot from a reasonably accurate sniper was all that was needed to make them keep their heads down. Five days later he flew back to Germany on a different false passport. This time he was accompanied by a volunteer. The promised phone-call to Murray had ensured that he was in the flat when O'D arrived. The volunteer had been lodged with the ex-soldier, with orders to be at the rendezvous point for briefing on the operation.

O'D relaxed instantly in Murray's flat. He dropped casually into an armchair while Jim covered much of the sofa with his ample body.

'What are the Germans like, Jim?'

'They're all good, kid, they're communists,' said Murray, joining the two clauses unintentionally so that it sounded as if their political affiliations made them infallible.

'Yes, but can they operate?' asked O'D a little more realistically. 'Have they been on jobs before?'

'Well, I don't know, kid,' admitted Murray doubtfully, 'but wait till you see them, they're all naturals.'

'I hope you're right, it's a bit late to change them now. Do you think they could panic?'

'No chance of that, kid, these characters are all fanatics. They hate the fuckin' Brits worse than the Provos do – and there's one of them could tear soldiers to pieces with his bare hands.'

Murray's optimism began to rub off on O'D. If it went on much longer he would begin to believe that these Germans really were superhuman. He asked when he would meet them.

'Whenever you like, they're all over at Wolfgang's place now.'

O'D was impressed with the three men. Wolfgang had arms like tree trunks, and gave the impression that he could stop ten-ton trucks. The other two were quiet and intense, treating every statement with an equal degree of gravity whether it deserved it or not. Never a smile crossed their faces; but Wolfgang more than compensated. All three spoke excellent English.

After the introductions and a short general chat about the political situations in Germany and Ireland O'D got right down to the heart of the matter.

'Do you know exactly what the job entails?'

'Ya,' said Karl, answering for the other two. 'You wish to rob an army barracks for rifles.'

'That's right. Do you realise what can happen if we are caught?'

'Ya, we realise,' said Karl, while the other two nodded in agreement.

'Right, that just leaves one problem,' said O'D solemnly.

'And that is?'

68

'You must get your hair cut.'

'That will be fine,' said Karl in his sing-song voice.

O'D's confidence was growing; there was an indefinable quality common to the three men which inspired trust.

On the way back to Murray's flat that night they stopped to inspect the warehouse. To gain access Murray simply hit the lock a smart crack with the heel of his shoe, assuring O'D that it would pop closed again quite securely. Inside the place was massive: it could have held twenty lorries on the ground floor and the same on the floor above. Satisfied, O'D turned his mind to the next problem.

'You know the road structure in Hamburg pretty well, Jim?'

'I do, kid.'

'Could you drive a lorry, say, from the southern outskirts to this warehouse without any problems?'

'Could you drive a lorry through Derry?'

'That means you could then?'

'No problem at all, kid, I could do it blindfold.'

The next day O'D made his way to a Hamburg address which only he knew. Here a bespectacled old man, who could have passed comfortably for a Jewish jeweller, furnished him with the materials for the operation. His English was very patchy, but he managed to get the idea across. Pointing at the box which he had just handed to O'D, he said with great gesticulations: 'Venn vinish, nicht return. Kaputt. Ya?'

'Okay,' said O'D, 'I know what to do with them.'

The old man smiled sympathetically.

That day was Saturday and as yet he hadn't set a final date for the raid. As he drove through Hamburg with the stuff locked in the boot, he decided that it would be used the following night. Army camps were like graveyards on Sundays.

The final part of the operation was the responsibility of a unit which O'D knew nothing about. His instructions were to leave the address of the warehouse with a certain hotel manager in Hamburg. It was to be in a plain envelope addressedsed to a Mr Kugn and, if possible, the estimated time of arrival of the goods was to be included. O'D estimated time of arrival at four the following Monday morning and, with a touch of embarrassment, included details of how to enter the warehouse with the assistance of a shoe.

Final arrangements for the operation were made with everyone concerned that night.

At eleven the following night the seven men drove south out of Hamburg in a minibus and a Mercedes. They carried six 9mm pistols and two military policemen's uniforms.

One hour after leaving Hamburg they were in their first jump-off positions. Wolfgang and Karl were parked in a quiet lane two kilometers from the camp. The other German along with Murray and the Saor Eire volunteer lay in a wood facing the guardroom. Their minds were concentrated on the only lit window. O'D and the ex-soldier drove to within a hundred yards of the guardroom in their hired Mercedes.

O'D switched the engine off and, as a heavy silence surrounded them said quietly, 'Ready?'

'As I ever will be,' was the nervous reply.

Both men left the car and walked casually to the camp. There was no one on duty at the gate so they mounted the guardroom steps. Three pairs of anxious eyes watched their movements from the blackness of the wood.

Once on the wooden veranda they tip-toed noiselessly to the door. O'D could hear voices but there was no knowing how many were keeping silent.

He opened the door and entered, one hand in his pocket holding his 9mm pistol. The Guard Sergeant sat behind a large desk, a Corporal sat in front of it and over the Corporal's head could be seen a Rifleman of the Third Batallion, Greenjackets. He was laughing at a joke the Sergeant had just cracked.

O'D instantly recognised the cap badge. The Greenjackets had earned a reputation of being fearless fighters in Northern Ireland, had even gained the grudging respect of the IRA. He could not hesitate now: if anything even appeared to go wrong he would shoot to kill.

The Guard Commander looked up as the two men entered. He sensed no danger as they both looked like soldiers with their short hair and neat civilian clothes. Until they produced their 9mm automatics.

'Don't move or you're a dead man,' said O'D quietly, pointing his weapon at the Sergeant's chest. The Corporal twisted in his chair to see who had entered and looked straight into the barrel of the ex-soldier's weapon. 'That goes for you too,' said O'D in case he had missed the message.

'What the hell's going on here?' demanded the Sergeant in a loud voice that was clearly intended to carry.

'The next word you utter will be your last,' said O'D with a cool violence which affected everyone in the room. He had just finished speaking when the other three men entered the guardroom with guns drawn.

O'D felt more in control of the situation now. He turned to the Saor Eire man and said, 'These bastards are Greenjackets so watch them if they try anything.' He turned back to the Sergeant, saying, 'You and your two mates on the floor.'

The three complied quickly and silently. Murray and the German were left to watch them while the others entered the room where the off-duty guard slept. Four soldiers lay snoring loudly on iron beds. O'D tapped the first man's cheek with his gun. The man opened his eyes and began to stretch his limbs, thinking it was his guard. Seeing the three figures in the dim, dark green room he stiffened. 'Don't make a sound or I'll kill you,' said O'D quietly. The soldier did not move. The other three were wakened in the same way before being herded into the presence of their prostrate Sergeant.

'Get the cell key,' said O'D, apparently to no one. The ex-soldier moved to a wall-board behind the Sergeant's desk and plucked a key from it. The seven soldiers were locked into a single cell. As the door closed, O'D spoke through the grilled window. 'We're going to be here for a few hours so don't get any ideas about escaping. The first one who tries it

71

will be shot dead. Have you got that, Sergeant?' The Sergeant nodded silently.

Returning to the guardroom, O'D dispatched Murray and the German to collect Wolfgang and Karl. The ex-soldier and the volunteer began changing into their MP's uniforms. There was nothing to do then but wait for the others to show up. The next fifteen minutes dragged slowly. As soon as they heard the engine of the minibus the ex-soldier, now dressed as an MP, left the guardroom to raise the security barrier to the camp. He was about to raise it when Murray called him in an urgent whisper. 'Watch it! There's two soldiers coming from the camp with rifles.' The 'MP' walked calmly to the driver's window. 'Show me a driving licence or something,' he said. Murray reached for the first thing in sight, which was the rental for the minibus, and handed it out the window. The 'MP' made an ostentatious display of reading it under the artificial light of the camp, speaking to Murray quietly. 'Where are they now?'

'About a hundred yards away and approaching, they look suspicious.'

'Okay,' said the 'MP', 'I better warn the others. Don't shoot, whatever you do: their guns aren't loaded. Just sit tight and I'll sort it out in the guardroom.' He stepped back from the van holding the form in view and said in a passable cockney accent, ' 'ang on, mate, till I check this out.' He walked towards the guardroom, pausing as if he had just seen the soldiers. He cocked his head in a gesture of surprise before waving his arm in a signal for them to come to him. Then he stepped through the door and spoke in an urgent voice to O'D.

'The other two guards are coming.'

'How far are they?'

'About ten seconds.'

'Christ!' exclaimed O'D.

He flattened himself against the wall behind the door and motioned the other two with his pistol. 'Make as if you're on the phone, we have to get them in here or they'll alarm the camp.'

The ex-soldier lifted the phone and began speaking – this time with his own accent as he knew he couldn't imitate for long an English accent at close quarters. 'Yes, sir, that's right,' he said into the mouthpiece. 'They say they have come from Nurnberg and that they were to report here. Their bus apparently broke down. . .' He looked up at the window, three feet from O'D's right shoulder, where the guard looked in at him. He waved for them to enter and returned to the phone. 'The stag are here now, sir. I'll see what they have to say.'

The door opened and the two guards entered reluctantly, looking both suspicious and confused.

'Hold on a sec, sir,' said the MP into the phone. He looked at the two men, saying, 'What's your names?'

'Higgins and Heath,' said the first, moving a little further into the room.

'It's Higgins and Heath, sir. Will I. . .'

As soon as the second soldier was fully through the door, O'D slammed it closed. Both men spun, startled, and stared at him. 'What's this?' said the nearest one, composing himself instantly.

'The camp has been taken over by a gang of IRA terrorists.'

O'D was just a little too flippant. The words were barely out of his mouth before the man smashed the butt of his rifle into his face; the movement was so fast O'D caught its full force. His head cracked sickeningly against the door and he slumped sideways away from the wall. He was still conscious as he reached for the rising floor, but only just. He sensed rather than heard the door being wrenched open and the two men scrambling through it. 'Drop them before they alarm the camp,' he muttered at the floor. The two men pounded out the door as the MPs drew their weapons. But there was no need. The fleeing soldiers ran straight into the tree-trunk arms of Wolfgang. Before O'D could raise himself both of them were lying unconscious on the guardroom veranda.

Murray took control of the situation while the volunteer helped O'D into a chair. The two unconscious soldiers were carried into the other cell while Wolfgang went for the minibus. 'How do you feel?' asked Murray, staring intently at O'D.

'A bit numb, but I'll be all right in a minute,' answered O'D gingerly fingering the sticky mess of his face.

'He busted you up pretty bad,' said Murray.

'It certainly feels it, but I don't think anything's broken, is it?

'Are you fuckin' jokin'?' said Murray. 'Your fuckin' nose is hanging under your right eye!'

'There goes my good looks,' O'D quipped. 'You will stop here as originally planned,' he pointed to the volunteer and the third German, 'but only the MP is to go outside.' The statement was directed at the German, but both men nodded. 'If there's any trouble from the guard, just remember that our lives depend on it so don't hesitate to shoot them. The noise won't travel far outside this place.'

Five of them climbed into the minibus and headed for the nearest three-storey building. Once inside they went to the Duty Corporal's room. In each building the man responsible for the armoury slept on the ground floor. The first door they came to was locked: O'D knocked twice before getting an answer.

'Who's there?' snapped a voice from inside.

'Duty Officer,' said the ex-soldier in a passable public school accent. 'Open the door.'

They could hear the man stumbling as he groped for his clothes in the dark, but he didn't argue. He had barely unlocked the door before it crashed in on top of him and the two men came tumbling after it. The one with the busted face grabbed him by the windpipe and placed the cold barrel tip of a gun against his ear. The Corporal blinked; he started to say something but changed his mind.

'Where are the keys to the armoury?' snapped O'D.

'Corporal Watson is responsible for them.'

'Where does he sleep?'

'At the other end of the corridor.'

'Show us the room. And don't try anything stupid or I'll kill you.'

The same play was successful on Corporal Watson. At the mention of the Duty Officer he was out of bed and had the door open in seconds, only to be shoved violently onto the bed again by O'D and Murray.

'Where are the keys to the armoury?'

'What do you want them for?' he answered stupidly.

'How would you like your balls left in the same condition as my face?'

'They're hanging behind the door,' he said timidly.

Once the armoury was located the two captives were bound and bundled into it as a replacement for the weapons. O'D was elated with the haul as it was far above their most optimistic estimates. As well as two hundred SLRs there were also four GPMGs, six Sterling SMGs, twelve Browning 9mm pistols and twelve thousand rounds of assorted ammunition. The second MP was left outside to guard the minibus while the others loaded it. Their only fear now was an unexpected appearance by the Duty Officer. But he did not appear. The minibus, loaded down with weapons and personnel, creaked back to the guardroom. It had taken exactly thirty minutes to empty the armoury.

When everyone was assembled O'D addressed them quietly. His voice did not carry to the cells. 'The two MPs,' he said, 'will stop here until five and then take off in the Mercedes. You have the address to go to and you know how to get there. As soon as you get clear of the camp area, tear the false number plates off the car and dump them with the uniforms and weapons. Your alibis will have to carry you from there. Any questions?'

'Just one,' said the volunteer. 'These characters who have a description of your busted face' – he nodded towards the overcrowded cells at the rear of the guardroom – 'will we nut them?'

Karl wasn't familiar with the colloquialism but he grasped the implications instantly. 'No killing unless it is absolutely necessary,' he said forcefully.

O'D agreed. 'Okay, Karl, we want as little pressure as possible. They won't be killed unless they are stupid. Okay?' he asked the MPs.

'Right,' came the answer.

The five set off for Hamburg as fast as the overloaded minibus could be coaxed along the autobahn.

At exactly five o'clock the two MPs walked briskly out of the camp and turned towards their Mercedes. Just over a hundred yards along the road, out of sight of the camp, they climbed into the dark-coloured car and sped away. Two miles later they stopped at the side of a deserted hedge-lined road and changed into civilian clothes. The uniforms, guns and false number plates they dumped into a deep, wooded valley. Then they drove off.

One hour after leaving the camp the three Germans were dropped off; O'D and Murray drove straight to the warehouse. O'D's face was beginning to hurt badly by then; but the pain kept his mind concentrated on one problem at a time, the next hurdle to be negotiated. When they reached Murray's flat he went straight to the bathroom and examined his face. What he saw shocked him: a jagged scar of torn skin mingled with dried blood and splintered bone. There was more blood on the outside of his face than under the skin, which was ashen. The sight made him weak with nausea. Maybe the volunteer had been right and the witnesses should have been killed. One thing was certain, he could not attempt any border crossings.

Five

AT SEVEN THE same morning a 32-ton articulated truck parked outside the warehouse and two men climbed out. After a minute's delay with the lock they entered the building; the massive doors swung open and the giant truck inched backwards. As soon as the doors closed the men fell silently to their task. A dusty morning sun filtered through the massive windows as they loaded their truck. An hour later the truck pulled in at a lay-by outside the city and both men got out to change the vehicle's English number plates for Irish ones. They gave the seal a final check in daylight and then the lorry was on the road again eating up the concrete in the direction of France.

The police were very much in evidence as they neared Hannover, but the traffic was only slowed to walking pace and waved on as it passed the roadblock. Only two trucks were being checked on the hard shoulder. Essen told the same story; they were slowed but not checked. They were speeding along the river Rhine to Frankfurt, Kaiserslautern and the border crossing at Saarbrucken with checkpoints getting lighter all the way. The border check entering France was more stringent than the others. A queue of traffic stretched for almost a mile, edging forward like a rusty conveyor belt. As the lorry came to a halt at the crossing its documents were demanded by a sweating customs official.

He checked the lorry's final destination, Dublin, and then checked the seals on the doors. All was in order. The lorry had left Austria the day before and driven straight to Hamburg for another load. The driver was invited to an overheated, overcrowded portakabin where the appropriate paperwork was completed. He continued on his journey.

By noon the following day the driver and his mate were safely lodged in London, where they went on the town, having parked the lorry, securely locked, on the property of a friend. In the morning they checked the lorry and found it exactly as they had left it, then climbed heavily into the cab and set off on the last leg of their journey to Holyhead. The ferry crossing was rough but they rolled off the boat in Dun Laoghaire in high spirits; the driver handed his papers over for inspection with a flourish.

'Did you stop in Germany?' asked the customs man after checking the route.

'I did,' answered the driver, just a little too ostentatiously.

'Pull into that empty bay over there,' said the official coldly before walking away with the papers.

The driver did as he was told and parked the lorry. As he climbed out of the cab he saw the official approaching with two uniformed colleagues and a civilian whom he recognised as a branchman.

'We're going to search you.'

'Search away.'

The branchman nodded his head and the officials climbed into the cab. They began to examine it a square inch at a time.

'How long did you stop in Germany for?' asked the branchman.

'Just for a night,' answered the driver reasonably.

'What did you stop for?'

'We had to pick up in Hamburg.'

'What did you pick up?'

'It's on the sheet in your hand there.'

The branchman did not look at the sheet, but stared coldly at the driver. 'Where did you stop?'

'Bed and breakfast.'

'What address?'

'How the fuck should I know, I only stopped there a night.'

'Don't get cheeky with me, son, or I'll lift ye,' the threat sounded like a challenge.

The seal was broken and the entire contents of the lorry unloaded and every box opened. Then the floor, walls and roof were checked. It was almost two hours later when the original official jumped from the back of the naked lorry and declared: 'It's clean.'

The branchman looked at the litter of cargo with a mixture of disgust and disappointment and mumbled angrily, 'Let them go, so.'

Fifteen minutes later the lorry was hurtling along the dual-carriageway into the sprawling suburbs of Dublin and the driver and his mate were still laughing.

'The fuckin' eejit didn't even ask about our stop-over in London,' spluttered the driver, wiping tears of laughter from his face.

That night an unmarked Special Branch car pulled into a deserted car-park in a quiet area of Derry. A figure walked quickly from the bushes and entered the car, which then drove to a quiet country lane on the outskirts of the city. Sergeant Taylor spoke as he switched off the engine: 'Well, what's new, Seamus?'

'Nothing's been happening since O'D went away,' said Seamus McLaughlin, Saor Eire explosives officer.

'When did he go?'

'The middle of last week sometime.'

'Do you know where he went to?'

'There was a rumour that he was going to Germany, but I don't know if it's true or not. The Staff didn't talk about it anyway. I think the only one who knows anything is Mulhern and he never says a word.'

'Did anyone else disappear off the scene at the same time?'

'Naw, no one. If he had taken anyone else, I am sure the Staff would have discussed it. Do you think he was involved in that raid in Germany?'

'Do you?'

'Don't know, but the rumours are beginning to start.'

'What jobs have you planned for the future?'

'None at the minute, but I'll let you know as soon as they plan any.'

The morning following this meeting with McLaughlin another report reached Belfast RUC Headquarters at Knock Road. The southern Special Branch reported that a member of a Saor Eire Active Service Unit could not be located and that rumour had it that he was in Germany. The collated information was quickly relayed to New Scotland Yard, who immediately relayed it to Interpol with a request that both men be located and put under surveillance.

O'D's face had become excruciatingly painful. The numbed nerves and the adrenalin shooting through his body had delayed the onset of pain, but when it came it came in spasms which threatened to become unbearable.

'What time is this contact supposed to arrive at?' he asked Murray.

'He should have been here by now. I don't know what's keeping him.'

'I think I'm going to need a doctor for my face. Do you know any sympathetic ones?'

'I know a nurse,' said Murray hopefully.

'What's she like?'

'She's as sound as a bell.' It was the best compliment Murray could pay.

The doorbell rang. Murray smiled to himself, answered it and a minute later showed a tall, slim German into the room.

'Heinz, das ist Henry,' said Murray, confusing O'D completely.

'Wie geht es Ihnen?' asked the German, doubly confusing him. O'D nodded his head and tried to smile away his crooked face. But confusion remained on both sides.

Murray didn't bother to explain. 'He's going to Italy for a month today so we not only have his flat but also his car.'

'That's great,' said O'D. 'Tell him I thank him.'

Heinz handed over his keys. Immediately after showing him to the door Murray returned and said to O'D, 'Let's get you to this nurse before you bleed to death. Heinz reckons you look as if you're about to faint.'

Murray drove the car to a quiet flat on the outskirts of the city. The nurse, called Ingrid, had just returned from night shift in a local hospital. O'D was introduced and they were invited into a comfortable two-roomed flat. It was lavishly decorated with knick-knacks and souvenirs from many corners of the world. Murray did not beat about the bush.

'Ingrid, me darlin', we have a problem.'

'I think I can see it, Jim,' she said in perfect English, looking at O'D's face.

'Hugh is over from Ireland and he's in a little bother,' said Murray with over-acted simplicity. 'He needs someone to look after his face and put him up for a few days.'

'That's new,' thought O'D, 'I don't need to be put up.' But then, he thought, it would be much more convenient if he was.

Ingrid approached O'D as he sat rigidly on her small sofa and took a close look at his face. 'He must see a doctor immediately.'

'Doctors are out, Ingrid, me darlin'.'

'Have you done something?' she asked without a hint of suspicion, as if she were asking him if he had cigarettes.

'Yes, we've done a lot,' said Murray gravely. 'We're going to be very unpopular for a while.'

Ingrid gave a peculiar and very individual shrug of her shoulders. It seemed to indicate that it did not matter to her. She took a closer look at O'D. 'But this face,' she cried with a gesture of hopeless concern, 'I can do nothing. It must be stitched. And the nose is broken badly.'

'We can do nothing until we at least hear the news,' said O'D looking at Murray.

Ingrid pouted her lips and raised her eyebrows to indicate that she thought the decision was insane. O'D began to find her mannerisms attractive; they gave her an air of innocence which was irresistible. He smiled a twisted smile and said, 'Could you get me something to kill the pain.'

'You have much pain?' She was interested in the degree as opposed to the fact.

'Yes, quite a lot.'

She disappeared into the kitchen and reappeared almost immediately with two tablets and a glass of water. 'Take these,' she ordered. 'Now I clean your face,' she said seriously.

'I better get back and make sure the flat is clean,' said Murray. 'Are you happy?'

O'D raised his hand in a gesture of satisfaction, and said, 'You'd be best to move out of the flat for a while.'

'I might go to Heinz's place now that you're lodged here. I'll keep in touch.'

Ingrid let him out and returned immediately to O'D's face. She cleaned it expertly and then, much against her profess-ional pride and in the absence of a needle and gut, closed the wound and held it together with sticking plaster. The tablets affected O'D within minutes and he became completely relaxed. He thought about the pain; it was still there, but he just did not seem to care.

At lunchtime Ingrid translated the German news and explained about the Irishman with the scarred face who had raided a British army barracks. 'But they didn't say how many guns you got,' she said disappointedly.

'I didn't count them,' said O'D. They both laughed.

After a light lunch, which he had difficulty eating, she said, 'You should rest now. You will be very weak. You will be more comfortable in the bed,' she continued, 'and I won't mind.' She made it sound like an important concession, but he thought this was a function of her accent rather than any ideas about sex.

'Not at all,' he said stupidly, 'I wouldn't dream of depriving you of your bed.'

'You won't be depriving me,' Ingrid answered patiently; 'the bed is big enough for two.'

'Oh, I see,' said O'D, who wasn't sure what he saw, but he hoped.

He stumbled naked into bed and wondered what was going to happen next. Ingrid looked to him like a beautiful German goddess, and he found it hard to accept that she hopped into bed with every scarred cripple she met. She had to be more particular than that. But on the other hand, she might just be talking about sleep. She was. Five minutes late she came from the bathroom in a black ankle-length nightdress which left no room for doubt. It showed off her full breasts and accentuated the delicate bulge at the bottom of her flat belly, but it was definitely just for sleeping in.

'If the tablets wear off and disturb your sleep, you must waken me that I get you more. Okay?' she asked.

'Okay,' agreed O'D as he lay back, closed his eyes and slipped immediately into thankful oblivion.

He awoke at six the following morning and thought it was the evening of the day before. His body ached and his face was angry enough to claw. He tried to get out of bed, but his head spun violently. He sat down heavily, then saw the note propped against a glass of water on the bedside locker.

Dear Hugh,
I have to go to work and I don't want to disturb you. Two more tablets are on the table and will do you until I return at 6.30. You would be better to stay in bed all the time as you will be weak through loss of blood.
Ingrid.

O'D took the tablets and slid between the sheets again. The pain had just begun to dull when she returned. She came straight to the bedroom.

'Ah, you are awake,' she said with a smile. O'D felt a surge of happiness at the sight of her, and for some indefinable reason he had the impression that she felt the same. 'Just,' he answered.

She sat on the side of the bed. 'I see you have taken the tablets. How do you feel?'

'They're just beginning to ease the pain.'

'Just beginning,' she began anxiously, 'but when did you take them?'

'Just before you came in.'

'You mean you did not waken?'

'Slept like a baby.'

'Good God! I am amazed, but it is very good. . . I've brought some sterilized material from the hospital so that I can stitch your face. Otherwise it will take so long to heal and the scar will be awful.'

'Whatever you say, nurse, you're the doctor.'

She prepared the materials in a surgical dish, scrubbed her hands and returned to the bed. 'Now, I think it's best that you lie on your right side so that I can work,' she said with precision. O'D obeyed and she worked with steady concentration. 'That's not very well,' she said, 'but at least it is better and will heal much quicker.'

'Feels fine,' he said diplomatically.

'Pooh,' she said, pouting her lips, 'I think you say that if it is falling off! Now I must clean it and then we bandage.'

He propped himself against the pillow as she washed the dried blood from his face and cleaned the wound. She was sitting on his right side and had to lie across him to get to the left side of his face. O'D could feel her body across his hips. She was not wearing perfume, but he caught the smell of her fresh sweat. He placed his right hand on her hip, letting it rest there. He felt a charge ripple through his body. He stared intently into her eyes, but she continued to work on his face. His hand applied the barest suggestion of pressure to her hip, further stimulating him but seeming to do nothing for her. He slid his hand casually up to her waist.

'You break my concentration,' she said huskily.

'Sorry,' he apologised, 'it's difficult.'

'There,' she said, beginning to move back, 'you look much

84

better now.'

'So do you,' he said, staring at her and forgetting about his face.

She stopped moving and returned his stare. 'You know, you are very weak.'

'I feel as strong as a bull,' he returned quickly.

'I feel as strong as a bull too,' she said, 'but I don't think you should be excited.'

'Ah,' he said. 'Does that mean you don't want to?'

'Oh, no, I want to, but I think of you.'

He raised his hand slowly and delicately touched the side of her face, and there was no more talking.

His hands glided over her body and occasionally assisted in removing her clothes; five minutes later both of them were lying naked on top of the bed. Her hand found his erect penis and as she massaged it he felt as if he were permanently on the verge of orgasm. After what seemed a blissful eternity she pushed him gently onto his back and began kissing down his chest, gently biting his nipples, licking his naval and taking his penis in her mouth. She began to run her tongue along the cord of his foreskin, but she had barely begun when his seed rose uncontrollably.

'Oh, Christ!' he moaned, almost out of his mind with pleasure.

They were wakened in the early afternoon by the doorbell. Ingrid put on a dressing gown and hurried to answer it. Murray entered the flat breezily. 'Well, kid, how's the face?'

'Not so bad now.'

Ingrid smiled and O'D chose to ignore it.

'Has my contact turned up yet?' asked O'D as Ingrid left the room.

'He did, and he's still prepared to take you by car if you want to go.'

'That's out of the question now with this face.'

'You're right,' agreed Murray soberly.

'Let's leave it for a day or two and see what happens.' Murray readily agreed, pleased to think that O'D had other things on his mind than escaping from the country.

It was two day later before he returned again, but this time his sharp edge had been blunted. 'Bad news, kid,' he greeted O'D. 'The two volunteers were arrested in England this morning.'

'Damn it!' O'D's voice held both anger and sympathy for the two men.

'I'll make some food,' said Ingrid quietly.

O'D scribbled on a piece of paper and handed it to Murray. 'Get to a phone at exactly seven o'clock Dublin time tonight and ring this number – it's clean so don't worry about what you say as long as your end is clean. Ask for John – he knows you – and tell him the situation. Tell him I can do nothing at the moment with this face and that I need a more secure route out of here. . . oh, and you better tell him you are calling for 'Hamster One'. That's my code word.'

'Thanks for telling me,' said Murray. They talked over a few more details and then, after Ingrid's hastily prepared meal, Murray repeated the instructions to make sure he had them word perfect and left.

Ingrid tended to O'D's face again and they fell into a comfortable conversation which lasted well into the evening. O'D experienced little surprise in discovering that most of their ideas were compatible. He found her thoughts and insights interesting and her mannerisms entertaining. When she departed for her last shift of night duty before a seven-day rest period he felt he had known her a long time. He woke in the morning to find her creeping in beside him. She dropped into his arms naturally and they made slow, passionate love as if nothing else in the world existed.

Afterwards they talked seriously about insignificant things, enjoying the sound of each other's voices until Murray interrupted again with the now unwelcome doorbell. Ingrid let him in as O'D dressed, and now after making coffee, she did not leave the room. Instead she handed round the cups and sat beside O'D on the sofa. He let his hand rest gently on her thigh and squeezed it occasionally to indicate something they were both sure of.

'Well, I got through on the phone,' said Murray.

'Was John there?'

'Aye, he sends his best regards and says not to worry, that he'll arrange something else. I have to phone him back tonight. He told me not to forget to give you his congratulations as well.'

'Did he mention the two men lifted in England?'

'Naw, didn't mention anybody, just said to tell you it was a good job well done.'

There was nothing to do after that but wait. O'D and Ingrid spent the rest of the day amusing each other. She did not go to bed at all, with the result that after they made love that night she fell immediately into a deep sleep.

Murray dutifully appeared with news the following morning. An alternative route was being arranged and would be confirmed in a few days. In the meantime he was to keep his head down as the police forces of the whole of Europe were apparently looking for him.

That night Ingrid said simply, 'I shall miss you when you go.'

O'D stared deeply into her clear blue eyes. 'I wish I could bring you to Ireland so that we could sleep in another bed.'

Suddenly she burst into tears, sobs shaking her body. He took her in his arms and whispered what he hoped were appropriate words of comfort. After a few minutes she calmed down.

'What was all that about?' he asked eventually.

'I think I love you,' she said, her face puffy and tear-soaked.

Three days later Murray arrived in a sweat and panted, 'You have to be ready to move in an hour's time.'

O'D felt a knife of disappointment slice through him. For an instant he toyed with the idea of refusing to go. The thought of wrenching himself away from Ingrid at such brutally short notice was a pain he did not wish to inflict on either of them. But he knew there were no options.

'How do I go?' he asked.

'Don't know, your original contact man just landed at the door and told me he would pick you up in an hour. I told him it would take me an hour to get in touch with you so he made it two hours, but he wasn't too pleased about it.'

'Fuck 'im, I've been waiting long enough for him', O'D said, aware that his reaction was completely out of character.

Ingrid had disappeared suddenly into the bedroom. He found her sitting on the bed staring blankly at the wall when he entered. She seemed to be in shock. O'D thought she probably was but all he knew for certain was what he had to tell her. He had been preparing the words for days so that it would all sound reasonable and logical and well thought out but when he began talking the words tumbled like potatoes out of a busted sack and he was left feeling empty, useless and deserted.

'I don't know how to say this, girl,' he began. 'You have been very good to me and very good for me and I would like it to go on. But if it did I would tear myself in two because I have dedicated my life to a cause and both of you would interfere with each other.'

'I understand,' she said simply, short-circuiting his complications.

They spent the hour ignoring Murray, talking to each other in the bedroom. When the door-bell rang they both emerged with red-rimmed eyes. There was no time for anything else after that. O'D left the flat for the first and last time and barely managed to kiss Ingrid a last goodbye before being bundled into the back of a large container lorry.

'Where the fuck am I going?' he asked with more than a little annoyance as the door was being closed on him.

'We will drop you off at the docks where you will get a boat to Ireland,' said the contact, closing the door and bringing an end to any dialogue.

O'D felt like kicking himself for having slipped. He knew

better than to ask questions about someone else's operations. There was an unwritten code of conduct which said that people in transit must have a blind faith in their contacts, otherwise the whole system broke down in disorder. He perched uncomfortably on top of some boxes and found his thoughts escaping back to Ingrid instead of forward to the docks and freedom.

The lorry worked its way through the flow of suburban traffic to the centre of Hamburg. He rocked gently in the back, his thoughts interrupted only by the occasional stops for traffic. In the throbbing darkness he could feel the muffled beat of his heart against his chest. He recognised the stop which signaled the entrance to the docks. They were stationary for a longer period and no traffic noises filtered through. He guessed they were not at their destination or his contact would have told him, but decided to take no chances. He climbed quietly across the awkward load to the front of the lorry and crawled into the best hole he could find. The lorry began to move again after what seemed like five or ten minutes and only then did he realize that he was sweating. Two minutes later it stopped again and he heard the driver climb out. Footsteps moved to the back, a few fumbled noises, and then a burst of blinding sunlight flooded the interior as the doors swung open.

'Okay, you can get out now,' said the contact.

O'D clambered into the brightness, blinking and squinting. It took him a few seconds to adjust to the light, then he noticed that he was standing between two long rows of deserted warehouses. The contact told him the next stage of the plan.

'At the other side of this warehouse', he pointed, 'is a ship called the 'Macushla'. You must go on board yourself and ask for Captain O'Sullivan. He is expecting you by the name of Lynch. I am sorry I cannot go with you. It would be suspicious for me.'

'That's okay, you've done enough,' said O'D extending his hand.

The ship was being worked by various gangs of dockers as he approached it. They hardly cast him a glance as he climbed the gangplank, perhaps assuming he was just another Irishman who had got himself badly mauled in a fight. A sailor with flaming red hair and freckles almost bumped into him as he stepped onto the deck.

'Excuse me,' said O'D, 'could you tell me where I'll find Captain O'Sullivan, please?'

'Sure, along this way.'

O'D followed, dodging the man's enquiries. They stopped in front of a door and the sailor knocked loudly.

'Come in.'

'There's a man here to see you Captain, says his name is Lynch.'

A stout elderly man in the uniform of a merchant navy captain appeared at the door and glared at O'D's bandaged face. 'Ah, Mister Lynch,' he said cheerfully. 'I was wondering when you were going to show up. Come in, come in. Take a seat,' he went on, pointing to a large armchair beside – O'D was astonished to notice – a blazing turf fire. 'How's your face? It looks bad.'

'It was bad,' said O'D, 'but the pain has left it now and I think it is on the mend.'

'Apparently there's a bit of a panic to get out?' said the Captain.

'How did you know?'

'I got a message to phone Dublin this morning and they asked would I take you.'

'I see. . . You know the form then?' said O'D

'I know the form, son,' said the weathered old man, smiling.

The ship sailed that afternoon, made one quick call at a port in France, and docked in Cork three days later. The only officials O'D came in contact with were customs officers and he was in the sick bay for the duration of their visit. They barely glanced at him, and were told by the Captain that he had burned his face in a galley accident and that a German doctor had advised him to keep the wound covered until they reached Ireland. The ship had hardly docked at Cork when the Captain entered his cabin.

'There's a lift ashore for you.'

O'D removed the bandages before leaving the ship, not that it made any difference to the man who greeted him at the bottom of the gangplank.

'Ow are 'ou, boy,' roared Finbar Barry, in a thick Cork accent, as if they were at opposite sides of the river. He grabbed O'D's hand, shaking it violently and slapped him on the back, almost breaking his spine. ''Tis glad I am to see 'ou, boy!' Every word was shouted at twice the normal speed and sound of language.

'Are you trying to alarm the dockside?' said O'D smiling, but still showing his apprehension.

''Tis a little late for that, boy,' shouted Finbar, seeming to vary his vocal cords an octave on alternate words. 'Sure don't they know already.'

O'D glanced at the dockers nearby as he entered Finbar's car: they were nodding and smiling at him and one old docker raised a bony hand and shouted: ''Twas a grand job, lad!' O'D felt he should have been angry, but such a surge of emotion filled him at the old man's reaction that he was incapable of anger.

'Finbar, I thought my arrival would have been a close secret?'

''Twas, boy, 'twas. Sure only the dockers knew of it,' came the reply.

There was no answer to that. 'Only two hundred dockers on the Cork docks,' thought O'D. 'Then all the pubs in Cork tonight – and tomorrow the world. Great ways we have of keeping secrets in Ireland.' It would have been futile to say anything to Finbar who would immediately have launched into the family background of every docker to prove their pedigree. Instead he sat silently until Finbar began pumping him for all the information he was prepared to impart. After a blow by blow account of the journey and a rendering of the recent history of his face, O'D was going to Limerick for a debriefing.

The fate of the weapons had been decided well in advance of the lorry reaching Dublin. In the early hours of the morning after its arrival in London a second lorry had reversed into the cul-de-sac where it had parked. The driver of the first lorry had been given explicit instructions to drive straight into the entry. With both lorries parked back to back, the four men in the second lorry had immediately set about opening the doors of the first. Five minutes of manoeuvring had located the crates in question. In a further five minutes they were in the second lorry. Both lorries had then been locked and the second lorry had driven off through a sleeping London.

That afternoon it boarded the ferry out of Stranraer and drove ashore at Larne just four hours later. Two hours after that it drove into Derry and unloaded its entire contents into the premises of a private haulage contractor. It had been travelling for seventeen hours without being stopped at any checkpoint.

Six

FINBAR DROVE TO a farmhouse in the fertile, rolling hills of County Limerick. As the car entered the farmyard the Soar Eire Chief of Staff and the adjutant general emerged smiling from the whitewashed house. The Chief of Staff did not offer to shake hands. 'I'm glad to see you, Hugh,' he said. 'How's the face?'

O'D was quickly briefed on the situation. The two volunteers were still detained, and obviously being interrogated, at an unknown destination in England. The good news was that the stuff had arrived and had been safely dumped in Derry. O'D gave his report on the operation.

The Chief of Staff returned to the practical problems confronting them. 'That last operation went very sour in Derry,' he said, shaking his head and wrinkling his face with distaste.

'I know,' said O'D solemnly. 'It looks as if it was a setup.'

John's slow, country drawl became even more deliberate. 'Do you think you might have an idea about who done it?'

'I have an idea, that's all, but it'll have to be worked out later.'

'There's something else you'll have to work out,' said the adjutant general joining the conversation.

'What's that?' asked O'D.

'We have information on a spy working in your area.'

'How good is it?'

'It's the best,' said the Chief of Staff. 'Some of his reports were intercepted in England.'

'Who is he?'

'A character by the name of Hanley, he lives in a mansion just outside Derry.'

'I know him,' said O'D quickly. 'We suspected him of spying over a year ago. He was seen driving about the area a few times for no apparent reason so we picked him up and questioned him.'

'Why did you let him go again?' asked the Chief of Staff.

'I think mainly because we were afraid of the consequences of shooting him at the time. We were very unsure of ourselves then and it was impossible to prove that he was spying. The only evidence we had against him was that he was a member of the landed gentry.'

'Well, we certainly have enough for shooting him now. I want you to put him down as soon as possible.'

'Right,' said O'D, 'I'll see to it as soon as I get back. Now, what about this stuff Dublin was supposed to get for us?'

'We have two bazookas and a rocket-launcher in Dublin,' said the adjutant, 'and there's half a ton of jelly in Limerick waiting to go up. In fact you'll be travelling with the scout car in front of it.'

'That sounds grand,' said O'D. Derry now had more stuff than his men had ever contemplated.

After a meal O'D was driven a few miles to another farm for explosives. They were stacked in the middle of a five-ton open-backed lorry and neatly surrounded by a load of turf. It looked like a common, everyday turf lorry. The procedure of the scout car which O'D travelled in was a well-practised one. The car drove as far as possible in front of the lorry while they both kept each other in sight. If they ran into an unscheduled roadblock, the driver of the car pumped the brake gently with his left foot while still pressing the accelerator with his right. Once the driver of the lorry saw the brake lights flashing he parked the lorry until the road was clear. The attraction of this procedure was that the lorry could stop at least one bend before a roadblock, and thus avoid detection. It did not matter how long it had to remain at the side of the road: no one ever noticed anything suspicious about a lorry-load of turf.

The trip passed without incident. There was only one permanent road-block to negotiate; it was a combined Army/Garda checkpoint on the Ballyshannon bridge and it was strategically placed to catch all traffic flowing into Donegal from the South. But this strategic position was the very factor which rendered it ineffective. Everyone bringing contraband materials across the bridge took precautions to counteract the check.

The scout car and lorry parked at the side of the road just out of sight of the bridge. O'D got out of the car and walked. He had just reached the bridge on foot when the two vehicles passed him together and halted at the checkpoint. The driver of the car presented a Northern Ireland driving licence.

'Who owns the car?' asked the Guard suspiciously.

'Friend of mine in Dublin,' said the driver with deliberate carelessness.

'Where are you taking it now?'

'Derry.'

'What's your business up there?'

'I'm just going up for the run to see some friends, like.'

'I see,' said the Guard. 'Just pull into the centre of the road there for a search.'

'Holy fuck!' exclaimed the driver. 'How long's this going to take?'

'Not long,' the Guard replied, and it was clear he did not mean it.

He turned to the driver sitting patiently waiting in the turf lorry and waved him through without a glance at his licence. As for the man with the badly scarred face walking across the bridge, he did not even see him.

Half an hour later the car stopped on the northern side of Ballyshannon and O'D once more climbed into the passenger's seat. The lorry pulled out of a parking space and fell in behind them as they passed. Once again the distance increased as they sped through the familiar countryside. Almost two hours later they drove into a farmhouse deep in the rugged hills of the Innishowen peninsula in north Donegal. The farm was a regular transit dump for army materials coming from Dublin. The explosives would remain there for a few days before being dispersed to other sites. While the lorry was being unloaded O'D was driven to a quiet border crossing where he walked into Derry.

Once there he went straight to Mulhern's house. The front door opened before he got within five yards of it and Mick greeted him with a startled expression. 'Jesus, you look awful.'

'Thanks, you don't look so beautiful yourself. What have you been doing?'

'Keeping out of the road mostly: the Brits are raiding for me.'

'Ah,' said O'D in an I-told-you-so voice.

'. . . and trying to keep the machine oiled.'

'I hope you did a good job because we have a big operation coming up.' They had moved into the empty living room now and O'D threw himself on the sofa.

'Hold on a minute,' said Mick taking the chair opposite him, 'I want to hear about the last one first. You did the German job, didn't you?'

'Aye,' and once again O'D launched into the details.

Mulhern was surprised and delighted with the story. 'Do you know a description of your face has been broadcast all over the world?' he said with childlike admiration.

'Stop exaggerating, Mick,' said O'D coyly, 'it was only all over Europe.'

'I stand corrected. But what I really mean is, do you not think you had better do something about it?'

'There's nothing I can do at the minute, and even if there was I wouldn't be able to do it as we have too much work here. Like, for instance, I want to put an operation on for tomorrow night.'

The adjutant was immediately deflected. 'What is it, a hit?'

'It's a nutting job.'

'Oh, fuck.' That meant it was a serious matter as opposed to a few wildly aimed shots fired at an unsuspecting foot patrol. 'Who is it?'

'A spy in the Waterside.' O'D explained the details and then named the people he wanted on the job.

That night a meeting of the Command Staff was held in Creggan, but the job wasn't mentioned. Instead everyone was informed of the German raid and told to prepare for an intensive period of training. The fact that the arms had arrived in Derry was also kept from the Staff.

Twenty minutes after the meeting had ended Sergeant Bill Taylor received a call at his home number.

'This is me here,' said a voice on the end of the line.

'I'm on my way,' said the Sergeant. He replaced the receiver and then lifted it again and rang the Strand Barracks.

'Give me extension thirty-two,' he told the operator on duty.

'Yes,' answered the extension.

'Bill here. I'm on my way to meet one of the Soar Eire informers, will you open a channel and keep your ear to the radio in case I call in?'

'Will do, Bill. Do you want any back-up?'

'Keep a car clear just in case, but do nothing unless I call. I'm meeting him at the usual place.'

'Right, Bill, I'll look after it myself.'

Sergeant Bill Taylor was taking no chances. He felt reasonably secure as he drove into the quiet car-park and picked up Seamus McLaughlin. 'Well, what's new?' he asked.

'O'Donnell is back with a busted face,' said the informer.

'That's interesting.'

'Yeah, he told us about the German job.'

'So it was definitely him then.'

'Aye. He told the Staff as well that they would have to prepare for an intensive period of training. He gave the impression that he was going to train the whole of the movement in Derry.'

'Did he say anything about the weapons?'

'Naw, but he left us in no doubt that we will be getting

97

some of them.'

'Did he say when?'

'That'll be decided by Dublin. They'll have a meeting and then allocate the weapons to the various areas. That's what they usually do.'

'Find out as much as you can about that and let me hear anything you pick up.'

'Good enough.'

'Has he got any more jobs in the pipeline?'

'Naw, he seems to be concentrating on this training thing.'

'That's good. Don't forget to let me know as soon as you hear anything.'

The following day all Saor Eire OCs were visited by the brigade adjutant and told to report for a meeting at eight. It was a top-security meeting, which meant they could tell no-one.

Thirty minutes before the meeting began a beat-up Ford Cortina, containing four men and a variety of equipment, crunched to a halt in the gravelled forecourt of Clive Sebastian Hanley's Georgian mansion near Greysteel, County Derry. The mansion was hidden on three sides by trees and shrubbery, but the driveway ran down an open slope of green lawns and multi-coloured flowerbeds and commanded a majestic view of Lough Foyle two miles away.

A tall figure came storming through the front doors and across the marble porch as the battered car crunched to a halt.

'I say, you chaps,' he called in an agitated Oxford accent. 'What the bloody hell do you think you are doing? Get that contraption off my property this instant.'

Four heads stared from the car, regarding him as if his existance were irrelevant.

'Do you hear?' he shouted, looming over them. 'Are you workmen or something?'

'Aye, that's right,' said one of the men, producing a Magnum revolver and pointing it at Hanley's stomach.

'Oh, I see,' said Clive in a voice that instantly hinted of courtship. He almost smiled, but could not quite make it. 'You are IRA chappies, are you?'

'Aye, that's right,' repeated the man with the gun.

'I suppose you want me to do this?' Hanley raised his hands into the air in an obvious attempt to warn someone in the house.

'Put them down again or I'll blast you all over your marble pillars,' said the gunman. And then to one of his companions: 'Liam, cover the back.'

Liam leapt from the car and disappeared at a trot round the side of the mansion. Hanley had turned white. His voice trembled as he spoke.

'I never agreed with the policies of the Unionist governments, you know. They gave the minority a shocking deal.'

'Fuck up,' said the youngest member of the group.

The gunman spoke again. 'How many people are in the house?' Then as an afterthought, he added: 'And you only get one chance to get it right.'

Hanley crossed his arms in front of his chest in an unsuccessful attempt to stop them shaking. 'Only my wife, my sister and two servants,' he said quietly.

'Are they watching us now?'

'They are probably on the phone to the police at this very moment.' Hanley was determined to put up some sort of fight.

'Mister, you don't have a phone: the Post Office just disconnected you five minutes ago.' The gun flicked towards the mansion. 'Let's go and meet the family.'

Hanley turned and began to walk as the gunman spoke to his two remaining companions. 'One of you come with me, the other get the gear.' Then to Hanley he said, 'Hanley, you know what sort of gun this is, don't you?'

'I thought it was a .357 Magnum,' Hanley answered.

'And you know what it'll do to you or your two lady friends if you are stupid?'

'I have an idea.'

'Good. Don't be stupid.'

They paused in the grand entrance hallway of the mansion, with the gun placed firmly against the small of Hanley's back. The second man, now sporting a Thomson sub-machine gun, moved to the bottom of the staircase and partly concealed himself behind the bust of an ancient Roman figure. 'Get everybody assembled here,' the gunman commanded.

Hanley called his sister and wife in a trembling voice. They emerged through a door on the left. Neither of them spoke; there were no protests, no enquiries.

'Where's the servants,' demanded the gunman.

'Probably in the kitchen,' returned Hanley.

'Tell your wife to get them.'

Hanley nodded and his wife disappeared. In less than a minute she was back again with two elderly servants. The gunman then ordered the five captives into the library. They were all ordered to sit down.

'Now,' said the leader, 'I'll tell you what's going to happen.' He paused long enough for everyone to accept the idea that he was giving orders. 'We are going to blow up this beautiful, artistic, stinking house of yours.'

Mrs Hanley gasped loudly and put her hand to her chest as if to steady her heartbeat. Clive Sebastian spluttered, 'Good God, man! are you mad? Do you realise what this house is worth? It's one of the most valuable houses in Northern Ireland and of enormous historical interest. You will be wiping out a valuable part of your own culture if you raze it.'

'Correction, Mister Hanley,' said the gunman, 'we will be wiping out a part of your culture, which is a lot different from mine.'

'At least let us save some of the paintings – there is a wealth of art here which will never be replaced if you destroy it.'

'You must be joking,' said the man derisively. 'Let you save an art treasure that is the exclusive possession of the upper class? An art treasure that me and my class would never set eyes on? Don't make me laugh – that's the first bloody thing that's going up! Eddy!' he called angrily, and the man with the Thomson SMG entered the room. 'Keep them covered and if one of them even moves from a sitting position – blast them.'

'Right,' said Eddy, and there was not a shadow of doubt that he would do it.

The last member of the team was in the process of negotiating two large sacks of equipment through the front door as the leader left the library. 'Sort the stuff out here while I get Liam,' he ordered.

A large well-kept lawn at the back of the house revealed Liam with his Sterling SMG pointed dangerously at a defiant gardener. 'So they thought they were pulling a fast one?' The leader took a step closer to the gardener and glared at him threateningly. 'How many people are in the house?' he demanded.

'I don't know,' was the obstinate reply.

'It'll cost you your life if you don't.'

'I wouldn't tell you even if I did know.' He spat the words bravely.

'Nut the cunt,' said the leader, turning on his heel and walking away.

'Kneel down,' Liam ordered, lifting the Sterling.

'You're not serious?' The leader was striding back to the house.

'Wait a minute,' the gardener called. 'Wait! I'll tell you!'

The leader turned and looked at him.

'There's six people,' said the gardener, a quaver in his voice. 'Sam and Sally, the two servants, the master, his wife and his sister, and then myself. That's all, honest.'

'Did you say "the master"?' asked the gunman in disbelief. 'Jesus Christ! I thought that went out with Queen Victoria. Bring the old idiot inside.'

The gardener was led to the library where Liam took charge of the captives. The other three set about the task of preparing the house for demolition.

They began with the twelve bedrooms. The inside corner of each room was drilled to allow a hole to the room below. When all the rooms were drilled explosives were placed in the

101

corners nearest the centre of the house. Detonators were placed in each charge and a length of cortex dropped through the hole to the floor below. Explosives were then attached to the ground floor and the cortex extended to the front door. The grand reception area of the mansion now looked like the inside of a telephone exchange. White strands of cortex crossed and criss-crossed along the floor to wind themselves finally into a single strand at the entrance.

'Give it a final check and make sure all the doors are closed, then take it half-way down the drive,' said the leader. He entered the library as the two men bent to the task. 'Everybody outside,' he ordered, 'and watch your step.'

The captives left the house in single file. Once outside they were halted in a bunch until the volunteers appeared with the cortex. The leader addressed them, 'All of you, with the exception of "the master" here,' – he indicated Hanley with a sarcastic wave of his weapon – 'are going to take a walk round the back of the house. You will then go straight up the hill until you come to the first farmhouse – that's about a mile away. When you get there you will not phone the police for one hour. If you phone them before that, Mrs Hanley, your husband will be shot. Is that clear?'

'What are you going to do with my husband?' asked a frightened Mrs Hanley.

'We are going to hold him hostage to ensure that you don't phone the police. Now get movin'.'

Mrs Hanley looked anxiously at her husband who attempted to smile reassuringly at her. 'Go along, my dear, I'll be quite all right,' he said. She attempted to move towards him, but a threatening gesture from Liam's Sterling stopped her. 'Go along,' Hanley said firmly, 'I'll be quite all right.' He almost managed to sound annoyed.

His wife turned and stumbled towards the back of the mansion, followed by the sister, the gardener and the two servants. As soon as they were out of sight the team in front of the house set off down the driveway, leaving their car behind and taking Hanley and the cortex with them. One hundred yards

102

from the mansion they moved off the driveway and took cover behind a large tree. As one of the volunteers stopped to prepare the cortex for detonation, the team leader turned to Hanley.

'Kneel down.' Hanley did so. 'Now tell me this: how long have you been spying for the Brits?'

'What?' said Hanley, his voice suddenly hoarse with real fear. 'I have never spied for anyone.'

'We know you're a spy, you bastard, so don't deny it!' the words were spat at him.

'I admit that I have a few friends in the British army and that I visit Ballykelly occasionally, but these are purely social visits, I assure you.'

'Say your prayers,' said the gunman without sympathy, staring into the upturned eyes.

Hanley fell into an eternal silence. His eyes dropped from the glare of his accuser and he stared at the blades of green grass between his knees.

'Ready,' said one of the volunteers, holding two contact wires between his fingers.

'Let her rip,' said the leader.

The blast lifted the roof off the house and hurled it at the sky in a thousand fragments. Simultaneously two shots rang out from two guns behind the tree. Both bullets entered Clive Sebastian's head, throwing him to the ground like a discarded rag doll.

The house caved in on itself and not a single marble tile landed in the forecourt. The explosive charges had been placed in such a way that the interior of the building had collapsed first. In the resulting vacuum the shell was dragged inwards. The mansion was razed to a six-foot pile of rubble. Both it and the man who had owned it lay as dead as if they had never been created.

'Let's get out of here,' said the group leader.

As the mansion exploded the Saor Eire meeting in Derry was coming to a close. Hugh O'Donnell was summing up.

'You have all got the picture now,' he said, glancing round the assembled faces. 'There is plenty of gear, but we must train the men how to use it properly before sending them out on the streets. There will be no cowboys-and-indians episodes round the area. No hijacked cars with weapons that no one knows anything about. From here on everyone will be an expert on the weapon he handles. And we must train all the men, not just a few elite ASUs. That's why this training course will be spread over three months with twenty men going on an intensive training course each week. Operations will still go ahead while this is taking place – that's essential to keep the Brits out of the area – but the main priority will be directed towards training more than anything else. I'll be in charge of the first week myself and I hope to see all the best section leaders there.' He paused to let the message sink in and then said, 'That's it. The day after tomorrow each of you will have four men at the pick-up point in Donegal at exactly eleven. I hope there's no more questions.'

The five Battalion OCs seemed satisfied. Their constant complaints were that they never had enough stuff and that their men were not properly trained. Now they conveyed their contentment and left the meeting place at staggered intervals. When the last man left, O'D turned to his adjutant. 'Well, Mick, what do you think?'

'That was dead-on. They looked as happy as a bunch of wanes on Christmas morning.'

'Good, what have we got to do now?'

'First thing is to get thirty SLRs out of the dump and get twenty of them across the border. The other ten will go to Con McDaid – and you have to tell him yet that he is taking over as OC while both of us are out of town. After that we head for Killybegs.'

'Let's get to it then.'

As soon as Mrs Hanley and her companions reached the nearest farmhouse, they explained their predicament and asked to use the phone. The first number she rang was that of Superintendent Len Haslitt whom she knew personally. He answered the phone himself.

'Lenny, this is Ann Hanley, I'm afraid something dreadful has happened.'

'Yes, Mrs Hanley, what is it?'

'Greysteel has been blown up and Clive has been kidnapped. I'm phoning from a neighbour's house at. . .'

'Good God!'

'Yes, the house is levelled, but I'm more worried about Clive. These people took him away. . . Heaven knows what they might do to him.'

'Of course, of course.' Haslitt was struggling to pull himself together. 'How many of them were there?'

'We saw only four, but I don't think there were any others. They were driving a box-type Cortina, a red one, registration number UI2908.'

Haslitt reached for a pen and scribbled the number. 'Right, Mrs Hanley, we'll get onto it straight away. You stay where you are until I come and see you. What address are you at?' She gave him the address and telephone number and he rang off to contact the barracks. He spoke rapidly and excitedly.

'Block all roads coming into Derry on the Waterside and look out for an old box Cortina, registration UI2908. And get all available cars out to Greysteel: the Hanley mansion has been blown up. Have you got that? And tell the army at Ballykelly to seal off the area. I'm on my way out there now.' He slammed the phone down and snatched his coat from a peg on the wall.

When he arrived at the Hanley mansion he discovered a police landrover blocking the entrance. The two constables on duty saluted as he approached. 'Are you the first here?' he asked.

'No sir, there's another landrover up at the house. Sergeant Hogan's in charge of it.'

He walked past them and entered the driveway. As he turned the first bend he saw a small group of constables at the base of a large oak tree just of the driveway: they were examining a body. Sergeant Hogan saluted informally as he approached.

'Who is it?' asked Haslitt breathlessly.

'Mr Hanley, sir. Shot in the head. Made an awful mess of him.'

The body lay crumpled, with knees bent, on the bloodstained grass. The face was still intact, but half the head had been shot away. Haslitt stared at it in shock and disgust. 'The bloody bastards,' he muttered.

'There's nothing left of the house only rubble,' said Sergeant Hogan, 'and there's a battered Cortina.'

'A red one with a UI registration?'

'That's right, sir.'

'That's the car they came in,' said Haslitt urgently. 'It must have broken down. That means they could still be in the area on foot. For Christ's sake! Spread your men out, spread out, Sergeant, and tell them to keep their eyes peeled.' He started running towards the gate, calling over his shoulder to the diminishing group. 'Check the car for a clue to who the bastards might, but watch you don't spoil the fingerprints!' He was entirely out of breath when he reached the landrover.

'Have you got a frequency open to the army?' he gasped at the young constable.

'No sir, just the barracks.'

'Get them on the air and tell them I want to speak to the superintendent in charge.'

The young constable ran to the radio and relayed the request. The radio crackled.

'Sunray speaking, what's up?'

'John, this is Len here. I am. . .' He ducked in a sudden reflex movement as a massive explosion ripped the air. Hundredweights of shrapnel went flying in all directions and the percussion of the blast, even at that distance, gripped his head.

Early the next morning Mulhern and O'D set off in a rented car for the County Donegal fishing village of Killybegs. The Saor Eire OC for the area was Pious Doherty, who lived on a small hillside farm on the rocky Atlantic coast about three miles from Killybegs. It was a tortuously inaccessible place, approached by a scarred track which was bordered alternately by boulders and bog. From the front door of the small, thatched cottage with whitewashed walls was a view of wild, dramatic landscape. Behind lay the wide expanse of the Atlantic ocean, and far to the south this was interrupted by the purple of the Mayo mountains which sat eternal and majestic on the horizon of Sligo Bay.

Pious was digging a drain at the side of the cottage when he saw the car approaching. He was leaning on his spade as it came to a halt.

'That's the classic stance of the Donegal peasant,' said O'D, emerging. 'Leaning on his spade watching the world instead of bending his back to the work.'

A welcoming smile cracked across Doherty's weatherbeaten face. 'By God, if it isn't an unemployed Derryman. I'm surprised that you know what a spade is.'

The three men greeted each other warmly with much handshaking and back-slapping.

'Did you get any word from Dublin?' asked O'D, coming straight to the point as he settled into an antique armchair in front of the open turf fire.

'I did,' was the reply. 'Is this plan of yours serious?'

'It is.'

'Christ! You really intend to take over Derry?'

'We'll do it in one night.'

'One night? I don't believe it.'

'That's all it will take. With the right training, and if everything goes according to plan, the entire city this side of the Foyle will be in our hands in the course of a night.'

'By God,' said Pious. 'I don't know when it's taking place, but I hope you're putting the Killybegs unit on it.'

For the rest of the day they toured the remote farmhouses

107

and cottages which would feed and house the entire member-ship of the Derry brigade over the coming months. The occu-pants were delighted at the prospect of housing two different volunteers from Derry each week. All of them, to a man and woman, adamantly refused to accept payment for their services but O'D persisted and finally got a tacit agreement from most houses to accept £10 per week. It was late that night when he and Mulhern set off for north Donegal again. At two o'clock in the morning they pulled into a cottage not far from the Derry border. It was to be the last sleep they would have in proper beds before the training started.

They rose early and in the village of Bridgend collected a furniture van and parked it at the rendezvous at exactly eleven. Twenty men, silent and sombre with anticipation, clambered into the back of the lorry and the doors were closed on them. The interior offered the spartan comforts of six mattresses and a single lightbulb, which dimmed and glared in harmony with the revs of the engine. Some of the men recognised familiar faces from different batallions, others were surprised to see people they did not suspect of being involved in the movement. Conversation came slowly in the unfamiliar circumstances. The only local OC to accompany the group climbed into the cab beside O'D, who wanted company for more than one reason: he wanted a first-hand account of the reaction in Derry to the shooting of Clive Sebastian Hanley. He had heard the news broadcasts, which had offered condemnations from the usual sources, but what he was really interested in was an account of the British army's activities. The army, it seemed, had raided numerous Provo houses after the shooting and picked up at least twelve, all of whom were released when the Saor Eire statement claiming responsibility had been received by the press. The OC, from Rosemount, suspected that some Saor Eire houses had been raided that morning but he was unsure; he had stayed away from his own home the previous night and all he had heard was rumour.

The lorry did not go near the billets in the surroundings of Killybegs. Instead it drove to a hillside forest about five miles from the area; everyone climbed out, stretching their limbs and stamping their feet. O'D assembled them in a clearing of sun-speckled leaves surrounded by gentle undergrowth, and though the talk was serious the atmosphere was relaxed and open. O'D, sitting with his forearms resting on his knees, might have been a country rambler resting against a tree for a midday break.

'You might as well relax as it's the last chance you'll have for a week,' he began. 'The rest of the day we'll spend talking and looking over the maps you have been issued. Then you will be given the grid references of your billets, and that's when the training starts.

'Just a word about the billets before I go any further: don't abuse them. These are ordinary people who are putting you up and they are putting themselves out a lot to do it. They will probably feed you more than they eat themselves – they always do. I want you to think carefully about this. The only food you will be getting will be in the billets; outside of that everyone, including me, will starve. So don't make pigs out of yourselves.

'Another point to bear in mind: after today you will be arriving at your billets at all hours of the day and night. I want you to use your heads about this. If you land into a farmhouse at four in the morning, don't go banging on the door looking for your bed. All the places you are stopping at have outhouses and some of them have haybarns, so think of the people who are putting you up and shack down in the outhouse or barn.

'Now the training itself. Everything you will be asked to do over the next week has been well thought out with a specific purpose in mind. Some of it won't make sense and will be hard to put up with, but it is all part of the course and it will all help to develop your thinking in the right way for what we intend to do in Derry. So, whatever you are asked to do, do it with a will.'

After detailed explanation of what the course entailed he asked for questions. They flew freely, provoking long discussions which stretched into the afternoon. Finally the gathering broke up and Mulhern gave each man the grid reference of his sleeping accommodation. Each pair had to make their way to their billet and report to a rendezvous point in the hills on the following morning. O'D and Mulhern walked to Pious Doherty's house where they stretched for the night in two sleeping bags before the open fire.

Next morning everyone assembled on time, chatting excitedly in the first flush of a new adventure. The rendezvous was an old ruined farmhouse surrounded by well-spaced trees. The place looked as if it had been abandoned since the famine; the roofs had long ago caved in but one outhouse had been repaired. It lay in a large bogland valley about three miles long by a mile wide. Green, barren hills surrounded the valley giving the impression of a deep, sunken bowl. Only one road crossed it, running north-east to south-west. The men lay in the deep grass in front of the ruins. There was a crispness in the air which seemed to sharpen even the songs of the birds.

'The first thing we want,' said O'D holding three walkie-talkies in the air, 'is three volunteers to operate these.' Twenty hands immediately shot up; he pointed to three, gave them the sets and directed them to Mulhern. A few minutes later two of the men were walking in opposite directions across the valley to cover the only openings to the single road; the third man stayed in the planting.

'Next we have to sort out what to do if we are raided,' said O'D. 'We have ten rifles here and whatever else we lose, we don't want to lose them. So here's the routine. The biggest ten men will grab the rifles if I give the word.' He carefully selected ten. 'You lot will follow me across the hills if we have to get off-side. The rest of you will stop here with Mick and fight off whoever comes so that we can get clear. Any questions?' There were none.

The training began at last. First every man was taught how to load, reload, strip and reassemble a rifle. They were paired off in twos again with a rifle between each pair which they pulled and prodded and persuaded to yield up its secrets until everyone could strip and reassemble the rifle blindfolded. A makeshift firing range was erected behind the ruins and each man was given two targets, one for his own use and one for assessment at the end of the period. The bog echoed to the sound of gunfire: nine men at a time lay firing into the eastern hillside; when they expended two full magazines their partners replaced them.

Next the squad was broken up into groups of five with the object of launching mock attacks on the ruins. Two men were allocated the task of defending, along with O'D and Mulhern, who perched themselves conspicuously on a mossy wall to observe the tactics of the three groups. Two groups stalled, unable to decide why their OC and adjutant were occupying such an exposed position. The leader of the third group moved to the tree-line where he spread out his men warily. Then he sent one man crawling forward in the long grass towards the two defenders on the ground floor of the ruins. Had it been a real attack the man would have killed one defender before the other had spotted him. As it was an argument ensued as to who saw whom first, and while this was being debated the leader ran his group into the ruins and quietly occupied it. The other groups, seeing the objective achieved, made an infantile charge on a crest of shouts and yells.

The analysis of the attack lasted for over an hour. Then three new leaders and two new defenders were selected and the process began again. A halt was called late in the afternoon to change the scouts, and the exercise resumed; by ten-thirty all were heading for their billets with instructions to report to the rendezvous at the same time the following morning.

Two people went astray on the way back and, ironically, one of them was Charlie Coyle, who had led the first attack on the ruins and who had received the highest marks of the day. His partner was navigating and it was almost midnight before Charlie realised that something was wrong, and quickly discovered that they were completely lost. After getting the general bearing by the stars, Charlie struck out for the coast and after a long and ill-tempered trek brought them both to the house. Not wishing to disturb the people of the house at that late hour they bedded down in the straw which lay between the cottage and the outhouse.

Some six hours later Mrs Sweeney went to fetch some straw for the hen-house. As she approached the wall she noticed a pair of feet protruding. 'Good Mary, Mother of God!' she exclaimed to herself. She drew closer until she saw another pair of feet and a denim-clad knee. At that she bolted to the back of the cottage where her husband was stacking turf.

'Mother of God, John,' she said breathlessly, 'come quick: I think the two young fellows have been murdered!'

John Sweeney dropped an armful of turf and strode in the direction his wife's finger was frantically pointing. 'In the straw,' was all she could say as he stormed past her.

He drew to a sudden halt at the sight of the two pairs of feet. For a moment he lifted his head like a dog sniffing the wind, then he glanced suddenly as the pile of straw moved.

'It's all right, Mary,' he called as he prodded the two figures. 'They're only sleeping. What are you doing out here, boys? Why didn't you come into the house?'

Charlie parted the straw, blinking, 'Hello, Mr Sweeney. We were late: didn't want to disturb you.'

'Sure, you wouldn't have disturbed us at all: I left the front door open and Mary left sandwiches on the table for you.'

For their breakfast they ate a pound of bacon, eight eggs and nearly two whole loaves. Mrs Sweeney watched as they consumed the meal. Two hands reached for slices of bread, buttered them, fed them into their mouths like paper into shredding machines; then the hands reached out again. When at last they sat still she asked doubtfully, 'Have you had enough boys?'

The second day was occupied with an elaborate initiative test. The furniture van was already at the camp when everyone arrived, and O'D addressed them from the tailboard.

'The object of this exercise is to see how well you'll handle

112

yourselves on the run. What we are going to do is close you into the back of the lorry and drop you off at intervals in quiet parts of the country. What you have to do then is get back here as quickly as possible by whatever means you can.'

'How are we going to know where we are when we are dropped off?'

'You won't,' said O'D with a smile. 'That's where the initiative comes in. Any questions? No? Good, let's go.'

Heads turned simultaneously to look at companions in disbelief.

'Oh, just one last thing,' said O'D as they began to move uncertainly towards the van. 'There is one rule on this exercise: no hijacking.' Everyone laughed except O'D himself.

The first stop was just south of Galway after a manoeuvre which had the lorry approaching the town from the south. The second pair was dropped on a mountain road in County Limerick. Others were deposited at points on a nationwide, erratic circle which stretched as far east as Dublin and as far north as Drogheda and Monaghan. After a winding route through counties Cavan, Leitrim, Sligo and Donegal, the lorries arrived back at the ruins just before midnight.

Charlie Coyle and Jim McCallion were dropped off on an anonymous back road. All they knew was that the time was seven o'clock in the evening.

'Which way do we go now?' asked McCallion, glancing up and down the road as if he were waiting for a bus.

'North.'

'North? Why north?'

'Because that's the way the lorry's going.'

'Why are we following the lorry?'

Charlie sighed. 'Because I think we've been travelling south most of the day.'

A mile later they reached a signpost which indicated that Balbriggan lay three miles to the east. McCallion wanted to head for Monaghan and take the shortest route, but Charlie wanted to stick to the busiest roads by first heading south to Dublin and then striking west towards Mullingar. After a few

113

minutes' argument he strode off leaving McCallion to stand and then to follow. It was almost dark when their first lift brought them into Dublin. They walked to the Mullingar road.

Two hours later no car had stopped. 'What do you reckon, kid?' asked Charlie as he stared at the disappearing tail lights of a car: 'Will we go back to Dublin and get the first bus to Derry?'

'What? You wouldn't do that would you?' McCallion was shocked.

'I'm sorely tempted.'

'We'd be shot.'

'It's either that or find some transport.'

Charlie walked in the direction of the city. Two hundred yards down the road stood a Triumph 1300 saloon in front of a detached bungalow surrounded by a wall. Charlie walked around the car checking the doors: they were locked. He tested the boot and it sprang open. A toolbox was neatly stored there and after rummaging in it for a few seconds he withdrew a heavy-duty screwdriver.

'You surely won't open the door with that?' asked McCallion glancing anxiously at the house behind the wall.

'Just watch me.'

McCallion did not take his eyes off him as Charlie inserted the screwdriver in the lock and turned it, opening the driver's door as easily as if he had inserted the key. McCallion's jaw dropped as he saw Charlie disappear inside the car and reach over to open the passenger's door. The ignition was already lit on the dash before he settled into the passenger seat.

'We're in luck, kid,' said Charlie enthusiastically, 'the bloody tank's full.'

The screwdriver turned again and the engine whined into life and a second later the car was rattling down the road towards Mullingar. It made one stop before the next village to remove the numberplates from a Fiat 600 parked near a roadside cottage and put them on the Triumph. At four-thirty in the morning they drove into the valley and parked the car in front of the path to the ruins. They entered the circle of flickering light where two figures sat beside a fire. The OC and adjutant looked up without surprise. 'Where'd you get the car?' asked O'D.

'Dublin.'

'Did you change the plates?'

'Aye.'

'Want a drop of rubbery tea?'

'Aye.'

The next bout of training began that afternoon. An hour on the firing range woke them up, then they split into two groups, one led by O'D, the other by Mulhern. When they were sorted out Mulhern led his group across the valley at a trot and within minutes they disappeared over the nearest hill.

O'D explained the idea to his own group. 'Mick is going to divide his section into two units. One of them will take up a defensive position about ten miles from here. The other will go to ground somewhere around the same area. What we have to do is attack and capture the first group's position and then find the second group.'

After a period in which he allowed everyone to throw out ideas, they set off at a leisurely pace. The country they travelled was rough, but the mild, summer weather made the journey more of a pleasure than a chore. A few songs at regular intervals along the route, mixed with some stories and a multitude of wisecracks, created a holiday atmosphere. It was early evening when they halted about a mile from the target; a disused slate quarry.

'Settle down and relax, we are going to be here for a while,' said O'D.

'Have you decided on a plan then?' asked one of the volunteers.

'Aye,' said O'D. 'We'll rest here for about eight hours and let them worry about us. Then when they are at their lowest ebb, about four in the morning, we'll hit them. That sound okay?'

The plan was acknowledged with nods of approval.

At three-thirty the following morning they broke camp, stamping the night's coldness out of their feet and marching under a sky pebbledashed with stars. Only four men were sent to cover the horse-shoe entrance to the quarry. The rest approached from the rear armed with bundles of bullrushes and pockets full of stones. The quarry was sheer at the back with only two relatively safe places where anything other than a mountain goat could descend.

They approached the edge cautiously and peered over. In the moonlight they could see the dark shadows of four men sleeping against one wall and a fifth sitting on a small boulder with his head hanging almost between his knees. O'D directed Charlie Coyle to take five men down one side while he negotiated the other. They began to descend in single file. The first man was on the ground before the dozing sentry realised something was wrong. He leapt from the rock with a hysterical scream which roused the camp. His companions scrambled frantically to their feet, but before they could orientate themselves they were further confused by a shower of burning bullrush torches followed rapidly by a hail of stones.

The battle had commenced now and past loyalties were momentarily forgotten. The object of the exercise was to sub-due the opposition and it was tackled with a fierce will. The fact that friendly obscenities were hurled from one side to the other, then amended and flung back again, did not diminish the ferocity of the affair. But from the beginning the defenders didn't have a chance. The light from the burning bullrush torches in their midst blinded them to everything beyond the glow, and stones raining out of the darkness ensured that they would suffer an early defeat.

'Do you give up?' shouted O'D above the insults and screams.

'Aye,' answered Mulhern with relief at the sound of the familiar voice among the attackers. 'Stop throwing for Christ's sake before you kill someone.'

The battle stopped and friendly relations were resumed with little animosity. Casualties were examined and sympathised with as if all had been injured by a common enemy. One man had an open wound on the left side of his temple and four more had bruises on their arms and legs.

At first light all fifteen men set out in search of the remaining five. There was only one valley where they could have been, but it was a large one. It was broken up into sections on the map for the purpose of searching each one systematically. They had just begun when Charlie Coyle's attention was caught by a group of bales of hay: they were stacked together in a block, while the rest were scattered singly about the field. Coyle and O'D approached the stack together while the rest of the group tagged along behind. The top bale was removed and they looked into the shelter to discover two pairs of bloodshot eyes staring up at them like those of trapped rabbits. 'You have just been captured by the enemy,' said O'D by way of greeting. The other three men were not as easy to flush out as they had concealed themselves in the deep ferns of the hillside. It was three hours before anyone saw a sign of movement. Once the alarm was raised, however, they were quickly captured.

The same exercise was repeated that night with O'D's squad being hunted. They were captured without any injuries being inflicted, though Charlie Coyle could not be caught in the follow-up search. He surrendered voluntarily on Saturday morning with nineteen voices echoing around the hillsides that the exercise was over and would he come out so they could all go home. The thought of returning to his billet and getting some decent food for the first time in two days brought him out of the ferns at a trot. The men arrived back at their billets lean, hungry and taciturn. Most of them ate the meals provided and collapsed into bed without even washing, some did not even remove their clothes.

The last training period of the week's camp entailed assembling and discharging molotov cocktails, making nail-bombs, handling explosives for boobytraps and, finally, a sample of night shooting. All of the men were already familiar with molotovs and explosives but this time they were taught how to handle them in the calculated, unheated way of the professional saboteur. On Sunday the course ended and the furniture van set off for the Derry border. It stopped at Bridgend and twenty-two hardened men, a little drawn but fit and cheerful, descended on the local pub. From there they were picked up in varying stages of drunkenness by a fleet of taxis and private cars which had driven from Derry to collect them.

Seven

THE DAY BEFORE the Donegal exercise ended Con Mulcahy was approached by his OC in the Finglas area of Dublin and told that he had to do a run the following day.

'Game ball,' chirped Con. 'What time and where to?'

'Ten o'clock,' said the OC, 'you'll be told where in the morning.'

'Can you tell me how long I'll be gone at least?' queried Con.

'You should know better than to ask a question like that,' said the OC severely. 'I don't even know where you are going myself, and if I did I wouldn't tell you.'

'All right,' said Con jovially. 'Don't get your jockstrap in a twist. I only wanted to know so's I could tell the mot, like.'

As soon as he left the OC, Con went straight to a public telephone and dialled a number in Dublin Castle; shortly after nine he was sitting in Inspector Porter's car in a quiet suburban avenue on the south side of the city. His small, wiry figure turned to face the burly Inspector.

'I have to do a run tomorrow,' he said.

'Where to?'

'I don't know, they wouldn't tell me.'

'Do you know what you're carrying?'

'Haven't a clue, but I think it might be stuff for the North.'

'What makes you think that?'

'The OC tried to tell me he didn't know where I was going,

119

but I know he was lying. The fact that he won't tell me makes me think it's the North.'

The Inspector tore a page from his notebook and scribbled on it.

'As soon as you know what it is and where you are going, give me a ring at this number.'

'What are you going to do, stop me along the road?' There was a hint of alarm in Con's voice.

'No way,' said the Inspector convincingly. 'We'll keep out of sight and watch what they do with the stuff at its final destination. You might be moving some of the rifles I was telling you about.'

'That's what I was thinking too,' agreed Con.

At exactly ten o'clock the following morning a taxi called for Mulcahy and took him to an upper-class residential area on the east side of the city and a leafy, Georgian mansion surrounded by what looked like a small forest of trees. There he was presented to the quartermaster general.

'You've done a few runs before?' was the only preliminary.

'Yeah.'

'Well, this is the most important one you've ever done. You will have a souped-up Triumph 2000 Estate and in the back of it will be two bazookas and two rocket launchers. And I don't want you to lose them.' The tone was like a sharp slap in the face to Con, an indication of what might happen if he did lose anything. The quartermaster general indicated a man standing at his side. 'Kieran here will be doing the dummy run for you. If he gives the signal I don't want you to just ditch the car, I want you to attempt to get it off-side. Your OC reckons you can do a handbrake turn no bother, so try that and get the car at least a mile away from any roadblocks before parking it. Kieran will come back for you as soon as he can. Got it?'

'Game ball,' said Con, wondering how he was going to make a phone call on the journey. 'Am I allowed to know where I'm going now?'

'You don't have to know where you're going,' said the

quartermaster general, 'just follow the car in front.'

Con sorted out the signal routine with Kieran and five minutes later both of them were driving west. They pulled into the car-park of the bar in Bridgend at three o'clock. Neither of them knew O'D, but Kieran had a vivid description of him as the man with the broken nose and badly scarred face.

At the counter they waited to be served, but no one appeared. Several hours before, the bar had been a madhouse of noise with over forty Derrymen either going to or coming from Killybegs. But they had departed now and only two silent figures remained, both of them engrossed in newspapers in front of a blazing fire.

'Where's this fucker with the broken nose, then?' said Con, beginning to feel uncomfortable in the comparative silence. The two papers rattled instantly into crumpled heaps.

'Is that the fucker there?' asked Mick Mulhern, pointing at O'D with his mutilated paper.

'You O'D?' asked Kieran.

'That's right. Are you Kieran?'

'Yeah. We didn't see you behind the papers,' he said by way of an apology.

'That's my fault,' said O'D, 'I didn't hear you come in. Where's the stuff?'

'Outside in the Triumph.'

'Good,' said O'D, 'we'll take it from here. You might as well have a pint and a pie till we come back.' He glanced at Mulhern, who immediately rose and went behind the bar for the order.

'Is there anywhere I can make a phone call?' Con blurted out.

O'D smiled with his teeth. 'This isn't the most tactful time to ask that. With the amount of paranoia in the country, the first thing everyone will think is that you want to phone the Guards.'

Con blushed and his Adam's apple gave an involuntary swallow. 'I only wanted to phone my mot,' he croaked lamely. 'I'm supposed to see her tonight.'

'What time?' smiled O'D coldly.

'Am. . . ah. . . eight o'clock,' stammered Con.

'In that case you don't have to worry,' said O'D losing the smile. 'You'll be home before that if you take the short road down.'

Mulhern placed two pints on the bar and removed two pies from the microwave oven. 'If the barman appears while we are gone,' he said, 'which is unlikely, just tell him that we'll be back shortly and we left you two in charge.'

'Left us in charge?' asked Kieran, looking from Mulhern to Con and back again.

'Aye, that's right,' said Mulhern, disappearing out the door behind O'D.

Kieran stared at the empty bar with mild curiosity, then said to Con, 'Trusting sort of characters, aren't they?'

'Fuckin' eejits if you ask me,' said Con lightly. 'Drink up and I'll buy you another one.'

'Yeah, but make it the last,' said Kieran in the voice of someone giving an order, 'we have a long drive back.'

Mulhern and O'D were gone only thirty minutes. They drove the two cars straight to the transit dump near Buncrana, checked the materials, dumped them and drove straight back again. The two Dublin men were nursing the dregs of their second pints when O'D and Mulhern returned.

As soon as Mulcahy was free in Dublin he rang Porter.

'What the hell happened you?' barked Porter angrily.

'They wouldn't let me make a phone call,' said Mulcahy lamely.

'Did you do the run?'

'Aye'.

'You stupid little bastard! Why the fuck didn't you make an excuse to go to the jacks in some bar and phone from there?'

'I tried that Inspector, honest, but they came with me and wouldn't let me phone.'

'Where did you go to?' he asked with a tone of patronising disgust.

'A place outside Derry.'

'Where about?'

'I'm not telling you over the phone. Will you pick me up?'

'I'm on my way.'

Porter was still in his office in Dublin Castle at ten o'clock that night. It had taken until that time to get through to Buncrana Garda barracks by telephone. And all he could do when he did get through was to tell them to keep a sharp lookout for any Saor Eire activity in the area.

As soon as they left the bar in Bridgend O'D and Mulhern drove straight to Derry on an unapproved road.

'What time is the Command Staff meeting organised for tonight?' O'D asked as they negotiated the road.

'Nine o'clock, I think'.

'We'll just discuss the training programme and leave everything else to a later date.'

'What about the object of the training, are you not going to tell them about that?'

'Not yet, I want to be more sure of my ground where Seamus is concerned.'

'He's a bit of a problem all right,' agreed Mulhern. 'Have you decided what to do with him?'

'No, but he will have to be watched.'

The Staff were content with a detailed report on the week's training. The new activity injected a sense of excitement into the meeting which made the thought of operations almost irrelevant for the moment. The excitement was further heightened by the news that another ten SLRs were coming into the city. Nothing else was discussed and the Staff left the meeting in a state of high spirits.

Less than an hour after they broke up Seamus McLaughlin and Sergeant Bill Taylor were parked on the Culmore Road.

'Well, what's the news?' said Taylor.

After McLaughlin had given a full report of the meeting

123

Taylor asked: 'Did he say where the rifles were coming from?'

'Naw, but it's obviously part of that German load.'

'Must be,' mused the Sergeant. He chewed his lower lip before speaking again. 'Concentrate on them and see if you can find out where they are being dumped.'

'Right.'

'Just one more thing. Do you know where the training camp is?'

'Naw, the normal procedure is not to tell anyone. Sometimes the people who go on the things don't even know where they are.'

Taylor dropped his informer off and rushed to the barracks where Superintendent Haslitt was working late on a report for the Chief Constable. Haslitt was in his shirt sleeves with a half empty bottle of whiskey at his elbow as Taylor entered the office.

'Sorry to bother you, sir, but I think I have something important.'

'I could do with something important to put in this bloody report, Sergeant; it wouldn't do for that, would it?'

'Afraid not, sir,' said Taylor smiling in automatic response to his boss's informal approach, 'but it is serious.'

'Let's hear it then,' said the Superintendent, pouring himself another drink.

The Sergeant told of his meeting with McLaughlin and offered an opinion of its significance. 'I think it would be a good idea for me to go to Dublin and have a chat with Special Branch down there. I have a feeling we are not getting all the information and I might just pick up a hint of what's happening. I'm in contact with Inspector Porter in Dublin Castle, sir, so I can arrange it myself.'

'Good, go to it.'

Just after eleven the next morning Taylor was shown into Inspector Porter's office, a ramshackled room with a large mahogany desk planted firmly in the middle of a lino-clad floor. A typewriter and a telephone were barely visible amidst a litter of scattered papers which threatened to overflow onto the floor. Six double lockers lined the walls, their doors exposing files, papers, reference books and a host of other paraphernalia. It was a masterpiece of disorder.

'It's a long time since we've seen you, Bill,' Porter said extending his hand. 'How've you been keeping?'

'Not too good, not too bad,' said Taylor equivocally. He shook the offered hand firmly before sinking into an armchair.

'I suppose you've come about the call I made to Buncrana?' said the Inspector.

'I didn't know you made one,' answered Taylor. 'We only have a weekly meeting with the Buncrana Guards unless something out of the ordinary comes up.'

'Have you got problems in Derry then?'

'Yes,' said Taylor, 'it's in connection with those guns that were stolen in Germany. I suppose you have no idea where they are?'

'Haven't a clue. We thought they might have come through Dublin, but we haven't heard a whisper of any movement. Not a whisper.'

'Same in Derry too. They must be well dumped. Have you any idea what they want them for?'

'The North obviously, they're hardly going to start using them down here.'

'I know that: what I mean is, have you heard any rumours of a big campaign coming off?'

'Heard nothing like that,' said the Inspector, 'you think there might be?'

'I think there might be something like that in the air. Saor Eire have started a massive training programme in Donegal. It's more intensive than anything they have ever attempted before: they intend to train over two hundred men in three months. The whole thing is being organised by O'Donnell.'

The Inspector whistled when he heard the name. 'That's the fellow that picked up the stuff yesterday.'

'What stuff?'

'Stuff that went up to Bridgend – that's what my call was about – two bazookas and two rocket launchers.'

'What!' Taylor was startled.

'Afraid so,' said Porter with affected sympathy.

'What the hell do they want them for?'

'To shoot at you, I presume.'

'Not with bazookas they don't. I thought there had to be something bigger going: now I know.'

'What do you mean?' asked Porter.

'It's a new campaign – it has to be!' Taylor was becoming more animated by the second. 'Saor Eire are going to launch a full-blown bloody campaign designed to kill God knows how many people. That's what the raid in Germany was for. It also explains this heavy stuff.'

Sergeant Taylor's mind was disturbed by many thoughts on the drive back to Derry. He knew that a monumental storm was about to blow across the province. He had a sickening feeling in the pit of his stomach which told him that all the intelligence he had gathered would be insufficient to prevent it. Something else was required, a new approach. O'Donnell had to be found and put out of action.

First thing the following morning, after a sleepless night, he was waiting at the office for the Superintendent to arrive.

'Well, how did the trip to Dublin go?' Haslitt greeted him politely.

'It confirmed my worst suspicions,' said the Sergeant following his boss into the office. 'Saor Eire sent two bazookas and two rocket launchers up from Dublin yesterday. They are probably dumped somewhere in the Creggan by now.'

'Good God!' The Superintendent jumped arrow-straight in his chair. 'What are they going to use those for?'

'Exactly my question. But combining them with two hundred SLRs from Germany and the intensive training programme that the volunteers are going through, we don't have to look far for an answer. I think they are going to launch a massive campaign within the next four months.'

Superintendent Haslitt was taken aback. 'There is no way

126

we can handle that, Bill,' he said worriedly.

'Absolutely not,' agreed Taylor, 'especially if Belfast and other areas are getting similar stuff.'

'Have you any idea how we can stop it?'

The Sergeant leaned forward in his chair. 'The first thing we have to do is find out where those rifles are. I think most of them are still in the one dump otherwise we would have heard something by now. Second, we have to find out where the volunteers are being trained and pass the information to the Guards so that they can break up the camp, and hopefully, nail the instructors. And thirdly, most important of all, I think we should put one of our own people inside Saor Eire.'

'Now that, Bill. . . I don't know. . .' Haslitt faltered, clearly alarmed.

'I realise that, sir, but it's the only way we are going to nail this character O'Donnell – and he is the man at the bottom of all the trouble. I think it's wishful thinking to hope that we will nail him on a job. The only way is to get someone in ourselves so that we can at least get him on a conspiracy charge.'

'You actually want someone to go into the witness box against him?'

'That's the only way we will get him for certain.'

'But think what that could mean for whoever gave the information.'

'We would have to guarantee that it didn't,' said the Sergeant, as harshly as he dared. 'If we can't protect our own people, then who the hell can we protect?'

'Yes, of course,' said Haslitt. 'Do you have anyone in mind if this is agreed to?'

'Not at the moment, but I'll get onto it right away.'

'Well, I'll think about it,' said the Superintendent. 'In the meantime you can take whatever steps you think are necessary to find out about the weapons.'

'I want to pull in a few Saor Eire members tonight.'

'Okay, whatever you think best. Work it out with Inspector Miller.'

At five-thirty the following morning all known addresses of the Saor Eire Command Staff were raided. Most of the detained men received routine interrogation, but Seamus McLaughlin was taken to a comfortably furnished office where he sank into a large armchair. He dragged deeply on one of Sergeant Taylor's cigarettes as Taylor spoke to him from a hard-backed chair.

'Sorry about this, Seamus, but I had to talk to you quickly and there was no other way I could reach you. Have you heard anything about this stuff that came up from Dublin?'

McLaughlin's eyes shifted their gaze uneasily around the room. 'Is it the rifles you mean?' he asked, staring blankly through the window facing him.

'No, bazookas.'

'Bazookas? You're fuckin' jokin'!'

'It's no joke, they came up at the weekend. What is this character O'Donnell up to?'

'Well, he wants everyone trained for operations,' began Seamus doubtfully.

'He wants operations all right,' Taylor gave a crisp ironic snort. 'He's planning another campaign as soon as the training is over.'

'He didn't tell the Staff about it,' said Seamus, defensively indignant.

'Well, I think it's about time he did, don't you? I want you to call a Staff meeting and ask him what he is up to. The Staff has a right to know what is happening, so get out of him exactly what he has in mind.'

By eight-thirty that night everyone had been released except the Rosemount OC who had been transferred to Ballykelly Interrogation Centre. For the other four, the first call was the Bogside Inn, and it was there, still comparing notes with boyish excitement, that O'D found them. A chorus of friendly obscenities greeted him.

'Is everybody out?' he asked.

'They held Rosemount,' said Dermot Donnelly.

O'D acknowledged the fact with a nod of his head. A shock-wave of pity rippled through his system but he did not dwell on it.

'What were they looking for?'

Three of the men attempted to speak at the same time, only McLaughlin remained silent. Observing this, O'D asked after some minutes, 'What about you Seamus?'

'Same thing,' said McLaughlin and O'D did not press the point.

'Well,' he said with affected cheerfulness, 'we don't have the rifles yet and none of you know where the camp is, so we don't have anything to worry about, do we?'

'Well. . . we do,' said Seamus before anyone could fill the pause which followed.

'How's that, Seamus?' O'D encouraged.

Seamus staggered on. 'I mean. . . all this training. . . every fuckin' unit. . . where's it all leading to? Are we going to increase our present operations or are we going to move into a bigger campaign?' The words rattled from him in the quietness of the lounge.

O'D had sensed his anxiety and tried to draw him a little further. 'I think,' Seamus continued, 'that we could increase our operations now if we had the stuff. All this training is a waste of time.'

'I agree with that,' said Sean Doherty before O'D could answer.

'Hold on, Sean,' said O'D quickly, sensing that the opinion could spread fast. 'We could increase our operations certainly, but we would also increase the pressure from the Brits. And I don't want to invite that until I am sure we can handle it without interfering with any future plans.'

But the poison had already been planted and taken root. The wariness of increased pressure did not seem to merit much consideration. Everyone was hardened to harassment as it was. They saw their sole task in the city as attacking the British army and the RUC wherever, whenever and with whatever they could; stalling until everyone was properly trained just seemed like a waste of time. Dermot Donnelly expressed the feelings of the others. 'I think we should tell Dublin to send up whatever stuff they are going to give us right now and let us get on with it.'

O'D found that he was being pushed towards choosing between two undesirable alternatives: agree to an increase in operations, or reveal the plan. A barman entered the lounge with another round of drinks leaving a connecting door open. A confusion of noise filtered through. He closed the door behind him returning them once again to silence. Everyone looked expectantly at O'D.

'We can't increase operations,' he said simply. 'This training programme is not just to keep us off the streets; there was a specific plan at the back of it. All the stuff from the raid in Germany, and a lot of other stuff besides, is coming to Derry.' There were gasps and shuffling as everyone settled into more attentive positions. 'GHQ has worked out a plan to attack all the army barracks this side of the Foyle in the one night – that's what the intensive training is directed at. I don't have to tell you how important it is to have the element of surprise for such an operation.'

'What do you think of this plan yourself, Hugh?' asked Con McDaid.

'It's a good plan, Con, but I think we had better leave off discussing it until we are ready to use it.'

Everyone agreed, with the exception of Seamus, who was ignored. The meeting continued informally over another round of drinks until O'D asked unexpectedly, 'By the way, can any of you put me up for the night? I lost my regular billet for a few days.' Everyone offered at once and he opted for Con McDaid's house.

Half-an-hour later Seamus McLaughlin was sitting in Sergeant Taylor's car. 'Didn't take you long,' said the Sergeant encouragingly. 'Did you find out something?'

'Everything you wanted,' said Seamus with a twisted smile.

'Let's hear it.'

'Well, he didn't say anything about a campaign, but I suppose that's what it amounts to – a change of direction would be more accurate. He says that the GHQ have a plan to attack all the army barracks in Derry in one night. That's what the training's for.'

Taylor stared at McLaughlin for several seconds before answering. 'Is he trying to commit suicide?'

'That's what he said.'

'He's a maniac – the whole movement will be wiped out in one go!'

'You'll hardly worry about that, will you?'

'I couldn't give a damn if they all destroyed themselves with fire, but I don't want them wrecking the town while they do it.'

'Oh, there's something else,' said Seamus, 'I know where O'D is sleeping tonight.'

'Where's that?' asked the Sergeant urgently.

'Con McDaid's house.'

The Sergeant removed the notebook from his inside pocket and began to write. 'Tell you what,' he said, 'don't sleep in your own house tonight and we'll lift the Staff again in the morning.'

'But then I will be the only one not lifted and that will look suspicious.'

'Not if you have a good alibi. Go and stop with one of the Battalion OC's or pick up a female volunteer for the night. Unless you want to be lifted with the rest, that is.'

Seamus ignored the insult and took the hint. 'I'll think of something,' he said morosely.

O'D strolled casually towards the Creggan with Con McDaid. 'Big Con' as he was known to most of the people in the area was only five feet ten inches tall, but he weighed over fifteen stone without an ounce of fat. He was almost as broad as he was tall, and for as long as anyone could remember his favourite sport had been weightlifting and his only hobby had been

131

hunting. A combination of both activities seemed to weigh equally on his personality: he had the will-power of a weight-lifter and the quiet concentration of a hunter. Most people underestimated his intelligence but O'D did not.

'I think we have a problem, Con,' he said as they walked away from the Inn.

Con's deep canyon of a voice boomed back, 'What kind of a problem, Hugh?'

'I think we have an informer on the Staff,' said O'D as casually as he could. He thought Con would have accepted it with a minimum of shock — there had been informers before and Con himself had assisted in disposing of one of them. But this time the reaction was different — this time Con was on the Staff himself.

'Jesus!' he exclaimed, 'you mean one of those three is an informer?'

'Yes,' O'D replied, 'I think so.'

'It must be Seamus then,' said Con with simple honesty.

O'D nodded. 'That's what I think too.'

'Christ! I never would have thought it. What do you want to do?'

'Well, for one thing, I don't want to sleep in your house tonight.'

Both of them stopped in the house opposite Con's. It was a narrow street, typical of Brandywell, no broader than fifteen feet from kerb to kerb, and the houses were no higher. O'D set the alarm for five o'clock, confident that there would be no raid before that time.

At five-thirty in the morning four landrovers rolled to a stop in front of Con's door. O'D shook Con awake just in time to see a soldier kick his front door in. The rest of them piled into the little house. Con was visibly angry as they saw the lights switched on one by one.

'How many is there?' he asked.

'Fifteen, I counted,' said O'D without taking his eyes off the house.

'They're not taking any chances are they?'

'Indeed they're not,' agreed O'D, 'which must mean, I suppose, that they want us a lot.'

The soldiers left ten minutes later as quickly as they had come, and five minutes after that Con was back in his bed snoring like a chainsaw. O'D lay awake with his thoughts. Seamus McLaughlin was the immediate problem, but O'D wasn't sure whether he had enough evidence. It was certain by now, of course, that the RUC knew of plans to attack the barracks, but that did not mean much. As long as he could stay free they still held the element of surprise. With two hundred well-trained and armed men he held the advantage.

As soon as he entered the Bogside Inn he heard that the rest of the Staff had been lifted in a general raid. A shadow of doubt instantly crossed his mind, but when he heard that Seamus had somehow escaped the raid the doubt evaporated. Outwardly he was unchanged towards Seamus when he entered the Inn later that morning. 'Yes, kid,' he said in his usual light-hearted manner.

'I hear you had a lucky escape as well,' said Seamus, trying to strike some sort of affinity.

'Yeah, we were steeped in it. Mick rang up from Donegal and I had to go across the border. Con came with me so he got the benefit of the luck as well. How did you miss it?'

'I was down in the bird's house. I sat there so long that she put me up for the night on the sofa. Mind you, when I think of it, I don't know which was worse, being lifted by the Brits or having to put up with her old lady this morning.'

O'D laughed appropriately and took a mouthful of drink to avoid an immediate answer. He could see all the strains in Seamus's performance now that he knew what to look for – the false smile, the nervous mouth, the shifting eyes, and even the bared teeth. There was something grotesque about this caricature look, but he wondered would he have noticed all these signs in Seamus if he had not known that the man was an informer? It was impossible to say.

'Did you get anything to eat yet?' Seamus asked.

'Not yet, I was going to scrounge a dinner somewhere.'

'Why don't you come around to the bird's house with me?'

O'D agreed. It was a good idea to keep close company with Seamus until he decided how to deal with him. He felt that the closer he was to Seamus the safer he would be. At least that way he could keep an eye on him.

The house was a small one, almost identical to Con McDaid's. Marie, Seamus's girl-friend, had been expecting him and immediately set about preparing food as they arrived. Seamus brought two cans of beer from the kitchen and he and O'D settled on the sofa with them. The thought struck O'D that this particular item of furniture would be damned uncomfortable to sleep on. Half-way through the beer, Seamus rose abruptly, saying, 'I'll just be a minute.' O'D thought he was going to the kitchen until he heard him shout from the hall, 'Marie, I'm just going down to the shop for fags, I'll only be a minute.'

'Will you get some coal for the fire before you go?' she called, but the door slammed an inanimate reply behind Seamus. O'D saw him passing the window on his way to the corner shop at the bottom of the street. He wondered automatically whether the shop had a phone, then felt guilty about the thought, then began to really worry.

'Where do I get the coal, Marie?'

'In the back yard, Hugh, you'll see the shed. Thanks.'

There were no back lanes in these old streets. Instead, the back yard of the house was separated by a six foot wall from the back yard of its neighbour's in the next street. Both streets were cul-de-sacs which ran off the main Brandywell Road. What O'D liked about the area at this moment was that it was extremely difficult for the army to cover the rear of the house he was in. He stood in the yard examining it. He stopped to look at an assortment of potted plants below the window. Marie smiled at him as he examined them. 'Who has the green fingers?' he called to her, pointing. He did not care in the least about green fingers or potted plants or even coal for that matter. He simply wanted to stall in the yard for as long as possible. He felt that he had a chance from there. If a pair of

134

heavy-duty boots kicked in the ancient front door he would be hopelessly trapped in the little cramped front room. He dropped to his hunkers and examined the plants under Marie's curious, half-amused eye. Then he heard the landrovers in the front street. He stood tensed looking at Marie, who froze. The sounds stopped. He moved towards the back wall. Marie was transfixed.

They did not bother to knock: one boot and the door splintered open. Marie waved excitedly for him to get away. As he turned to flee he wondered whether the raw terror on her face was for him or herself. He ran a few steps, leapt and cleared the wall into the next yard. The yard was identical to Marie's and he covered it in four strides, praying that the back door was not bolted on the inside. He tore it open and raced through the house. At the front door he poked his head out. Luck was with him.

'Here! What the hell's goin' on here?' demanded a woman's voice.

'Sorry, missus, the Brits are after me,' was all he had time to say before tearing towards the dead end of the street.

'Ah,' said the woman with understanding, but he was too far away to hear.

He leapt one more wall at the bottom of the street, and dropped into comparative safety; then he trotted towards the city cemetery, Creggan and sanctuary.

But the safety of Creggan was not quiet: before he was out of the cemetery he heard the gunfire rattling in the distance. At first he thought it was coming from Brandywell and his thoughts automatically sympathised with Marie's plight. But then he heard more clearly: the firing was in front of him. He stopped to listen: by the sound it seemed to be coming from somewhere on Creggan Heights. He started trotting again; he was half-way between the cemetery and the Heights when Con McDaid pulled up in a car.

'You look as if you are in a hurry to get yourself shot,' he grunted.

'Or prevent someone else from getting shot,' said O'D,

135

climbing in. 'It sounds serious, doesn't it?'

'Aye, I heard it in the Bog.'

Their first task was to find the ASU responsible for the Heights. It proved easy, they simply followed the sound of gunfire. The first volunteer they saw was standing on top of a coal shed firing across a pigeon loft. He looked like someone at a carnival trying to ring the bell on a rifle range but for the fact that he was firing a .306 sporting rifle.

'Who's your section leader?' called O'D, recognising the man's face but not his unit.

'Charlie Coyle,' came the reply.

'Where is he?'

'Next block.'

They found him in a back garden drinking a mug of tea with one of his volunteers.

'What's happening?' asked O'D.

'About twenty Brits tried to come in the back of the Heights,' explained Charlie. 'We thought it was a daylight raid so we opened up on them. We hit two and the rest fell back.'

'Well done,' said O'D forcefully.

'Fuckin' right it was,' answered Charlie, without a trace of modesty. 'They're all over the place now.'

'You mean there's more of them?' asked O'D.

'Fuckin' hundreds of them – they're all over the place,' Charlie repeated.

'You're exaggerating,' said O'D, more in hope than in certainty.

'Think so? Follow me.' Charlie entered the house, placed his mug on a table and tramped upstairs to a back bedroom with O'D and the volunteer behind. From the bedroom window he pointed to at least twenty positions which the soldiers had occupied in the surrounding countryside. 'And there's more of them up on the back road in Saracens,' he said with authority. 'I don't know whether they are reinforcements or whether they intend to dive in once these fuckers have a toehold.'

136

'Good Christ!' said O'D in astonishment, 'it looks as if they are trying to swamp the place.'

'Looks like it,' agreed Charlie casually.

'Think you can keep their heads down there, Charlie?'

'No problem. They can't get near these houses without losing at least a dozen men, and they're not going to risk that.'

O'D swung the entire Derry Brigade into action. All OCs were contacted and told to muster as many men as possible. A small fleet of cars left Creggan in convoy and covered the city in ever increasing circles until everyone who could be contacted was informed that a battle was in progress in the Heights. They flooded from all areas: some came by bus, others got lifts, some hired taxis and others hijacked cars, some walked and some ran and there were very few who didn't make it. The only exception was in Bogside where the OC was told to put all his men on patrol around the perimeter of his area and shoot or burn anything that moved in a uniform. O'D made some of the contacts himself in a hijacked bread van which he threw around corners in his haste. He blushed as he handed the keys back to the breadman telling him Saor Eire would pay for the damage to the stock. He felt nothing but relief as he walked from the van to face almost a hundred volunteers at the back of the Creggan shops.

He quickly gave them a run-down on the situation without creating any illusions: the Brits were on the edge of the area in strength and they were trying to get in – but they were not going to. He attempted to convey his own determination to the motley bunch of freedom fighters collected before him, but somewhere in the middle of it he wondered whether he really wanted to. After all, most of them had already laid their lives on the line before now for the same cause, and sometimes in far worse circumstances.

He was about to continue when Seamus McLaughlin walked round the corner. O'D's heart skipped a beat and he was unable to continue with what he was saying. His train of thought deserted him like steam from a broken boiler, and was replaced by a dilemma: he did not know whether to reach for one of the many weapons surrounding him and shoot McLaughlin on the spot or give him a little more rope to hang himself. O'D handed the briefing over to Con.

'Jesus, I'm glad you got away, kid,' said McLaughlin to O'D.

'Yeah, me too,' said O'D, 'what happened to you?' The dilemma had resolved itself by default.

Seamus went on rapidly. 'I was just coming back from the shop when I saw the bastards coming down the street. I couldn't do a bloody thing but stand and watch them raid the house. I thought they were going to come out with you, but, by Christ, I was glad when they didn't. Marie told me that you had gone over the back wall into Mrs Hasson's as they were coming in the hall. She told them that someone had called for you in a car a couple of minutes earlier. . .'

'You mean they asked for me by name?' O'D jumped at the slip like a hunter snapping the last trap closed on his prey.

'Yeah, they asked for both of us,' said Seamus blundering on through his panic.

'How did they know I was there?' The trap had snapped now. But his prey was still struggling.

'That's what I was thinking too. Someone must have seen us going into the house and rang the bastards.'

Once again O'D's mind reached readily for the excuse. He found himself surprised by his own decision. Why he did not shoot this man, whom he would readily have shot just an hour earlier, he did not know. He simply felt more comfortable ignoring the problem, as if the decision would have destroyed some idea he cherished. His focus shifted from Seamus, blurred a little, and stared blindly into middle distance.

'Yeah,' he said dreamily, 'I guess we were lucky.'

'Damn right,' said Seamus.

But a sense of revulsion both at himself and Seamus was rising in O'D. He wanted the man out of his sight before the dreadful decision forced itself upon him.

'You better go along with Con,' he said. It was the only way out he could think of.

Five groups ranged in a semi-circle around Creggan, covering its northern, western and southern perimeters and leaving one group in reserve to patrol the estate and mount internal roadblocks. Con's group worked out of St Peter's school on the south of the estate. The battle raged into the long summer evening. Once the news spread that the battle was in progress, people started converging on Creggan Heights from all areas, like children attracted by the magnetism of a circus.

Out of all the ensuing confusion, one old man in his seventies made his way to the headquarters of Con's group in St Peter's school. He confronted Con in a heavily congested but determined voice. 'You in charge here?'

'Yes,' said Con thinking it was another irrelevant interruption.

'The army are behind you. . . in the nun's field.'

'What?' Con was startled. 'How many of them?'

'I counted six. . . but there's more.'

Seamus, standing beside Con, took the initiative. He picked up a rifle saying, 'I'll check it out.'

'We'd better get O'D first,' said Con, unsure of Seamus's status.

'Yeah,' agreed Seamus, 'send someone to tell him and in the meantime I'll have a look at the set-up.'

O'D arrived at St Peter's in a rage after a volunteer had conveyed the message. 'Why the fuck didn't you stop him?' he flung angrily at Con.

'Jesus, I tried to, Hugh, but he just lifted the rifle and took off before I could say anything.'

'How long is he gone?'

'Only about five minutes.'

'Where does the old man live?'

'In High Park.'

'I know that! What's the address?'

'I don't know,' said Con desperately.

'Oh fuck! That's great!'

But Con's spirits lifted with the birth of an idea. 'He has to live in a flat because he's an old pensioner' – O'D was almost tempted to smile at the description – 'and there are only two blocks of flats down there so he shouldn't be hard to find. I'll come along with you,' he said in an attempt to redeem himself.

'You stay here and make sure the Brits don't get near the place,' said O'D, pulling a luger from his waistband and cocking it.

Two minutes later he was in High Park trying to figure out which flat Seamus was in. One side of the small square estate faced an open field which was an ideal approach for the army. He decided to walk along the front and check the windows. He was just beginning to wonder what Seamus would do when he heard the shot.

Seamus had seen the soldiers as soon as he entered the flat. He could have hit all six of them before their mates discovered his firing position – it would have been like shooting ducks in a pond. But then he saw the Special Branch car. It could not have been anything else, parked as it was between an army landrover and a Saracen. He searched frantically for a glimpse of its owner, and spotted him where he stood almost concealed behind a high hedge which lined the field. Bill Taylor's bulldog profile was unmistakable, even at a distance.

The sight sent contradictory thoughts flashing through Seamus McLaughlin's mind. But a strong feeling of sympathetic identity shifted the subtle forces influencing him. He raised the SLR in a trancelike movement to the open window and fired a single shot which landed harmlessly, fifty feet away from the nearest soldier. He was still thinking of the delight it would give him to explain this to Sergeant Taylor when O'D appeared behind him.

'Did you get any of them?' the voice asked calmly.

Seamus leapt as if he had been bitten. His single thought as he spun away from the window was that O'D has seen the six soldiers scrambling safely over the hedge.

'I think I got a Branchman,' he lied.

'A Branchman?' asked O'D. He glanced cautiously out of the window. 'Oh, yeah, I see the Branch car. Give me the rifle.'

Seamus handed the weapon up without a thought. Even as it was levelled straight at his chest he did not understand, until O'D spoke.

'You're a dead man, Seamus.'

'What are you talking about, O'D?' he said, searching for a last, hopeless attempt at escape.

'Seamus,' he answered wearily yet firmly, 'don't try to con me again or I will blow your head through the window.'

'What do you want me to do?' he whispered.

'Talk, Seamus. Talk. That's the only thing that will stop me shooting you.'

'I don't know where to begin,' said Seamus, still exploring for possible sympathy.

But O'D drew the final line over which he had to surrender or stand and fight. 'Who are you informing to, Brits or Branch?'

Seamus crossed the line in one leap. 'The Branch.'

'Who is it?'

'Bill Taylor.'

The name exploded in O'D's mind with a burst of painful memories and he almost shot Seamus in raw reaction. Only when his mind calmed did he realise that his finger was rigid on the trigger. His jaw was clamped like a vice.

'How do you give him the information?' The voice was barely audible.

'He picks me up in a car and drives to a spot on the Culmore Road.'

One by one the sentences tumbled from him, building up a picture so damning that O'D wondered how he was still alive let alone free. He had known the Brits on many occasions to shoot men for less than he had done. For the first time he felt that his days were numbered. Before it had been easy to feel confident about the future: the unknown was a double-edged sword which worked in his favour in the no-go area. But Seamus's treachery had ripped away the protection of the area leaving him naked in the midst of his own illusions. The

141

Branch, he thought with horror, are not dealing with suppositions – they know all the facts!

If he had known that in Ballykelly. . . ? The end of the sentence was pushed violently from his mind: too near, too much and too uncomfortable to contemplate.

'I'll give you one chance to save your neck,' he said in an almost casual voice.

'How?' said Seamus anxiously, eagerly.

'By setting up Taylor.'

McLaughlin breathed in great gulps of air before asking: 'What do you want me to do?'

'Get him to the pick-up point and let us take him. After that I'll make sure you get out of the country and no one need know that you were informing.'

'You mean you wouldn't tell the Staff?'

'That's right, we'll tell them that you have to go on the run for shooting a Branchman.'

'What about the Branch? They'll hunt me down.'

'That's a sight better than the problem you'll have if I court-martial you.'

'Will you give me money to get away?'

'I'll get you to America and then you're on your own.'

'Okay,' said Seamus, wiping sweat from his forehead and licking parched and cracked lips.

The battle was still continuing spasmodically at ten o'clock that night when Sergeant Taylor answered the phone. He had just come off duty less than an hour earlier, after eleven and a half hours.

'Yeah,' he said curtly into the phone.

'I've got to see you straight away,' said McLaughlin's voice.

Taylor's senses snapped into focus. His tiredness was forgotten as all sorts of dangerous possibilities flashed through his mind. He knew by the tone of McLaughlin's voice that he had something urgent, and on this particular day McLaughlin's was the kind of help he needed desperately. The strain he had been under, combined with his excitement, made him ask something he had never asked before. 'Can you tell me anything over the phone?' He was like an alcoholic asking for his first drink of the day.

'No way!' came McLaughlin's sharp reply. 'Either you turn up or we forget it.'

'Okay, okay,' said Taylor anxiously. 'I'll be there in ten minutes.' He cursed himself for asking the question. His mind dwelt on his own stupidity. All the way to his pick-up he speculated on the information. Not once did he think of asking the barracks for cover.

He drove into the car-park just before ten-fifteen and crept slowly towards the bushes where McLaughlin usually waited. The car-park was dimly lit. He saw McLaughlin's figure emerge from the bushes. Pulling the car to a halt beside him, he took it out of gear and leaned across to open the passenger's door. 'Here,' he called, pushing the door open. But McLaughlin failed to move.

Taylor squinted into the murky shadows. Then he saw a second figure emerge from behind McLaughlin's shoulder. His foot slammed the clutch. He groped for the gear lever but the adrenalin shooting through his body made him erratic. His foot slipped off the clutch. The gear-stick crashed uselessly against reverse gear. A screaming, grinding noise filled the car.

It was his last mistake. He tried again but his foot didn't make the clutch a second time. A volley of shots exploded and he was flung violently against the driver's door.

He was confused by the initial impact but still alive. As the noise fell away into the still, lamp-lit night his mind settled into a state of numbed shock. He closed his eyes and sighed, unable even to think about his gun. A series of images passed across his mind, some pale, some colourful, but all of them distant and meaningless. His mind lay in a cold, functionless limbo, oblivious to everything outside a vague consciousness of his existence.

O'D approached the car with a cocked carbine.

Taylor heard his footsteps on the gravel, but was unable to

turn his head. He sensed rather than saw the image with half-glazed eyes. The image intensified as it leaned inside the car. For a fraction of a second Taylor's mind became lucid and the terrible reality was clear to him. But he could do nothing. In that same instant the carbine was placed against his head and fired.

O'D spoke to McLaughlin almost casually. 'It is Taylor, isn't it?'

'Of course it is,' said the informer, 'that's his car.'

'Just make sure,' said O'D, 'and get his weapon while you're in there.'

McLaughlin was reluctant to go anywhere near the car, but one look at O'D's face forced him to overcome the revulsion. The single shot from the carbine entered the base of his skull, exiting above the hairline of his forehead and throwing him across the body of the Sergeant. He lay there like some macabre doctor vainly searching for a heartbeat in the corpse of a patient.

With a nod of acknowledgement O'D turned and crashed through the bushes. Charlie and his crew were anxiously waiting in the getaway car, its engine running. Within two minutes they were safely in the Bogside.

Superintendent Haslitt heard the news at midnight. He had just arrived home after a relaxing evening spent in the company of a few local businessmen. His wife informed him before he even entered the house, which sent him staggering towards his car in a drunken fury, his mouth frothing with alcohol and rage and his feet scattering gravel wildly in all directions as they ploughed across the even surface of his driveway.

The barracks was electric with activity when he arrived, but he hardly noticed. As he sank into his chair he squinted at Chief Inspector Mervin Wall with bloodshot eyes. 'What in God's name happened, Mervin?' he gasped.

Wall stood formally as he answered. 'He went to meet the informer McLaughlin and both of them were ambushed.'

'Is the informer dead too?'

'Yes, it looks as if the bastard set Bill up and then his mates turned on him.'

'How did they do it?'

'They riddled him with automatic weapons, probably two or three of them.'

'Bastards!' exploded Haslitt, sending a shower of spittle across the desk. 'This maniac O'Donnell has to be stopped, Mervin. Why the hell have you not picked him up yet anyway?'

Wall decided to knock the ball firmly into his superior's court. 'We are doing everything we can, sir. In fact, all our energies are directed towards cornering O'Donnell. But, I must say, I think we could have avoided this catastrophe if we had taken Sergeant Taylor's advice.'

'What was that?' said Haslitt, concentrating on the bottle of whiskey he had pulled from a drawer.

'That we put one of our own people inside Saor Eire,' said Wall crisply. 'Tonight has surely proved that these informers are just too dangerous for us to rely on.'

'Oh that.' The pouring continued, making Wall feel that the whiskey was being poured insultingly over his head instead of into the glass. He could not resist, in the circumstances, a personal swipe at his boss. 'Bill told me that he mentioned the idea to you and that you seemed to be in favour of it.'

'Yes, now that you mention it, he did say something like that, but we certainly didn't come to any firm decision.' Haslitt was defensive but not drunk enough to commit himself on anything serious.

'Well, I think we should now,' said Wall quickly.

'Do you think it will work?'

'Well it will at least prevent our best men from being gunned down in car-parks.'

Haslitt saw it was time to pass the buck again. He recognised an energy in Wall that was beyond his control and thought the best way to handle it was to give it its head. 'That's a point no one in the force would want to argue with, so go

145

ahead and plant your man.'

'Yes, sir,' said Wall formally.

'By the way,' said Haslitt as Wall opened the door, 'did anyone inform the wife that the man was dead?'

'Yes, sir,' said Wall backing out the door.

In the corridor he thought, 'He can't even call Bill by his name.' As he walked into his own office the feeling of revulsion grew, especially when he contrasted the Superintendent to the determined loyalty of Sergeant Taylor, a loyalty which had cost him his life. It was a bitter irony that Taylor – the main expert on terrorist groups in Derry – should be the one to get killed, while the Superintendent, who should have been retired years ago on medical grounds, was still misdirecting the show.

For the first time in his career Wall had difficulty concentrating on his work. He moped about several offices trying to take an interest in things which were none of his concern. He eventually ended up going home early. The following day he arrived for work in the same frame of mind. But it quickly changed when he heard that Haslitt had been called to the RUC Headquarters in Belfast for a dressing down by the Chief Constable. He actually smiled at the young Sergeant who gave him the news. A flow of ideas began to tumble through his head. The thing to do was to get the ball rolling while Haslitt was gone.

The first person he turned to was Tony Miller. Now that Taylor was gone, Miller was the main expert on Saor Eire. He rang his extension and told him to drop everything and come to the office. Miller arrived in less than a minute and Wall offered him a seat.

'How's Bill's wife taking the news?'

'Pretty bad,' said Miller. 'She seemed to go into a state of shock when I told her and has hardly reacted to anything since. Her mother will be staying for a few weeks, but I wish I could do something more.'

'Is there anything we can do that isn't already being done?'

'Well, you could call out and see her yourself on a personal

146

basis, sir. Outside of that, everything is being taken care of by the welfare officer.'

'I'll do that this afternoon, Tony, and if you think of anything else in the meantime, let me know.'

'Right sir.'

'And cut out the "sir".'

'Right.'

'Now, you know about the plan that Bill had to infiltrate Saor Eire?'

'Yes, we both discussed it, in fact, we even agreed on someone for the job.'

'Oh? That's good. Who was it?'

'Dympna Colhoun. She's a young policewoman who hasn't been with us for very long, but she's got top marks in her passing-out class at Enniskillen and she is excellent material for this sort of operation.'

They summoned the policewoman to the office there and then. When Wall suggested the idea she agreed to it eagerly and immediately surprised him by offering her own ideas on how Saor Eire could best be infiltrated. He found that her personality seemed to defy the very uniform she wore and transform it into something less inanimate than it actually was. After fifteen minutes of conversation, Wall had no doubt that she was the person for the job.

'You can consider yourself assigned to this operation and nothing else. Tony here will give you a file on all the relevant Saor Eire characters and brief you on anything else you need to know. But remember this, the sole object of the exercise is to nail O'Donnell. We need something concrete to charge and convict him with, preferably something that will put him away for a long time, but right now we will settle for possession of an imitation revolver just to get him out of the way. Bear that in mind. Tony will tell you anything else you need to know, okay?'

'Fine, sir,' said Dympna, giving the Chief Inspector her best smile.

That night she curled up on her sofa and read the bulky

dossier on Hugh O'Donnell and his organisation. She had seen O'Donnell once in the barracks – the day he had returned from Ballykelly – and she had formed the opinion that he was a narrow-minded fanatic incapable of seeing past his home-made political blinkers. But now as she read his career she began to change her mind. O'Donnell was far from a mindless fanatic: he was a pragmatic activist who had shown that he was capable of withstanding the strongest pressures; he was also a highly trained and ruthless killer. By the time she had finished reading, Dympna had developed a healthy respect for the scar-faced man whom she planned to meet within the next few days. It was four o'clock in the morning before she climbed between the sheets and set the alarm on her travel clock. She had an uneasy sleep.

It was two days later before Superintendent Haslitt returned from Belfast. His two interviews with the Chief Constable had not been comfortable: both of them had resembled interrogation sessions in which he had had to defend the record of the force in Derry. They left him with no illusions about the difficulty he was in: Derry was a disaster area as far as the rule of law was concerned, and he was the man being held responsible for it. That idea left him helpless in front of his boss in Belfast, but now that he was back in his own barracks it filled him with nothing but anger. As he poured Black Bushmills in a glass at his desk, he decided that someone was going to pay dearly for getting him into such a mess. After a reassuring gulp of raw whiskey he lifted the phone and barked at the internal operator: 'Get Chief Inspector Wall in to my office immediately.'

Wall arrived instantly, a little puzzled as to why the Superintendent didn't ring his personal extension as he usually did. But one glance at the man's face warned him to say nothing.

'What progress have you made in this Saor Eire business?' Haslitt snapped. Wall knew without asking that things had gone badly in Belfast. A fleeting feeling of elation brushed across his mind at the thought. But he would have to be careful: in this foul mood his superior was capable of anything.

'We have got the ball rolling at last, sir: our girl should make her first contact tonight.'

'A girl?' Haslitt straightened in his chair. He did not like the idea of a woman doing the job.

'Yes, sir,' said Wall, 'Policewoman Colhoun. She is very good, and in many ways she is ideal for the job.'

'Colhoun?'

'That's right. She got top marks in her training class. She is very keen and very capable.'

The Superintendent was unimpressed. 'Why the hell did you not get a man?'

Wall was hardly surprised at this attitude, but as he watched Haslitt lift the glass from the table and sip his drink almost sulkily, he realised that the man just was not well. Suddenly an answer to the problem popped into his head. 'Sergeant Taylor picked Policewoman Colhoun for the job because he thought she was ideal and I'm prepared to stand by his judgement.'

Haslitt placed his glass on the desk, sensing mutiny. 'I see,' he said, slowly raising his face to the ceiling. And then, after a pause, he said, 'In that case I suppose we will have to let the decision stand, but I want to see the girl myself. Where is she now?'

'We thought it best that she stay away from the barracks until the operation is over so we lodged her in a flat in the Northland Road,' Wall replied.

The eyes snapped back from the ceiling: 'Have you got it under observation?'

'No,' said Wall, 'that would be highly dangerous. Any hint of police involvement and she's in trouble.'

The Superintendent reached for his glass again, seeming to lose interest, but contradicting the expression with his words. 'I want a full run-down on Policewoman Colhoun's position up to now: what her cover is, where she is living, what she has done to date, what she is going to do, how she contacts you; in fact, the lot. Everything. Get it on my desk as soon

149

as possible.'

'Yes, sir,' said Wall rising. He was convinced now that his boss was severely debilitated. He had noticed a marked deterioration since the Hanley shooting, but that trip to Belfast had pushed him over the edge. Now he was nothing more than an unstable wreck, liable to destroy every operation which sailed close to him. And Wall realised there was nothing he could do about it.

Eight

JUST AFTER NINE-THIRTY that night Policewoman Colhoun entered the upstairs lounge of the Bogside Inn. She was a striking and attractive figure, dressed in sky-blue denim jeans and jacket.

'Haven't seen you in here before,' said a dark, good-looking young man, moving to her side at the bar, and instantly feeling he was out of his depth.

'It's my first time: I've just come back from England.'

'Ah, so you were in England, were you?' said the man thinking he had stumbled upon a common experience. 'What part?' Dympna encouraged the conversation. She felt conspicuously out of place in the noisy, smoke-filled lounge and began to think that half the people were looking at her and the other half were talking about her without looking. Chatting to someone she would look less conspicuous. So she suffered the chauvinism of her companion for thirty minutes. They were in the middle of a conversation about the deteriorating standard of television programmes when O'D entered the lounge.

She recognised him instantly and her heart pounded in anticipation. The scarred face stood out like a ruined monument in a modern shopping centre. Then she experienced a shock of disappointment as he held the door ajar: he was looking for someone and it appeared he would leave at any moment. She realised she had to act immediately or she might not get another chance. She excused herself from the bar and walked to the door. O'D absently pushed it open, but she

151

stopped squarely in front of him.

'What happened to your face?' she said in a very familiar tone.

'What?' said O'D in surprise and confusion.

'Your face,' she pointed. 'What happened to it?'

'Oh that,' he said, still confused but also strangely thrilled; 'I cut it shaving.'

'Don't you recognise me?' she asked blatantly, her brilliant blue eyes on a level with his, cold and shining.

'Should I?' He let the door swing closed and smiled warmly at her.

'Well, you used to.' She smiled coyly and then frowned, just a little, just enough. 'Your name is Pat McGuire, isn't it?'

'Well, to tell you the truth, I was thinking of changing it.'

'Oh, to what?'

'Pat McGuire.'

'Oh, dear,' she said, with just the right degree of embarrassment.

'If you let me buy you a drink,' he said, taking her arm, 'I'll tell you all about it.'

'You really look very like Pat,' she said, taking a drink from him at the bar. 'I can hardly believe the resemblance except for the scar, of course.'

'Does he come from the area?'

'He lived in Rosemount, but that was years ago before I went away.'

'I thought I hadn't seen you around here before,' he enquired gently.

She nodded her head over the poised glass. 'I went to England five years ago.'

'Found someone you know then?' the voice of her original drinking companion called loudly over her left shoulder.

She turned with a mildly surprised expression and then smiled at him, 'Yes, this is an old friend I haven't seen for years.'

She turned to O'D again. 'This chap bought me a drink when I came in, we were chatting for a while.'

O'D nodded and turned to the intruder. 'Will you have a drink?'

'Stick it up your arse,' answered the handsome fellow aggressively and turned to shoulder his way out of the bar.

O'D smiled at Dympna and said with obvious deliberation, 'So, what did you say you were doing in England?' The door of the lounge slammed closed and someone shouted something about ignorant bastards.

'I didn't, but I was nursing in London.'

'A very agreeable occupation. And what brought you back here, masochism?'

She laughed engagingly. 'A combination of things really. I wanted to see how the place had changed. As well as that, I felt guilty about all the suffering that was going on here. I got this feeling that I should be back home trying to help instead of having a good time in London. It's an illusion really, I suppose. I don't even know what I could do. I don't even know who I could ask even if I did know what I could do. But I will have to live with it.'

'Are you serious?' asked O'D in surprise.

'Oh, yes, quite. Why, don't you believe in fighting?' She made it sound like a challenge.

'Well, that depends on what you're fighting for.'

'What about the overthrow of the state?'

'In that case we can't get enough of it.' He finished his pint and waved at the barman for another round.

The conversation became agreeable, isolating them from the noise of the crowd and the dreadful abuse of music emanating from the stage. By closing time they felt they had known each other longer than a few short hours.

'Where do you live?' asked O'D.

'Northland Road.'

'Which end?'

'The top.'

'I'll walk you to the bottom.'

She gave him an ironic look, saying: 'You can come up for coffee if you like.'

153

'I would like,' he said seriously, 'but unfortunately I can't.'

'Why?' she asked with just the right amount of surprise and irony, 'do you have to be in early or something?'

'It's more a case of not being able to go out,' he said lightly.

'You're confusing me,' she said.

'I can't go outside the area.'

'Why not?'

With his fingers he imitated a gun, pointing playfully like a child.

She stopped dead and stared at him with surprise on every wrinkle of her frown. 'You're joking?'

'Afraid not,' he said with a casual shrug of his shoulders, 'I'm on the run.'

'Oh, I see,' she said quietly, without asking for an explanation.

He did not offer one and they strolled in silence, each wondering what the other was thinking. O'D started the conversation again on a different track and they avoided politics until they parted. She left him with a promise to be in the Bogside Inn the following night.

The next morning he woke at eight o'clock feeling fit to challenge the world. As he showered and shaved he felt a new energy flowing through his body. He felt like doing something irrational, whooping at the top of his voice or dashing down the stairs and kissing Ma Murphy, who was seventy-two years old and at that moment standing in the kitchen of his current billet cooking his breakfast.

His mood continued throughout the day as he toured the no-go area and consulted with OCs. Later that day the two Staff members who had been held on seven-day detention orders were released. He listened to the accounts of their interrogations before telling them the reasons for McLaughlin's execution. They were shocked, but readily agreed with the action in view of the evidence. Both of them were shattered after their ordeal of continuous beatings. O'D suggested that they take a break over the border for a few days. When he left them he went straight to his mother's house and changed into a clean jumper and jeans. At eight-thirty he entered the upstairs lounge of the Bogside Inn and saw her standing at the bar.

'Yes,' he said.

'Hello,' she answered, 'I didn't expect you to be on time.'

'Sometimes I am. Are you waiting long?'

'Just a few minutes.'

'Do you mind if we go somewhere else?'

'Not at all,' she said, feeling a momentary stab of anxiety. She wondered whether he trusted her and unconsciously signalled it with her face.

'I just have to go and see someone for a few minutes and then I'm free for the rest of the night.' He had missed the significance of her look.

'I'm not interrupting anything, am I?' she asked with relief.

'No, just one of the hazards of the job.'

She lifted her bag and led the way to the door, saying lightly over her shoulder, 'Are you fellas always kept so busy?'

'Didn't you know there was a revolution going on here?'

'Oh, I know, I know.'

Outside he led her to a three-and-a-half litre Rover and opened the door with more than a little ostentatiousness.

'This isn't yours?' she said incredulously.

'Goes with the job,' he said, closing the door behind her.

'I don't believe it,' she said as he settled behind the wheel. 'How can you afford cars like this?'

'Easy,' he said: 'we hijack them.'

'What?' she said in a spontaneous reaction which almost betrayed her instincts. 'You mean I have the privilege of being chauffeured in a hijacked car?'

'In fact,' he answered, starting the engine, 'you have the privilege of being chauffeured in the most expensive car we ever hijacked.'

'I feel honoured.'

When he drove to the Brandywell and parked the car she could not see where he went, as he disappeared round a corner. 'Are you sure I'm not interfering with your work?' she asked

155

when he returned.

'No, don't worry about it,' he said settling into the seat again. 'I had to go and see this old chap myself because he refused to see anyone else.'

'Oh, I see,' she said, probing a little, 'he's a friend of yours.'

'No, I never met him before, he just heard my name and refused to talk to anyone else.'

'That sounds impressive, are you supposed to have a famous name or something?'

'Famous and infamous, depending on your geographical location.'

'Tell me more.'

He thought for a moment and then said, 'Are you seriously interested in the movement?'

'Oh, yes, very much so.'

He could not get her off the subject after that, and before the night was through he had told her more than he wanted to about the history, development and future plans of the movement. She seemed so interested that he just kept talking. He put the reason down to one recurring fact which kept revolving round his head: she had strong similarities to Brenda. She promised to come to a lecture the following afternoon on the structure of the movement.

Policewoman Colhoun felt exhausted as she climbed the stairs to her second storey flat in the old Victorian building in Northland Road. As she opened her door she saw the air mail envelope which was part of the signal system worked out with Inspector Miller. She hoped as she tore it open that she would not have to leave the flat again that night. The thought of negotiating the dark, treacherous stairs for a second time and then hunting the city for a taxi did not cheer her up. She sighed with relief as her eyes flew across the paper.

I called but you weren't in so I'll try again at 9am. Mother.

'Mother': that meant the Altnagelvin Hospital meeting place. Well, at least it was in the morning.

It was just before nine when she left the bus at the stop before the hospital and walked towards the nurses' home. It was a fresh and lively sun-speckled morning. The recently cut grass filled the air with a summer fragrance. Her thoughts were interrupted by a car drawing alongside the verge. The passenger door opened and a head and shoulders appeared. 'Get in,' said a falsely bearded and outlandishly dressed Inspector Miller.

She was tempted to comment on the ludicrous disguise but feared that he might be offended. She settled for a formal greeting and sat with her mouth tightly closed and her smiles well suppressed until he parked the car in a deserted farmhouse two miles away.

'How's it going?' he finally said.

'Very good, so far,' she said confidently. 'At the moment I'm almost a sworn member of Saor Eire.'

'That was quick,' he said, looking at her with a mixture of pride and concern.

'It was quite easy,' she said without pride. 'The slob fell for me after a little feminine pressure. He now thinks that I will be an invaluable asset to the movement.'

'That's good, but I have a feeling it is not going to last.'

'Why shouldn't it?' she said with a hint of indignation. 'It's working perfectly so far.'

'The problem is,' he said, averting his eyes, 'that the Super is worried about you – he wants to put a man on the job.'

'That's silly, Inspector,' she said, balancing the liberty against formality. 'There's no way a man could get as close as I have.'

'You don't have to convert me, I agree with you. What we have to do is placate the Superintendent.'

'Great, how do we do that?'

'I haven't got a clue. How long do you think it will be before we can pick up O'Donnell?'

'That's hard to say,' she pondered, 'but it shouldn't be too long. As soon as he proposes anything that can be used as evidence I'll let you know.'

'What about setting him up now? I'm sure the DPP would agree to a long remand on the slightest evidence. We might be able to get him out of the way for a couple of years.'

'I think that would be disastrous in the long run,' she said, forcefully.

'Why?'

'Listening to O'Donnell talk, I get the impression, despite our view of it as a one-man organisation, that the movement could function perfectly without him. They have strong support from the locals, and in two years time it could still be intact and it might even have flourished.'

'Two years is a long time, Dympna.' Miller was discovering a new respect for his protégé.

'I agree, sir, but I don't think it is enough for this man O'Donnell. If he were on remand I'm sure he would find some way of influencing Saor Eire from his cell. We have to get him for something concrete and put him away for a long time, otherwise he will continue to be a menace.'

Miller felt a large dilemma appear on his horizon. Colhoun was right, of course, and she was doing an excellent job; he even thought he would resign rather than see her replaced on this operation. But the Superintendent was becoming more obstinate. The situation was getting to the stage where Haslitt was an obsolute hindrance to all operations: he bullied the men, demanded to know everything, refused to sanction anything that he did not have personal knowledge of. He was becoming paranoid, and Miller felt increasingly uneasy about the way he was reacting to Dympna's mission. But he had to agree with her reasoning.

'Right, I'll talk to Mervin Wall and both of us will put pressure on the Super to ease off. In the meantime give me a rundown on what you have found out. Do you know where he is sleeping at nights?'

'Not for certain, but he mentioned someone by the name of Ma Murphy in Creggan Heights several times. I got the impression that he was staying there.'

Miller scribbled the information into his notebook as Policewoman Colhoun continued to recount the intelligence she had gathered.

As both of them sat in the car, O'D was sitting in Ma Murphy's living room talking to Con McDaid.

'Your man Sweeney gave me the information last night,' said O'D sipping a mug of tea. 'He seems to be a sound old character.'

'Aye,' answered Con, 'he's as sound as a bell. I think he was involved himself in the twenties.'

'Is that so? Do you know what he told me last night?'

'Naw,' answered Con, 'he wouldn't tell me when I asked him.'

'He reckons he knows what Len Haslitt's route is every Sunday morning.'

'Superintendent Haslitt?' said Con, sitting bolt upright in his chair. 'You're fuckin' joking!'

'I'm not,' said O'D continuing to sprawl. 'The question is, is he joking?'

'No way,' returned Con quickly. 'If he says he knows, then he knows. I'll bet my life on it.'

'Would you be prepared to bet half-a-dozen lives on it?'

It was an unfair question: Con always had the severest inhibitions about ordering people to risk their lives. But O'D wanted to see his companion's reaction. Con raised his head fractionally as if he had been mildly jolted by a cramping pain, and said slowly: 'If it was my decision, O'D, I would be prepared to take the old man's word.'

O'D knew the answer to the next question, but he had to ask it anyway. 'What are the chances of him setting us up, Con?'

'Absolutely zero,' returned Con confidently, 'there is as much chance of me and my mother setting you up.'

'That decides it then: we're going to have a few words with Mister Haslitt this Sunday.'

Inspector Miller dropped Policewoman Colhoun off in the grounds of Altnagelvin Hospital.

That night she met O'D in the private lounge in the Bogside Inn where he ordered two whiskeys and a bottle of ginger. She drank hers half and half. As she took the first sip, he said: 'I won't be able to see you for a few days.'

'That's a shame,' she said, sounding genuine. 'Do you have to go away or something?'

'Well. . . I have to do a few things which are probably going to keep me busy until Monday or Tuesday.'

'I see,' she said, smiling knowingly at him. 'Is there anything I can do to help?'

'I wish there was,' he said genuinely, 'then I would be able to see more of you, but unfortunately there isn't.'

Her next statement surprised him: 'I don't mind helping out, you know. I'm a very good driver.'

'I'm sure you are, too,' he said smiling, 'but I would be beheaded for letting you.'

There was a sincerity in his voice which prevented her from pursuing the point. Instead she said, 'In that case will you do me a favour?'

'Sure.'

She pulled a small notebook and pen from her shoulder-bag and scribbled on it. 'This is my address: will you promise you'll send for me if anything happens and you can't come yourself?'

O'D stared deeply into her eyes and imagined for a fraction of a second that there was something there that he wanted to see. 'You have got a promise,' he said.

On the following morning O'D drove a hijacked car to meet the three men he had hand-picked to carry out the Haslitt operation. The pick-up point was the house of the Bogside OC. He parked the car out of sight of the Masonic observation post and walked the last fifty yards to the house. The door opened before he reached it and the nervous face of the local OC, Terry Donaghey, appeared.

160

'Where did you park the car?'

'Don't worry, Terry,' said O'D, passing into the living room, 'she's well out of sight.'

Terry could not resist a quick glance into the street before closing the door. When he entered the living room he sat on the arm of a chair, glancing frequently into the street.

O'D spoke to Charlie Coyle who was sitting on the sofa beside another volunteer. 'Did Con tell you anything about the operation?'

'No,' said Charlie, 'he just told me to meet you here today.'

'Well,' said O'D, deciding to give them a minimum of information, 'we hope it is going to be a kidnapping operation.'

Charlie gave him an ironic look. 'We hope? Couldn't we be sort of definite about it?' Charlie had a simple, disarming directness.

O'D smiled as if he had been caught sneaking up the back stairs after midnight with his shoes in his hand. 'We'll try to be definite Charlie, but that will depend on the man we are trying to kidnap. He is a big noise and he will certainly be armed, so if he is going to fuck about we are not going to take any nonsense.'

'What's the alternative?' asked Charlie as if he were asking a swimmer what the water was like.

'We nut him.'

'That's nice,' said Charlie, still in his ironic mood.

'That's essential,' said O'D, making sure there was no hint of irony left in the situation. 'If he refuses to come quietly or goes for a gun, he will be nutted on the spot.'

'Am I on this operation too?' asked Terry, dragging his eyes away from the street for an anxious second.

'You will be providing the back-up with two ASUs,' said O'D.

'That's grand,' said Terry, taking another lightning glance out of the window. 'Will we need much firepower?'

'Probably not,' said O'D, speaking to the back of Terry's head, 'but we'll bring it along just in case.'

The third volunteer arrived overflowing with apologies for

161

holding them up. He was taunted with good-humoured sarcasm by Charlie and the other volunteer as they followed O'D out of the house. Before they had gone ten yards Terry was back at the window.

Five minutes later the four men climbed out of the hijacked car in the car-park of St Peter's School in Creggan. O'D was carrying a holdall as they jumped the low fence into an adjacent field. He squatted on the ground, opening the bag, and produced three identical handguns. He passed one to each of the men. 'Any of you ever handle one of these before?' he asked.

'Yeah,' said Charlie, 'I have.'

'You know what it is then?'

'Yeah,' said Charlie, bouncing the gun in his hand as if he were trying to guess its weight. 'It looks like a machine-gun and it feels like a sledgehammer but it is really a .455 Magnum.'

'That's near enough,' said O'D. 'Just remember this,' he said to the two volunteers, 'this is the most powerful handgun on the market and if you don't hold it properly it will break your bloody wrist. Got it?'

The two men nodded, a taciturn pair who always operated together. He had no doubt that the two immature faces staring up at him belied the characters of the two men who owned them.

'What I want you to do,' he said, including Charlie again, 'is fire these things until your arms get sore holding them. We'll do some target practice later, but first I want you to familiarise yourselves with the weapon.'

The three loaded and began firing into a small ditch at the top of the field. The noise thundered and ricocheted through the streets but the inhabitants seemed unperturbed. A few people came to their doors and a few pedestrians stopped to stare for a minute or two but they quickly grew bored. Only one group attempted to stop work for the duration of the practice, the pupils of St Peter's school.

One incident interrupted the routine. Charlie Coyle was lowering his sights onto the ditch when a small figure appeared in the middle of his V aperture. He immediately released the trigger and opened both eyes. In the middle of the field behind the ditch a man was charging towards them.

'Hold your fire,' said Charlie to the two volunteers. O'D was kneeling on the grass sorting out ammunition.

'What's wrong?' he asked looking up.

'There's a maniac charging down the field.'

The four men watched as the stranger approached. He would have moved more quickly had it not been for the wellington boots which appeared to be four sizes too big. At first O'D thought it might be someone to warn them of the presence of a patrol but something about the way the man's elbows were digging into the air, like an angry navvy digging a trench, and something about the way the feet were leading the attack told him he was wrong. As soon as the man had dropped clumsily into the lower field, almost losing a boot in the process, he began shouting at the practising gunmen. 'What the bloody hell do you think you are doing?' he screamed in a high-pitched voice.

O'D sighed as he handed the box of ammunition to Charlie. 'Sorry about this,' he began apologetically, 'but we have to practise here for an hour or two. I hope we are not bothering you too much.'

'You bloody well are bothering me too much,' screamed the farmer. 'There are people living at the other side of that hill, you know. Are you trying to kill them or something?'

O'D recognised the man, a wiry, waxen-faced farmer in his mid-forties; he owned a small farm about half a mile away. 'There's no danger of killing anyone,' he said calmly. 'All our rounds are going into that ditch and no further.'

But the man was determined to have no marksman's logic. 'That's all very well for you, but I've got a wife and weans on the other side of that hill and I'm damned if I'm going to let you shoot at them.'

'We're not shooting at them,' said O'D reasonably.

'You're not fucking going to either!' returned the farmer.

'Look,' said O'D. 'There's no way I would risk a bullet going

163

over that hill because I have relatives living there myself.'

The farmer looked at him evenly. There was one thing he prided himself on: the fact that he was a hardened market dealer who was not easily conned. And O'D looked to him like a typical, ignorant layabout.

'Is that so?' he asked sarcastically. 'Is that so? Who are they then?' He barked the question out.

'The Craigs,' answered O'D in the silence that followed. 'Alison is my sister.'

The farmer took a step backwards and blinked. 'The Craigs? Sure, they're Protestants,' he stammered stupidly.

'That's right,' confirmed O'D, 'so what?'

'Well. . .' stalled the farmer, a host of thoughts evidently battling for prominence in his confused head. 'Well, . . . ah. . . I thought you were IRA,' he finished timidly.

'We are,' said O'D, 'Saor Eire, a non-sectarian organisation.'

The farmer's face registered a cautious disbelief. 'Okay, what's Mr Craig's husband's name, then?'

'Bill,' answered O'D without hesitation. 'And their two sons are called William and Trevor and the dog is called King. And if you still don't believe me,' he continued, withdrawing a photograph from his pocket, 'here's a photograph of me with them in their front garden.'

The farmer's confidence was badly shaken but he still managed to maintain a severe look. 'That's them all right,' he said grudgingly, 'but I don't recognise you.'

'Try to imagine me with my hair shorter and without the scar,' said O'D helpfully.

The man glanced from O'D to the photograph. 'You've changed a bit, haven't you?'

'Yeah, I had an accident.'

The farmer returned the photograph and stood awkwardly staring at O'D.

'Are you convinced now that we won't risk any stray shots? And after all, their house lies directly in the line of fire, whereas yours is a little to the left.'

'Oh, you know my house, do you?' asked the farmer, jumping at the chance to change the subject.

'Known it all my life,' said O'D. 'In fact, you caught me stealing apples in your back garden once.'

'Is that a fact?' And the farmer smiled for the first time.

The situation was defused. The only remaining problem was that getting rid of the man proved more difficult than calming him. He took an avid interest in their guns, explaining that he had never seen their like before, enquiring as to their weight, design, feel and muzzle velocity. He was eventually encouraged to go when O'D explained diplomatically that he would probably get in their way if a patrol came along and they had to open fire.

When the training finally ended that afternoon the guns were dumped in Creggan and the men were reminded to be at Creggan HQ at eight for a meeting.

As soon as he had dropped the last man O'D went to look at the site of the operation. He knew the spot as well as he knew his own street but he had never looked at it with such a particular idea in mind. He had to satisfy himself that it was as suitable as he imagined it to be.

Magazine Street lay next to the Bogside, separated only by the towering masonry of the city walls. Fifty yards from the front gate of the church was the main city centre entrance to the Bogside. O'D parked the car before reaching the gate and made the rest of the journey on foot.

The church gates were locked, but this made his decision easier, for he now had only one option: the kidnapping would have to take place outside the church. The street was empty and completely shadowed by the walls as the evening sun dipped below their parapets. But the next day would be different. As he let the atmosphere filter into his consciousness he began to think that the Sunday crowd would be an asset, especially if, as was likely, there were armed police in the congregation. So, the more people. . . well, it would hardly be merrier, but it might prevent a lot of shooting.

He spent two hours walking around the area memorising

165

every doorway and the angle of every corner. He checked the escape routes and worked out alternatives at every turn where an unexpected factor could enter the operation. He imagined himself as a grand master treading a giant chessboard before the pieces had been set up for a complex and perilous combination. Finally, when he felt satisfied with his observations, he drove to the Creggan meeting.

'We'll get straight to the point,' he began as soon as everyone had arrived. 'The quartermaster is out of town until tomorrow afternoon so the weapons will be arranged by the training officer. He will have them at the Bogside OC's house at eight tomorrow morning. So you two' – he indicated two section leaders – 'will have your sections there at that time. That's when everyone will be told what the operation is. In the meantime I can tell you that it's a relatively simple one and in all probability you won't even have to fire a shot. You will be taking up two different positions. The task of the first position will be to ensure that the army doesn't enter the area for a given length of time – it won't be too long. Which of you wants the job?'

Both men raised their hands and O'D pointed to one of them. 'You've got it.' The task was simple: if any army patrol approached the area the ASU was to open fire and make sure it stayed where it was for five minutes.

'What if they just stall about without coming into the area?' asked the section leader.

'In that case leave them alone: this operation is more important than a couple of dead Brits.'

'Good enough,' said the section leader. 'How do we get out?'

'It'll be one of two ways,' said O'D. 'If you have to open fire then give it exactly five minutes and pull out. If you don't have to open fire then watch for us passing your position in the operation car. If that happens it means the operation is over and you can safely pull out.'

'What if the other position starts firing first?'

'You're way ahead of me,' said O'D. 'In that case, give it five minutes again and pull out regardless. If we haven't arrived by then we won't be coming.'

'And if the car passes in the meantime, we pull out behind it?'

'Right, you seem to have the picture okay. Don't worry unduly about this briefing tonight; I am keeping it as general as possible. Tomorrow evening will be the final briefing and that will be much more detailed.'

'Just one more thing,' said the first section leader, 'what's the chances of the Brits coming in behind us?'

'No chance,' said O'D definitely. 'You will be right on the edge of the area, so they will only be coming at your front – that is, unless someone is chasing them, and in that case they won't be interested in you.'

Everyone laughed, more in relief than in humour.

O'D turned to the second section leader. 'Your section will be under the Bog OC so you can take your orders from him. You will be covering the actual operation itself – and your task is to make sure we don't get trapped by the Brits. The job is a kidnapping but we don't know whether the target will have any protection. I don't think he will, but I don't know for certain. What makes your part of the operation tricky is that you will only be able to see one member of my group at a time. Whatever you do, make sure you don't shoot at us if we come running round the corner. But we'll sort those details out in the morning: you will have to know the position to appreciate them. And that is more or less as much as I can say right now, unless any of you have general questions.'

'What about weapons?' said one of the volunteers.

'I'll sort them out tonight and have them at the pick-up in the morning. Anything else?'

There was silence as everyone shook their heads and glanced at their neighbours.

'That's it, then,' said O'D. 'I want you all to think about this tonight – don't fantasize, just keep it on your minds. And I'll see you at eight o'clock in the Bog OC's house.'

Everyone filtered out. O'D was the last to leave. As he closed the door a chill wind blew through his threadbare jacket; he shivered involuntarily.

It was a strange evening, he felt, as he drove to Con McDaid's house. It had the dying brightness of a long, summer day, but there was a chill in the air which harked back to early spring. He wondered about the operation and suddenly he felt uncomfortable with the idea. Perhaps it was the men: the only two he felt really happy with were Charlie and the Bog OC. Most of the others he had heard good reports about, but he didn't know them personally. That was becoming a problem with the movement: it was so big now that he could not know everyone on a personal basis. But that was not what bothered him either, he was prepared to accept them on the strength of their records. The trouble was that they all looked so young. Their average age was about nineteen, but most of them looked fifteen.

He was wondering whether it would be wiser to call the operation off for a week and pick a different team. He had reached the junction of Southway and Lone Moore Road and had to negotiate a left turn. He nosed the car out into the main road, and then saw the convoy. It was about a hundred yards away, heading straight for him. He paused in a second's indecision: he could take a chance and attempt to pass it; but he was in a hijacked car – a recently hijacked car. He swung the car in a wide circle across the road, mounted the footpath and drove away from the convoy as fast as he could.

The police landrover leading the file noticed the irregular turn and immediately sounded its siren. O'D flung the car out of the Lone Moore Road on two wheels and tore into the maze of Brandywell streets with a screech of tyres. By the time the police reached the turn-off he was out of sight. The RUC Sergeant in charge of the landrover guessed that O'D had entered the Brandywell, but he did not want to find out for certain: it was not the first time a combined police and army convoy had been lured into the area and ambushed. The convoy headed for the barracks.

O'D parked the car in a hurry two streets from Con McDaid's house. The adrenalin trickling through his body had one good side effect, he thought: it decided him with absolute certainty that the operation was definitely on in the morning. He could not imagine why he had thought of calling it off.

'Good God! Are you all right?' said Mrs McDaid the instant she opened the door. 'You look as if you've seen a ghost.'

'Do I?' said O'D. 'I feel fine.'

'Well, you don't look it. Come in and sit down.' She led him unprotesting by the arm, closing the front door with a flick of her wrist.

Con was sitting on a small sofa eating fish and chips off a plate on his lap. A half-pint mug of tea was poised precariously on the arm of the sofa and a piece of half-eaten buttered bread lay beside it. 'What happened you?' he mumbled with a frown.

'I ran into a convoy on the Moore.'

'I knew it,' said Mrs McDaid with authority. 'You're as white as a sheet.'

O'D dropped into a chair smiling at her.

'Did they chase you?' asked Con round a mouthful of fish.

'I don't think so. I didn't give them a chance to.'

Con munched contentedly, nodding his head as Mrs McDaid said, 'I'm sure you wouldn't say no to a wee cup of tea?'

'You're dead right, Mrs McDaid.' She disappeared into the tiny back kitchen as Con's sister Sheila squeezed past her on the way out, rubbing her hair furiously with a towel.

'Yes, Hugh,' she greeted, manoeuvring her way round the few pieces of furniture which cluttered the little room. It only measured twelve feet by eight and contained a sofa and two armchairs, a dining table and three chairs, a television and a cage containing a budgie. Sheila pulled a dining chair from the table and placed it strategically in front of the range so that she could dry her hair at the fire. Con had to remove his legs to facilitate this operation, and he had to move carefully in case he spilt his tea in the process.

'Yes, Sheila,' said O'D.

'I hear Brenda's gone to England, did you get any word from her?'

The thought flashed into O'D's mind that rumours had started to circulate about himself and Dympna. Sheila and Brenda had been close friends in the past.

'Not a word. I expect she's too busy infiltrating the BBC.'

'That's a good job she has,' said Sheila.

'Yeah, I suppose it is,' said O'D humouring her. 'How's Harry getting on?'

'Don't talk to me about that loafer,' she said disgustedly, shaking her hair at the open fire. 'If he ever gets a job the shock'll kill me of a heart attack.'

Con nodded his munching face in sympathy with Harry, but he was careful to do it behind Sheila's back. Mrs McDaid arrived with a half-pint of tea and enough sandwiches to feed five starving men.

'Good God, Mrs McDaid,' protested O'D, 'do you think I'm an elephant?'

'Sure, you don't have to eat them all,' she answered unabashed, 'just leave what you don't want.'

'Leave nothing,' warned Con, reaching for his tea, 'give me what you don't want.'

'Listen to that pig,' said his mother lightly, 'he would eat the sofa if we let him.'

'I wonder what it tastes like?' said Con, looking at it in mock hunger.

'And another thing,' said his mother with affected severity, 'if you're bringing any guns into the house tonight make sure you don't put them under the stairs like the last time. You nearly gave your father a heart attack. He put his hand in for a shovel to get some coal and came out with a rifle. He was worried sick about it all day – spent two pounds of the rent money in the pub trying to calm his nerves.'

Con groaned as Sheila said: 'Don't believe that, Ma, he was only looking for an excuse for a drink.'

'He certainly needed a drink when he came back again,' said the mother.

170

'What happened then?' said O'D, picturing Con's father staggering drunkenly through the front door to negotiate the cluttered furniture.

Con groaned again and sank further into the small sofa.

'He found wee David playing cowboys and indians with the rifle behind the sofa.'

'Oh, God,' said O'D, laughing with the two women while Con squirmed. 'He's only about ten, isn't he?'

'Nine,' said the mother. 'He couldn't even hold the rifle it was that big, he had to lean it on top of the chair.'

'What's this he said to me Da?' said Sheila, giggling tremendously, encouraging her mother.

'Oh, that's right, he pointed the rifle at him as he came in the door, and says, "Don't move, Paddy, or I'll part your hair!"'

'Oh, Jesus,' roared O'D, breaking into uncontrollable laughter.

Con smiled weakly from the sofa and looked as if he wished he could crawl under it.

'Me Da's lucky he didn't demand a rise in his pocket money,' cried Sheila with tears of merriment streaming down her face. 'The wee get would have shot him if he hadn't coughed up.'

'The gun wasn't loaded, was it?' asked O'D, trying to show alarm through the laughter.

'Naw, but Paddy didn't know that,' said Mrs McDaid.

Con dragged O'D out of the house, leaving a plate of half-eaten sandwiches behind.

'You never told me about that one,' said O'D, still laughing intermittently as they walked along the street.

'I hear enough of it in the house to last me a lifetime,' said Con. 'My Da's in his element worrying about it. It's the best excuse he ever had for staying in the pub and those two love telling it to everyone who comes into the bloody house. It's become the resident joke of the street.'

'What about your young brother?'

'He's the worst of all,' said Con in a voice heavily loaded with depression. 'After me Da nearly killed him he went straight out and told all his mates about the rifle. Tried to bring them into the house for a private viewing only the old man had sobered up. I came in the other day and found him and his two wee mates searching the place. "What are you looking for?" says I. "Guns," says he and keeps on looking.'

'What did you do?' said O'D, straining to keep his face straight.

'I nearly broke his hole and told him he'd get me ten years if he kept it up.'

'So your house is definitely out of bounds for dumping from now on then,' said O'D with some irony and a little spluttering.

'Aye, unless we want some of our neighbours shot.'

'Or your Da.'

'Or the Ma.'

The weapons for the operation were dumped in a pensioner's cottage on the edge of the Brandywell. The back garden of the cottage opened onto waste ground which could be negotiated by car. O'D backed the car up to the gate and then went to the back door with Con. It was opened even before they could knock. An old lady greeted them with a smile.

'Hello, Sally,' said Con, 'we're not disturbing you, are we?'

'Not at all. Come in, come in.' She stepped back into the hall, holding the door open, gesturing with an elaborate wave of her hand for them to enter. Con led the way, pointing to O'D. 'This is O'D, Sally, he's the boss.'

'O'D what? What's O'D?' said Sally excitedly.

'O'Donnell,' said O'D following Con, 'Hugh O'Donnell.'

'Oh, O'Donnell,' said Sally, closing the door. 'I see. You're nothing to the O'Donnells from Rosemount, are you?'

'I don't think so,' said O'D. 'We come from the Bog originally, but we live in Inniscarn Road now.'

'Ah, them O'Donnells is it? You must be Mary's son then?'

'That's right,' said O'D smiling. He had followed Con right through the bungalow to a small bedroom where they now came to a halt in front of an ancient wardrobe.

172

'Your father was a docker, wasn't he?' continued Sally as she lifted a small jar from a dressing table and began searching for the wardrobe key. Before the weapons were loaded into the car, O'D had received a full rundown on his family history since his grandfather had arrived in Derry half a century earlier. Sally was acting like a long lost aunt before he left. They drove to a lock-up garage in the Bogside where the weapons were transferred to the boot of the operation's car. This car was in turn driven to the back of the Bogside OC's house and parked. The two men then went their separate ways.

Nine

THE MORNING WAS one of the best O'D had seen that year. A brilliant, crisp sunshine splashed the streets with a unique freshness as he made his way to the Bogside. He arrived at the OC's house at eight to discover everyone already there. They were sitting or lying around the front room talking quietly and he felt the tension immediately: it was a tangible force which he knew could act as either a barricade or a boost.

After greeting them he launched straight into the briefing, keeping his voice low in deference to the OC's family who were still asleep upstairs.

'The target is Superintendent Len Haslitt.' There was a collective intake of breath at the mention of the name. He kept to the essentials of the operation and explained them as clearly as he could. First he gave an outline, then he went over it in minute detail, and he finished by taking each man quickly through his own part. Finally there was a question and answer session where everyone aired their opinions.

The entire process took over an hour. Only when everyone was satisfied with his own role did O'D leave with three men to collect the arms from behind the house. The car was parked at the end of a laneway which provided ideal cover. Once the weapons were out of the boot and into the laneway, the only things that could be seen by the neighbours were the heads of four men walking along the lane. Back in the house, each man took his weapon and immediately began to check it, bringing an abrupt end to all quietness. O'D glanced at the OC and raised his eyes towards the ceiling but all he got in reply was a shrug of the frail shoulders. The men tried to keep the noise to a minimum but the house echoed to sliding bolts, cocking weapons and hammers falling on empty chambers.

The rattle of shoes from the bedroom above was followed by a clump of feet across the ceiling. Everyone stopped working and listened to the descending feet, all eyes on the door. The OC's younger brother entered the room wearing a pair of faded jeans and heavy, black, brogue shoes. 'Good Jesus,' he said, stopping at the doorway to survey the scene, 'it's the entire membership of Saor Eire going on an operation. What are you going to do, rob a church collection?'

Another pair of feet was heard crossing the ceiling.

'This, for those who don't already know, is the young brother,' said the OC casually. 'He's the local Provo and thinks he knows everything. Just ignore him.'

The younger brother ignored the OC and made straight for one of the SLRs. 'So this is the SLRs you stole in Germany, eh?' It was still only a rumour in Provo circles, but it was ready ammunition for the rivalry between the brothers. The door opened again and the eldest brother appeared, slightly better dressed than the younger member of the household, in a heavy jumper and slacks. He was a member of the local battalion staff of the Official IRA.

'I thought the Brits were raiding with all the noise,' he said in an agreeable tone, eyeing the arsenal of weapons.

'This is the sticky of the house,' said the OC.

'Fucking United Nations here,' mumbled one of the volunteers.

The older brother nodded at O'D whom he knew, saying, 'Do you need a hand with anything?'

'Thanks for offering,' said O'D, 'but everything's under control.'

The brother nodded again, 'Sound. Take it easy so.' He passed across the room, putting his arm around the youngest

175

as he did so, saying, 'Come on, junior, and let me see what sort of breakfast you make on a fine Sunday morning.'

When the OC's mother and sister arrived they were just as casual. His mother took in the occupants of the room and their weaponry in one glance. O'D was the only one she knew. She greeted him and turned to her son.

'What time are you going at?'

'About quarter-to-ten.'

She glanced at the clock on the mantelpiece. 'That's half-an-hour yet, will you take some tea before you go?'

'If you feel like making tea for the ten of us.'

'That's no problem,' she said, turning to the daughter. 'Charlotte, put the big kettle on.'

Charlotte turned as crimson as her Sunday dress. She appeared from behind her mother's skirt to dash across the tangle of arms and legs towards the kitchen. The volunteers moved instinctively out of the way, most of them avoiding her face in the hope of saving her further embarrassment. As she closed the kitchen door her mother went to a cabinet in the corner of the living room. Opening the drawer, she removed two candles and a small bottle of blessed water. She placed the candles in two holders on the mantelpiece as everyone watched, and lit them. Then she turned to face the room and began sprinkling the water over the volunteers, mumbling a prayer as she did so. Some of them accepted it casually, others looked embarrassed and a few blessed themselves. O'D looked her levelly in the eye as she dosed him.

'I hope you don't mind,' she said.

'Not at all,' he answered.

None of them had much of an appetite. They drank the tea and picked at the sandwiches, and were glad when the half-hour crawled to an end and they could get moving. As soon as they had gone the mother entered the living room by herself and knelt in front of the cushions. She remained praying in that position.

As Superintendent Haslitt entered the church he was unaware of being observed by four pairs of eyes. He was preoccupied with other problems and did not even notice the service. He wished he had broken the habit of twenty-five years and stayed at home. At least there he would have had more time to think. Or perhaps he should have gone to the barracks.

He had come to the conclusion that the infiltration of Saor Eire was not a good idea. Policewoman Colhoun had done her job better than anyone expected, but he felt that while infiltration could offer a long-term solution, O'Donnell represented an immediate problem. He knew the man was up to something at that very minute – he never seemed to stop – but what it was Colhoun had been unable to discover. He felt in his bones that it had something to do with the weapons from Germany and the camp across the border. He still had no idea where that camp was. The Rosemount OC certainly knew where it was, but he would not tell. Well, he would pay dearly for that little pleasure – at least a year on remand. What was it they had charged him with? He could not remember, but Mervin had assured him that it was sufficient. If only they could do that with O'Donnell – pick him up and charge him and hold him for a couple of years on remand. They had not been able to charge him with anything the last time, but surely the DPP would bend the rules in their favour this time. It had certainly been done in other cases outside the city. And it was beginning to look as if O'Donnell would not be got any other way.

'Damn it!' he declared to the astonishment of his wife. She turned her head and stared at him aghast. But he did not realise he had said anything. He watched the minister's mouth speaking the words of the sermon he did not hear and decided finally what would be done. He would pull Colhoun out and pick up O'Donnell; either that or he would send the SAS in after him. The conviction settled firmly on his mind as the service ended and people began to file noisily out of the pews.

The activity made him conscious of having reached a vital decision. As he rose to his feet it occurred to him that he was happier than he had been for days. He looked around the little church and noticed how beautiful it was. The entire interior was an elaborate display of highly polished wood; he had never seen such fine wood in any other church before, beautiful. He felt exultant as he left the building: he could not quite put his finger on the sensation, but he felt he was about to make a significant impact on the world that glorious morning. He ushered his wife through the little, green gates and turned with the congregation in the direction of the two men standing in a doorway.

Charlie Coyle stood beside O'D on the steps of a large Victorian building which raised them nine inches above the footpath. The first volunteer was six feet away, half-standing, half-sitting against the window of the house. The second volunteer stood across the street in the mouth of Butcher Gate, in full view of the ASU in the flats behind him.

O'D recognised Haslitt immediately: his features were unmistakable even though there were hundreds of people pouring out of the church. Haslitt moved along in the flow at the edge of the footpath; he could not step into the street which was lined with cars parked bumper to bumper. The solid body of people shuffled along and O'D realised that they were going to have difficulty: Haslitt was in the middle of a sea of bodies. There was something else he had overlooked: almost every male in the congregation could have passed for a policeman. He had no doubt that some of them were policemen, and they would probably be armed. Two thoughts flashed through his mind in quick succession: the first that he was an idiot for not having an SMG; the second that he should call the operation off and walk quietly away.

He had time to explore neither. Haslitt was in front of him, walking beside a small, plump, grey-haired woman; his wife. O'D pushed determinedly into the crowd and grabbed Haslitt's coat tightly with his left hand. Haslitt attempted to take a step backwards, but O'D put the Magnum against his throat and said in a chilling voice: 'Do exactly as I tell you or I'll blow your fucking head off.'

The crowd in front moved on with the flow and those behind drew back in fear. Haslitt went rigid but his wife reacted quickly. 'Why you!' she shouted, lifting her leather handbag and aiming it at O'D's head.

She had extended her arm to its full length when Charlie Coyle stepped forward and pushed her violently in the chest. She tumbled into the couple behind her, taking the woman to the ground in a flash of petticoats and white legs.

'Clear a way to the gate,' said O'D to the volunteer behind him. And to Charlie, now behind Haslitt waving his gun threateningly at the audience: 'Cover our backs.' And to Haslitt: 'Start moving towards the gate, and don't be stupid or you're a dead man.' Haslitt stumbled forward as he began to shake uncontrollably, but O'D kept a vice-like grip on his coat. Around them shouts emerged from the crowd.

'That's a policeman they're kidnapping!'

'They must be the IRA!'

'Somebody do something!'

'Leave him alone you cowards!'

People were beginning to slide over the cars onto the road and soon O'D found himself surrounded by a jeering mob prepared to fight in defence of a fellow parishioner. Even the crowd in front were not intimidated by the volunteer and were beginning to advance.

O'D twisted and faced the advancing crowd. One man was only three feet away and trying to shout the young volunteer into submission. O'D stepped forward quickly and brought the barrel of his gun crashing onto the man's skull. He then stepped back and resumed his hold on Haslitt. It was done so quickly that Haslitt did not have time to run. The injured man crumpled to the ground unconscious. But it was a mistake: the act seemed to anger the crowd rather than subdue them.

The man who had been knocked to the ground with Mrs Haslitt made a lunge for O'D's ankle in an attempt to topple him and almost succeeded. Both O'D and Charlie were alerted by the sudden movement, and both of them shot him

179

simultaneously without a second's hesitation. The body leapt violently, crashing along the ground, spilling blood in a rapidly spreading pool along the footpath and into the screaming Sunday gutter.

Panic and confusion exploded. The front-line spectators turned and fled from the bloody mess, trampling or dragging any obstacle out of their path. Many of them leapt over the parked cars and dived like swimmers into the crowd or scattered in all directions on the road. Some women and a few elderly men had been trampled. Some realised the futility of rising to run and lay where they were, staring cataleptically at the kidnappers. Some lay with their eyes closed and their ears covered. For the rest it was flight and panic.

A path to the gate was clearing quickly. O'D dragged Haslitt over the human obstacles. No one attempted to grab at him. He passed between two cars and began to cross the road.

Two shots rang out. He saw two flashes from behind the railings of the church and he felt a bullet pass his left ear. A moan sighed from the volunteer behind him; O'D heard him fall. He turned to look but nothing could be done: the youth lay staring blindly at the sky with his brains scattered on the road.

Charlie Coyle was now firing back at the railings of the church. The volunteer at the gate had also sighted his weapon, but he could not shoot as O'D and Haslitt were in his line of fire. O'D was exposed: Charlie, himself and Haslitt were the only three people standing in the middle of the road. Everyone else was either lying on the ground or crouched behind a car. He tried to make Haslitt move faster by dragging at his coat. But Haslitt had recovered from the initial shock. He sensed his only chance of escape. He knew that once he went through the gateway he was doomed. Now was his only chance, he had to take it. He pushed O'D with all the strength he could muster. At the same time he twisted his body away. His coat ripped with a tearing sound. O'D went sprawling on the ground, half a coat in one hand, his Magnum in the other.

The marksmen in the church immediately gave Haslitt

covering fire. They concentrated on O'D. Charlie had emptied his weapon and was recovering the dead volunteer's gun. Bullets bounced around O'D, chipping the tarmac as he lay on his back. He raised his Magnum and took aim at the crouched, running figure of Haslitt.

One shot was all he needed. The body slammed and skidded onto its face, leaving no doubt as to its condition. Charlie retrieved the Magnum from the dead volunteer and returned fire at the church with deadly accuracy. The volunteer at the gate was also firing now. O'D joined in, ensuring that no head appeared above the church wall as he scrambled to his feet. Firing alternately both men backed towards the gate. As soon as they reached it all three took off as fast as they could towards the car and as O'D ran he waved a spiralling signal at the flats for the ASU to pull out.

Charlie drove the car with O'D in the back. As they moved away O'D noticed that the seat was wet. He felt it thick and oily under his hand and, looking down, he saw it was blood.

'How the fuck did that get there?' he asked.

Charlie turned his head at the enquiry and saw the pool of blood. 'You're hit,' he said almost casually.

'You're right,' said O'D just as casually. 'I didn't even notice.'

'Is it bad?' asked Charlie, changing down a gear and throwing the car into the first corner.

'Don't know,' he said, pulling his clothes away in search of the wound, 'but there's an awful lot of blood.'

The car sped on towards Creggan as the ASUs began to beat their own hasty retreats.

Chief Inspector Mervin Wall was enjoying a quiet Sunday morning in bed when his phone rang. He swore softly as he lifted the receiver. 'Yes?'

'Tony here,' said the metallic voice of Inspector Miller, 'you better come in.'

'Trouble?'

'Yeah, big trouble, the Super's dead.'

'Oh no! How did it happen?'

'You'll hear all about it when you get here,' said Miller cautiously.

When he arrived at the barracks, Tony Miller was questioning the two constables who had opened fire from the church grounds. They related their story to Wall who then turned to Miller. 'Bloody bastards,' he said emotionally. 'Do we know who the dead one is?'

'Not yet,' said Miller, 'but wait till you hear the description of the ringleader.' He nodded to one of the young constables.

'He was about six foot,' said the constable, who was still visibly shocked, 'medium build, dark hair, swarthy looking in his late twenties and he had a heavily scarred face with a broken nose.'

'O'Donnell,' said Wall heavily. 'How come you couldn't hit the bastard?'

'Both of us reckon we did, sir,' said the more formal of the two. 'We reckon we put at least two slugs in him.'

'Yet he still got up and ran away?' said Wall sarcastically.

'That's right, sir.'

'Without limping?' he said in the same tone.

'Yes, sir.'

'Could you get up and run if I put two slugs out of a P38 into you?' he hissed.

Both constables stared at him without answering.

'All right,' said Wall, 'you can go and make out full reports, and don't leave the barracks until you are told.'

Both men filed quietly and quickly out of the office.

'Go easy on them, Mervin,' Miller said as the door closed, 'they are just what we have been looking for. They have given us O'Donnell on a plate. Both of them are eye witnesses who can put him away for life.'

'Good God,' said Wall, hitting himself a blow to the head, 'you're right. I never even thought of that.'

'A case of not being able to see the wood for the trees,' said Miller. 'What about Mrs Haslitt?'

182

'She's in hospital suffering from shock and a broken wrist.'

'Is there anything else I don't know?'

'Yes. The Chief Constable should be here in just under an hour.'

The Chief Constable was met by Chief Superintendent Jacks, the man in charge of the entire barracks. After thirty minutes of kicking their heels in a corridor Chief Inspector Wall and Inspector Miller were ushered into his presence. They found him seated behind a large, bare desk. Their own boss was relegated to a hard-back chair in a dimly lit corner: he obviously intended to stay out of the proceedings. 'Sit down,' ordered the Chief Constable. He was a small man with a large nose and very close-set eyes, the combined effect of which made him look like a hawk. He had a long neck in proportion to his body and a peculiar way of manoeuvring it which made him look even more like a bird of prey.

'I'm told that you two are the resident experts on Saor Eire and that you worked directly under Superintendent Haslitt, is that so?' The words were forced out in a series of small barks.

'That's right, sir,' said Wall soberly.

The Chief Constable nodded his head in apparent satisfaction at the answer and began drumming on the desk with the index finger of his right hand. It sounded like a distant jackhammer rattling out a warning. 'Superintendent Haslitt was also an expert on this organisation,' he began the instant the pecking stopped, 'as was Sergeant Taylor. Do you think there is any significance in the fact that both of them were murdered within a short space of time?' The pecking resumed.

'Well, sir,' said Wall doubtfully, 'there's significance in the fact that Saor Eire had opportunities to shoot both of them.'

The Chief Constable stopped pecking, ignored the answer, and asked, 'Is there a remote possibility that Saor Eire knows who is conducting the investigations into their organisation?'

'They certainly know the team of investigators, sir, that's inevitable when we have to question them, but I doubt if they

183

could single out the most important men. And I'm sure they don't know anyone outside the questioning team.'

'Two possibilities present themselves to me, Chief Inspector,' continued the Chief Constable, again without acknowledging the answer. 'One is that police security as far as Londonderry is concerned is virtually non-existent. And the other is that Saor Eire knows every bloody move that is being made inside this barracks. And I can tell you that neither of these is going to be tolerated any longer. This state of affairs is going to be sorted out or I'll know the reason why.'

The Chief Constable launched into an assault on the record of insubordinate clannishness which the Londonderry force had earned for itself. He ended with: 'What we have here is a penny-ante organisation which is turning Londonderry on its head. And if my information is correct – information which has come from you, I might add – it is all being orchestrated by one man. Now that is a ludicrous situation, so ludicrous that it is beyond words. Don't you agree?' He glared accusingly at the two men and resumed his drumming on the desk.

Wall could see his future crumbling like a papier-maché castle under the beak of a very angry Chief Constable. He could never have been accused of over-adventurousness as far as his career was concerned, but now he felt instinctively that some sort of radical action was called for. He had been pushed into a corner and he obviously wasn't going to get out of it until he offered some initiative.

'The sequence of events has been disastrous so far, sir, but that has been because our hands have been tied.'

'What do you mean by that?' said the Chief Constable sharply.

'Quite simply, sir, we know the ring-leaders of Saor Eire but we haven't had enough evidence to convict them in the courts. I suggested to Superintendent Haslitt that we pick them up and hold them on remand but he was against the idea. That in my opinion is the only way we are going to bring this violence to an end: by taking these people off the streets and making sure they don't come back for a long time.'

'But,' said the Chief Constable, pausing in his drumming, 'you have been trying to pick this man O'Donnell up for weeks and you haven't got him yet. What am I to think of that?'

'The situation has changed now, sir. I think we can pick him up any time we want.'

'Well, do so then,' said the Chief Constable aggressively without a moment's hesitation. 'Lift him and anyone else you think of significance in Saor Eire and charge them and I will see to it that the Director of Public Prosecutions agrees to the remands. But, mind you, after those people have been arrested there better be no more Saor Eire nonsense in Londonderry. Have I made myself clear?'

'Yes, sir,' said Wall, 'if we can put these people away the trouble will stop.'

'I need hardly add,' said the Chief Constable, whose anger seemed to be on the wane now, 'that if you can get statements out of the buggers it will be all the better.'

'We'll do our best, sir.'

'Good, that's all I have to say. You have a free hand from here on, Wall. And you, Inspector.'

'Thank you, sir,' said both men automatically.

Back in his own office Wall said to Miller, 'I don't know which is worse: being shot at by Saor Eire or being set up by the Chief Constable.'

'You think he's setting us up?' said Miller in surprise.

Wall thought for a second, then said, 'I think he's trying to panic me into taking some sort of extreme action which he couldn't sanction himself.'

'Such as what?'

'I don't know, perhaps wreaking havoc in the town unless we destroy Saor Eire.'

'What are you going to do?'

'Everything I can do to get this bastard O'Donnell. And the first thing is to find Policewoman Colhoun.'

O'D was bleeding badly in the car and he began to black out.

185

Charlie wanted to drive straight across the border, but O'D insisted on being taken to Ma Murphy's house.

Ma was working in the kitchen when they stumbled into the living room with him and as soon as she saw him she went into action like a one-woman emergency unit. He was ordered to lie on the sofa. While she pumped Charlie on what had happened O'D blacked out and Ma was talking to him when he came around a few seconds later.

'Do you know where you're hit, son?'

'I think it's in the leg, Ma, but I'm not sure.'

'I'll have to take your trousers off to see,' she said and began undoing his belt. In the middle of the operation she glanced out the window and said to Charlie, 'Is that the car you used out there?'

'Aye.'

'Well, you better move it in case the army come lookin' an' find it here.'

Charlie handed the keys to the young volunteer saying, 'Leave it behind the shops and come straight up again.'

Ma was examining O'D, his left leg a mess of blood. The wound was eventually located on the back of his thigh.

'That won't kill you, I don't think,' said Ma, wiping the blood away and examining the wound closely, 'but it shouldn't cause you to black out. Was it a big bullet?' she asked Charlie.

'Not very big,' said Charlie. He held his finger and thumb about half-an-inch apart, saying, 'about that size.'

'So it's a shortarm then,' said Ma. 'What calibre?'

'Thirty-eight,' said Charlie.

Ma looked at the wound again. 'Well, that won't go far, so it must be something else that's causing the blackouts.'

She looked at O'D's blood-soaked underpants, then snipped them open with a scissors. A second bullet had entered his groin just above the pubic-hair line. Bright red blood oozed from the wound.

'Oh, Jesus!' exclaimed Ma, alarming everyone including herself. She examined the wound closely and declared firmly, 'He'll have to go to hospital.'

186

'That's out,' said O'D.

'You'll have to, son, you'll bleed to death inside and out if you don't.'

O'D looked at her for a few seconds, an expression of deep concentration on his face, then spoke to Charlie. 'Phone a doctor and tell him to come to the shops. As soon as he arrives, lift him and bring him up here.'

'Right,' said Charlie. 'Where's the nearest phone, Ma?'

'Just across the street, son, that house on the corner.'

Halfway across the street Charlie realised he did not know which doctor to ring. As he lifted the receiver he decided to phone his own doctor. The receptionist connected him immediately. 'Listen, Doc,' began Charlie as convincingly as he could, 'there's a man up here at Creggan shops who has just taken a fit. He says his name is Coyle and he refuses to go to hospital without seeing you.'

'What happened to him?' said the doctor.

'He just took a fit and fainted,' lied Charlie. 'Now he's sitting on the floor with a cut on his head and he can't move. Will you come and see him?'

'I think it might be best if I send an ambulance,' said the doctor cautiously.

'That won't work,' said Charlie quickly. 'He refuses to go to hospital and just keeps asking for you.'

There was a pause for a few seconds and Charlie held his breath. 'What did you say his name was?'

'He says it's Coyle and he seems to think you're his doctor.'

'Okay, I'll come,' said the voice, 'where is he?'

'Come to the Creggan shops and you'll see someone there.'

Five minutes later the doctor arrived. As soon as the car came to a halt, Charlie got into the passenger's seat. 'Listen, Doc, I'm sorry about this, but we have an emergency and we need your help. A man has been shot and he won't go to hospital. Will you take a look at him?'

'It looks as if I don't have much option, Mr Coyle,' said the doctor coolly, staring at the gun in Charlie's waistband. Two minutes later they entered Ma Murphy's living room.

O'D was propped up on his elbow when they came in, obviously in pain but in complete control of his faculties.

'Sorry, Doc,' he said weakly from the sofa, 'but you're going to have to give me two minutes with this lad before you examine me.'

The doctor's outraged expression faded as Ma, who happened to be one of his oldest patients, took him firmly by the arm and led him to the kitchen.

'Charlie,' said O'D urgently as soon as the door had closed, 'go to the Bog OC and tell him what happened. Then tell him to get someone over the border to stop the camps. Mick Mulhern will be in Bridgend this afternoon and I want him here as soon as possible, got it?'

'Got it. Is that all?'

'That's enough,' said O'D, forcing an unnecessary smile.

Charlie took the keys of the hot car, saying to the volunteer, 'You stay here and keep an eye on him and I'll be back in half-an-hour.' The volunteer looked uncomfortable as he nodded his head silently.

The doctor was ushered in by Ma. One glance at the wound told him what had to be done: 'I'm afraid there's nothing I can do for you, you'll have to go to hospital.'

O'D stared quietly into his eyes as he answered. 'There's no way I can go into hospital. Either you fix me up or I die on this sofa.'

The doctor was startled: immediately he began to examine the wound more closely. But the diagnosis was the same. He shrugged helplessly. 'It's out of the question,' he said gravely. 'This wound on your leg looks relatively minor – that's only a guess, mind you – but this one in your groin is extremely serious. You will have to be x-rayed to see where the missile has lodged itself and then you will have to be operated on to have it removed and see what damage it has done. I'm sorry, but that is the only way it can be.'

'I'm sorry too, Doc, because that's the only way it can't be. Will I die for certain if I don't get it seen to?' O'D sounded as if he were asking what the medicine would taste like when it arrived.

'I would say most certainly you will.'

'How long will it take?'

'Are you serious?'

'Very.'

The doctor stared at him incredulously, trying to figure out whether he was insane or just delirious from the wound. 'The fact is that you are dying right now from loss of blood – that's leaving aside your internal injuries, which are more serious. . .'

'How long, Doc?' interrupted O'D.

'I think there is every possibility that you could bleed to death before the night is out.'

'Will I be conscious till midnight?'

'That's impossible to say,' said the doctor, 'you could black out at any moment.'

'And there's no way I could persuade you to operate on me here?'

'Absolutely none. I couldn't do it in a properly equipped hospital, that's a surgeon's job.'

'In that case, Doc, I'm sorry for having put you to all the trouble. Will you give me a few painkillers before you go?'

The doctor tried every argument to get O'D into hospital, any hospital, but nothing worked. In the end he stopped the bleeding from both wounds and produced four strong painkillers. 'I'll come back again this evening and see you if I may?' he said, rising and closing his bag.

O'D paused with a glass of water in his hand ready to drop a painkiller and eyed him steadily. 'Have I got your word that you won't tell anyone about this?'

'You have,' said the doctor with a frankness bordering on insult. 'I'm an Irishman too, you know.'

O'D smiled at the emotional answer, which he estimated to be as much a longing for recognition as it was a statement of beliefs. 'Right, Doc, I'll be here,' he said almost cheerfully.

Ma Murphy showed the doctor out, fussing over him like a hen leading one of her chicks from the coop. She returned to find O'D examining his dressing.

'Ma,' he said, 'you'll have to marry me after what you saw today.'

'If I was fifty years younger, son,' she said, with reflected light dancing off her moist eyes, 'I'd take you up on that.'

Charlie Coyle arrived fifteen minutes later. 'How do you feel?' he asked, before he had even closed the door.

'Great,' said the invalid.

'Balls,' said Charlie.

'Well, I can feel the pain,' O'D corrected himself, 'but these tablets are so strong that I just don't care about it.'

'What did your man say?'

'Usual crap: I might die if I don't get to the hospital. Did you see the OC?'

'Aye, he sent someone across the border to collect Mick and call off the camp. He wanted to come up here but I told him to collect all OCs and double the patrols in the area. The Brits are obviously going to raid the night so I thought the more trouble we could give them the better. Was that okay?'

'Couldn't have done better myself, Charlie,' said O'D with genuine admiration. 'You've a good head on you.'

Just a little over two hours after the doctor left Ma's house Dympna Colhoun was reading a novel in her flat in Northland Road. She was interrupted by a quick, nervous knock. She anxiously left her book down and opened the door, allowing Inspector Tony Miller to enter. 'Something wrong, sir?' she asked urgently, closing the door behind him.

'Never mind the formalities, Dympna,' he said curtly, 'call me Tony.'

'Okay,' she said, following him into the room. Both of them sat before Miller spoke.

'The Super's dead,' he said bluntly.

'Oh, God.' She sighed like someone receiving the news of the death of a distant relative. 'How?'

'Saor Eire murder squad, coming from the church this morning.'

The truth suddenly surfaced in her mind. 'So that's what he had planned for today,' she said vehemently.

'This puts your operation in a different light now, you realise?' He was tapping his fingers together in front of his chest with the elbows resting on the arms of the chair, like a university don contemplating an intellectual problem.

'It must put everything in a different light,' she said uncertainly. 'What do you want me to do?'

'Mervin Wall is in charge now and he wants O'Donnell picked up as soon as possible. He's in the process of mounting an operation right now. What we want from you is where we can find the bastard.'

'I don't know, Tony, not at the moment anyway, but I think I could find out. Do you think the Chief Inspector will hold the operation until I go into the no-go area and see if I can locate him?'

'I think he might if you're certain you can find him.'

'Well, I can't guarantee it but I think there's every chance.'

'How long will it take?'

'I don't know, a few hours perhaps.'

Miller snapped a quick glance at his watch. 'Right, I'll tell you what: I'll stall the operation until eight o'clock tonight, that should give you plenty of time to locate him. Once you do, phone the emergency number and we'll come straight in. If it happens that you can't get to a phone then try to ensure that he is somewhere in the vicinity of the Bogside Inn at exactly eight o'clock. We will mount a major roadblock there at that time and if he comes through it we'll lift him. Okay?'

'I've got that.'

Thirty minutes later she was walking past the Bogside Inn wondering what to do when she saw Con McDaid. Hailing him, she called across the street, 'Have you seen Hugh about?'

'I seen him earlier this morning,' said Con crossing to her, 'but I haven't seen him since.'

'Have you any idea where I might find him?' She made it sound as if she had some vitally important information to impart.

'Not off-hand,' said Con in a low pensive drawl, 'but I'll find out if you like.'

'That would be great, Con, would you?' She linked her arm in his and smiled into his eyes.

They weaved their way through the new council houses and old tenements of the Bogside until they came to the OC's house where Con had left the weapons the previous night. The place was a hive of activity when they arrived and people were overflowing into the street. Con elbowed his way into the living room. 'What the fuck's going on?' he demanded.

Everyone fell silent allowing the Bog OC to answer.

'Haven't you heard? O'D's been shot!'

'What!' bellowed Con. 'You're joking!'

'No way. He's lying in Creggan at this minute bleeding to death.'

'Is he not going to hospital?' asked Con automatically.

'Don't know, we have only been told to double the patrols in the area and expect the Brits.'

'I'm going to see him,' Con announced, 'I need a car.'

The OC knew better than to argue. He fished a set of keys out of his pocket and handed them over: 'The green Cortina.'

Con did not speak as Dympna trotted along behind him and let herself into the passenger seat.

O'D was lying on the sofa, very pale but quite lucid. Dympna went immediately to his side and knelt on the floor. 'Oh, Hugh,' she said, 'what happened to you?'

'Slight accident. How did you get here?'

'I glued myself to Con.' She gave a nervous little smile.

O'D looked at Con. 'How many people know where I am?'

'Don't know,' shrugged Con. 'They know you're in Creggan, but they mightn't know you're here.'

'Who are they?'

'The Battalion OCs, but I don't think they know for sure.'

'I hope not,' said O'D; 'whatever happens, I have to see Mick Mulhern.'

'Hugh, you look bad,' said Con.

'I don't feel so bad, Con, just a little weak. Don't worry

about it.'

'I think you should go to hospital.'

'No way, Con. If I go to hospital I won't come out of it alive.'

'But they can't shoot you in hospital,' said Dympna quickly.

'Can't they?' was the cold, flat, sardonic reply.

'Letterkenny Hospital then,' said Con hopefully. 'I could carry you across the border and we could have a car there.'

'Maybe, Con,' said O'D dodging the subject, 'but first I have to see Mick.' Con's shoulders slumped as he stood in the centre of the floor like a defeated fighter.

'How are your wounds?' asked Dympna. 'Do you want me to have a look at it?'

'The doctor's already looked at it and said there's nothing much he can do.'

'Ah, so you've seen a doctor?' She breathed a slight sigh of relief. 'What did he say about the hospital?' she asked.

'Never mind, there's nothing I can do for him.'

'Could you do it for me?'

'Sorry.'

She nodded her head to signify her understanding, then said, 'Did he give you painkillers? I could get you some.'

'Yeah, he gave me some which are doing a pretty good job.'

She fell silent. It was obvious he did not want to talk. His Magnum revolver was lying on the sofa close to his head. She could have killed him without a doubt, the thought crossed her mind, but she had little hope that she could also kill the rest before they reacted. And she did not know how many more there were in the house. The old lady made an occasional silent appearance round the kitchen door and disappeared again as quickly as she had come. There was also at least one young volunteer who had access to the room. And there was Charlie.

'Look,' she said, 'I want to stay with you, but my mother is coming to the flat to visit me and she hasn't got a key. Would you mind if I went out and rang her up and came back again?'

193

He looked at her through very tired eyes. 'There's no reason for you to go through all this, why don't you go and see your mother and then come back again tonight?'

She seized the opportunity. 'I'll tell you what I'll do, I'll go and see her and then come straight back again.'

'Okay,' he said, too tired to think about it. He could feel himself slipping into unconsciousness.

She rose and turned to Con. 'Could you give me a lift to the Bogside? The sooner I get down the sooner I'll be back.'

Con was thrown into an open-mouthed dilemma as he looked from her to O'D's prostrate form and back again. He was about to offer her the car keys when Charlie spoke. 'I'll drop her down, Con, if it's okay. I want to go to the Bog anyway.'

'That would be great, Charlie,' said Con with obvious relief. Then, by way of an apology to Dympna, said, 'You don't mind, do you?'

Dympna touched his shoulder. 'It's okay, Con, I understand. In fact, I'm really glad you're staying.' Her smile almost brought tears to his eyes.

As the car pulled away from the house, Charlie said, 'I can get you a phone at the shops if you just want to phone, you know.'

'You don't know my mother,' said Dympna, just a little too sweetly for Charlie's seasoned ear. 'If I don't see her and give her the key to the flat she will take hysterics over the phone.'

Instead of driving her to the checkpoint at Waterloo Place as he had originally intended, Charlie drove to the back of Rossville Street flats about two hundred yards away and parked the car. 'I don't want the Brits to see the car,' he said curtly, 'so I'll drop you here.'

'This'll be fine thanks,' she said. 'Tell Hugh I'll be up again as soon as I calm my mother.'

He turned the car slowly as she walked out of the car-park then parked it and switched off the engine. He watched her from the car, then climbed out and followed her towards the city centre. Close to the Waterloo checkpoint he remembered the Magnum revolver, still loaded and lodged in his belt but he marched right up to the searcher and, smiling, said, 'Lovely day.' The man patted his sides and waved him through.

Dympna walked towards the main Post Office building in the centre of the city, then turned into Custom's House Street. As Charlie came to the corner he saw Dympna being driven away in a blue Opel Kadett. Hurriedly pulling a pen from his pocket Charlie scribbled the number in the centre of his hand. He did not hear the soldier approach.

'Excuse me, chief,' said the English accent, 'what's your name?'

Charlie leapt involuntarily. 'Good God!' he said, instantly disguising his voice, 'you frightened the life out of me. Do you make a habit of creeping up on people like that?'

'Sorry, sir,' said the soldier doubtfully, 'I didn't mean to frighten you, but could I have your name please?'

'You certainly could,' said Charlie flamboyantly, 'Sebastian Goldsmith.'

'Do you have any identification, sir?' asked the soldier.

'I'm afraid not,' said Charlie, patting his jacket. 'Unfortunately this is an old jacket I use for working.'

'I see,' said the soldier. 'What do you work at?'

'I'm an engineering research student at St Columb's College,' said Charlie brazenly.

The soldier looked undecided. 'What's your address, sir?'

'St Columb's College, Bishop Street.'

'I see, you live in the college then?'

'That's correct.'

'Just hang on a second, please.' He turned and walked a few yards to his nearest companion. They exchanged a few unheard sentences and then one of them spoke into a radio, asking their base for instructions.

'What's your date of birth, chief?'

'I'm over twenty-one,' he said with forced nonchalance.

'I guessed that, chief, but what's your DOB?'

'I believe I am only obliged to tell you whether or not I am over twenty-one.'

The soldier turned without answering and rejoined his companion with the radio.

'I'm sunk now,' thought Charlie, surprised to discover how calm he felt with a fifteen-year jail sentence stuck down the back of his belt.

After two minutes of intermittent conversation over the radio the soldier returned, and there was a swagger in his walk as he announced, 'I'm arresting you.'

Charlie saw that the third member of the patrol was standing across the street with his rifle trained on him.

'Is that so?' said Charlie, 'under what law?'

'What?' said the soldier confused by the unaccustomed question.

'Under what law are you arresting me?' repeated Charlie. 'You are required to name the statute under which you are taking away my rights.' The accent was improving with every sentence.

'No law,' said the soldier, shifting his stance, 'I'm just arresting you.'

'Well, I'm damned if I'm standing for that,' said Charlie indignantly. 'I demand to know why and under what law you are arresting me.'

The soldier with the radio began to approach as Charlie raised his voice. Curiosity also began to get the better of the soldier across the street who was just out of earshot and who slowly began to cross the empty street, throwing his long shadow on the overheated tarmac.

'The chief here,' said the first soldier sarcastically to the other two, 'wants to know what law we're lifting him under.'

Charlie clasped his hands behind his back and let his knuckles rest against the barrel of the gun.

'He don't need no law,' said the soldier who had just crossed the street, 'he can arrest you as a member of Her Majesty's forces.'

'Well, there must be a law to say that he can do that,' said Charlie, stalling and hoping that the three of them would put their heads together for just a second to discuss it.

196

But they didn't, instead the patrol leader said, 'Oh, there is, but we don't 'ave to tell it to you.'

Charlie looked at the ground for a moment, then, stretching his neck as if he were looking over their heads, he said, 'Well, here comes the police, let's hear what they have to say about this.'

The three soldiers turned simultaneously and Charlie grabbed for the weapon. For a second it caught his jumper as he pulled it from his jeans, but he ripped it through the obstruction. The three soldiers were still looking for the police when he levelled the gun. He shot the patrol leader in the back of the head from a distance of three feet. As the other two turned, he shot the radio operator in the mouth. The third one took off as fast as he could run, and had taken six steps before Charlie's next bullet caught him in the base of the skull and flung him to the ground like a discarded sack of coal.

Before his body had settled Charlie was running. He could not take the shortest route through Waterloo Place as the checkpoint there had obviously heard the shots – it was only fifty yards away from where he stood. Instead he ran up Magazine Street on the inside of the walls, a route which took him back towards the church where Haslitt had been killed only a few hours earlier. As his heart attempted to punch its way through his chest he came as near as he ever had to praying, willing that the police, who would certainly have been swarming round the church after the shooting, would by now be gone. He reached the exit half-way up the street without hearing the sound of approaching feet in either direction. The Castle Gate which led to the relative safety of the Bogside was the kingdom of heaven.

Policewoman Colhoun had been surprised to see Inspector Miller's car as she turned into Custom's House Street. 'I was just going to ring you,' she said, climbing into the passenger's seat.

'That's what I thought,' he answered, 'so I decided to save

you the bother. You see, I saw you getting a lift. I was in the army observation post on the walls.'

'Oh, I see. I thought for a minute you had a tail on me.'

'Did you find him?' he asked, as the car pulled away from the kerb.

'Yes, and he's injured.'

'That's good,' said Miller, 'I hope it's nothing trivial. Where is he?'

'The woman Murphy's house in Creggan Heights.'

'Ah,' sighed Miller with satisfaction, 'we were going to hit her anyway.'

'There are three other men in the house and I would say that at least two of them are armed. And O'Donnell has a gun by his side constantly.'

'That's nice,' said Miller with affected nonchalance.

Chief Inspector Wall listened to Dympna's account of the situation with single-minded concentration. He sat slumped over his desk, head in hand, and saw a small living room in a council house in Creggan with a wounded man lying on the sofa and two others lounging about the room, all of them probably armed. He questioned her closely, piecing together a minutely detailed map, pinpointing and circling the house. He asked her to describe the layout of the gardens, hedges and parked cars in the area. The operational briefing took almost an hour to complete.

Wall sat quietly considering whether he had chosen the best method of approach. He did not like the idea of attacking a house containing three gunmen, but he wanted O'Donnell. Finally he called Miller on the phone. 'Get Major Barry Down up here. We're going straight in for the bastard, shooting or no.'

Ten minutes after Dympna and Charlie had left the house Mick Mulhern arrived, having been briefed during his short drive from the border. 'How's it going, kid?' he greeted O'D with a mixture of lightheartedness and concern.

'I'm beginning to get dizzy spells, but I'm okay at the minute. . . I want to talk to you yourself.'

Mulhern glanced at Con and the young volunteer. Both filed silently out of the room. He crouched beside the sofa so O'D would not have to raise his voice.

'I mightn't make it out of this, Mick,' said O'D matter-of-factly.

'Don't be talking daft, Hugh,' said Mulhern, 'of course you'll make it.'

'Don't you be fooling yourself as well as me – just listen. It's of no importance whether I make it or not, the important thing is that this operation is carried out. If I do kick off I want you to take over as OC.' Mulhern was about to speak, but O'D stopped him. 'Now don't interrupt, just listen. As soon as you do take over the first thing you must do is go to Dublin and see the GHQ Staff – and tell them that I said the operation should come off as soon as possible.'

'But why as soon as possible, O'D?'

'Two reasons, Mick. The more we delay at this stage, the less chance of success the plan will have. I was wrong about the training: all these volunteers are beginning to cause too much talk. And, secondly, if Dublin are allowed to stall on this for a fortnight they will forget all about it and redistribute the arms. Belfast will be clamouring for them to do that right now anyway as they didn't like the idea of us getting them all in the first place.'

'They wouldn't do that,' said Mick with defiance and indignation.

'You can be sure that they will. As soon as I go off the scene they will try to call the whole thing off unless you convince them that you are determined to go through with it.'

'But only half the men are trained,' said Mick.

'Doesn't matter,' said O'D, falling back on the sofa and staring at the ceiling as if he were watching the progress of some invisible play being enacted there. He seemed to lose the idea for a second, then continued though still staring at the ceiling. 'Doesn't matter. What you do is take the men that are already trained and make them section leaders.'

Mick was startled. It crossed his mind that O'D was beginning to hallucinate. 'Wait a minute, Hugh,' he said, 'some of those men couldn't even lead themselves never mind lead a section.'

'Doesn't matter,' said O'D, 'they will be okay on the day. Just get them to out with the guns and point them in the right direction and the fire will do the rest.'

'Fire? What fire?'

'The petrol bombs,' said O'D insistently, like a small child explaining the simple operation of a new toy to an ignorant adult. 'I told you about them.'

'You didn't tell me about any petrol bombs, Hugh,' said Mick.

'I told you the plan,' O'D said almost mournfully with a heavy glaze on his eyes.

'You told me what barracks we were going to take over and how many men should be used on each, but you didn't say how we were going to do it, and you certainly didn't mention anything about petrol bombs.'

'How the fuck do you think we are going to do it: with bullets through brick walls?'

'I don't know,' said Mick simply.

'With fire, that's how. We're going to burn the bastards out.' He slipped into unconsciousness and Mick rose to call Con.

'What do you think?' he asked in alarm.

'I think he should go to hospital,' was Con's predictable reply. Ma was called. She examined O'D and adjusted the dressing where it had slipped from his groin, then took his pulse before giving her opinion. 'If he doesn't go to hospital right now he'll die.' Con and Mick agreed, but they were still debating when Charlie Coyle arrived.

'I just nutted three Brits,' he exclaimed as he burst into the room.

'What the fuck!' said Mick, leaping three inches in the air. 'How?'

Charlie told the story, hardly able to believe it himself. Mick asked about the car and Charlie looked at the forgotten scribble which was almost erased from the centre of his hand. He squinted and repeated it slowly.

'Oh, Christ,' sighed Mick, 'an Opel Kadett? That's a fucking Branch car!'

'Burn the fuckers,' shouted O'D in a sudden unexpected cry. Charlie stared at Mick, confused. 'And no one suspected that bitch,' said Mick. 'We better get him out of here before the bastards arrive.'

'Where to?' asked Charlie.

'Altnagelvin,' said Con, thinking of the nearest hospital.

'No way,' said Charlie aggressively, 'the cops will get him if we put him in any hospital in the North. It will have to be Letterkenny or nowhere.'

'Right,' said Mick, 'you and Con get him into my car and I'll tell Ma to expect visitors.'

The car was just crossing the border by an unapproved route when the first Saracen screeched to a halt outside Ma Murphy's house. Soldiers tumbled onto the street, backed up by two more Saracens, two landrovers, and a police jeep. Soldiers were running everywhere, jumping into gardens, lying on footpaths, rolling under stationary cars. Ma Murphy's front door was kicked off its hinges and a burly sergeant went thundering along her front hall, closely followed by three more soldiers.

'Who is it?' called Ma from the kitchen. 'The key's in the front door.'

He slowed to a walk as he crossed the deserted living room and entered the kitchen. Ma was standing at the sink washing her cushion covers.

Chief Inspector Wall did not take part in the operation. He had other problems to contend with: three of them; all dead, and they had been killed in what was supposed to be the most secure area of the city. He crouched over his littered desk, trying unsuccessfully to console himself with the fact

201

that he at least had the man responsible for most of the anarchy in the city. Inspector Miller interrupted by entering the office and closing the door noisily. 'Sit down, Tony, and tell me the worst,' said Wall, combing loose strands of hair from his forehead with his fingers.

Miller was economical with his words. 'The three of them were shot virtually at point-blank range with shortarms. It must have happened seconds after I left the post office.'

'How many gunmen?'

'There was only one seen, but there must have been more than that. The strange thing is that the soldiers seem to have been standing in a bunch.'

'There's no way that could happen,' said Wall with authority, 'they're too well trained to bunch up.'

'That's what I thought too, but they were all standing within ten feet of each other.'

'My God! Do you think a decoy was used?'

'Looks like it at the minute.'

Wall leaned back and looked at the ceiling as if he was expecting it to fall on him.

'Have we got O'Donnell yet?' asked Miller.

Wall pushed himself forward, listlessly reaching for the phone. 'Haven't heard anything yet, but he should be on his way in by now.' He dialled an internal extension and asked, 'Any word from Major Down yet?' He paused a few seconds listening to the answer and then roared into the mouthpiece, 'He what!' Then after another pause: 'What the hell happened this time?'

'We missed him?' Miller asked as Wall replaced the receiver.

Wall had a dazed look in his eyes as he answered. 'The bastard thinks he got the wrong house. Says it was empty when he got there. I'll bet he didn't think to look next door or across the street, the stupid idiot!'

'It certainly hasn't been our day,' said Miller finally.

Ten

IT TOOK THE car forty minutes to reach Letterkenny Hospital. O'D was unconscious for the entire journey, on pot-holed back roads. The hospital had been warned of their arrival and staff stood expectantly in the forecourt as they rolled through the gate. O'D was transferred to a trolley with a minimum of ceremony and wheeled away. Charlie and Mick looked on like redundant workers. Only a porter remained at the entrance to the hospital.

'How long will it take before they know the score?' Charlie asked him.

'Hard to say,' said the porter, regarding them with caution. 'You friends of his?'

'Yes,' said Mick.

'No,' said Charlie.

'I see,' said the porter before Charlie hastily added: 'He knows him slightly, I just drove him down here.'

'Shot by the army, was he?' asked the porter suspiciously.

'Aye,' said Charlie, repeating, 'Will it take them long to find out how he is?'

The suspicion seemed to wilt slightly. 'Hard to say, he seems to have lost a lot of blood.'

'Aye,' Charlie said carefully, 'apparently he's been bleeding all day and wouldn't go to hospital.'

'That so?' said the porter. 'When was he shot then?'

'I'm not sure,' lied Charlie, 'sometime in the morning, I think.'

The porter shook his head doubtfully in a long-practised portrayal of polished diagnosis. The act was so convincing that Mick was afraid to hear his opinion.

'It'll be all right if we wait, won't it?' he asked hopefully, almost pleading.

'Surely,' said the porter, raking out another few ashes of sympathy. 'Ye can wait if ye like.' Then he added as an afterthought, 'The Guards will want to question you anyway on how he was shot.'

'What?' said Charlie a little too quickly.

'The Guards, I said, they'll want to question you.'

'Do they always do that?'

'Aye, they always question people who bring people over the border.'

'When do you think they'll be here?' Charlie asked, trying to sound off-hand.

'They usually come as soon as they've been told, but I don't think they've been told yet.'

'In that case,' said Charlie, 'I think we'll go and get something to eat and then come back and see them. We won't have any word from the doctors for half an hour anyway, will we?'

'I wouldn't think so,' said the porter, but the two men were already climbing into the car.

They were on the main road driving down the hill towards the centre of Letterkenny before Mick spoke. 'What'll we do now?'

'Get off-side!' said Charlie without a moment's hesitation. His clothes were saturated with cordite and a single paraffin test could have provided conclusive evidence for a murder trial.

'What about O'D?' asked Mick as they hit the open road on the other side of the town.

'We can do no more for him now. We'll ring up when we get back to Derry.'

'Aye,' said Mick, resigning himself to whatever Charlie had in mind, and putting on his safety belt as the car sped on.

204

They avoided Garda and army checkpoints on the way back by using the same series of unapproved roads. The odds were in their favour and they arrived in Creggan without incident thirty-five minutes after leaving the porter at the hospital. Their first stop was a cautious one at Ma Murphy's house. They parked the car and walked the last hundred yards, checking as best they could that the house was not under surveillance. One glance at the splintered front door hastily patched and nailed into position told them the damage had been done and the culprits fled. They entered by the back.

Ma as usual was busy in the kitchen. But all tasks stopped when Mick and Charlie entered. She listened to the details of the trip before recounting her own ordeal with profound understatement. 'What are you going to do now, son?' she enquired.

'I don't know yet, Ma,' answered Mick honestly.

'You'll have to call a Staff meeting,' said Charlie, taking the initiative again.

'That's a good idea,' said Ma. And the matter was settled.

A severely depleted Staff, consisting of the two men just returned from Killybegs and Con McDaid, was rounded up by Charlie while Mick phoned the hospital. The Staff anxiously awaited his report at Frank McGuire's house.

'The hospital says he went through a successful operation, but is still seriously ill,' reported Mick.

'Thank Christ,' said Charlie, 'that means he'll live.'

'How do you know?' Con McDaid asked.

'Because,' explained Charlie patiently, 'if there was any immediate danger of him dying they would have said "critical" or "gravely ill". All "serious" means is that he will be okay as long as no other complications set in.'

Everyone seemed satisfied with the explanation and the meeting got under way. But it did not succeed in dispelling the air of depression in the room. Mulhern related O'D's last wish that the operation go ahead as soon as possible, but that was quickly explained away as the ravings of his delirium. Charlie was the only one who agreed with O'D's idea but he

205

had no vote. When the Staff decided to halt the training camp Charlie argued that it should continue now that the operation was off. His opinion was listened to but not agreed with. It was a dispirited group that parted at the meeting's end.

Late the following afternoon O'D was taken off the seriously ill list. He became fleetingly conscious in the evening without knowing where he was. But of one thing he had no doubt: the dark-suited figure sitting beside his bed was a Special Branch officer.

'Where am I?' croaked O'D.

'Ah, so you're awake at last,' said the man.

O'D dimly recognised a brogue through the buzzing in his head and his spirits soared a little at the thought of being over the border. The Free State, he thought, was relative freedom.

'Where am I?' he repeated. He felt nauseated and his throat was raw. He knew instinctively that he was very close to extreme pain, but he was determined to find out where he was.

'Letterkenny Hospital,' answered the cheerful branchman. 'Where did you think you were: Altnagelvin in Derry?'

'What happened?' O'D asked, ignoring the taunt.

'Would you believe,' said the branchman, 'that was the very question I was going to ask you?'

'Fuck off!' said O'D.

He was heavily sedated for the first few days. Until the end of the first week he was only half-conscious of the activities around him but still vaguely aware of a constant stream of visitors and a succession of Special Branchmen – all mixed up with the pain which racked his body and left him too weak even to think. Gradually the pain subsided into a dull, throbbing numbness. In the first coherent conversation with his mother he was surprised to discover that she had been visiting him every day. He vaguely remembered her appearing in his thoughts occasionally but was never quite sure whether it was a fantasy or fact. The only fact he was sure of was that the police were going to interrogate him as soon as he left the hospital. His mother was able to give him no news concerning any activities in Derry, but he was able to surmise from her general conversations that very little was happening. Her concern was to stuff him full of food which she brought into the hospital. It was the best way, she insisted, to make him well again, and she had no faith in hospital cooking. So she travelled the twenty-two miles from Derry every day with her basket of food and meekly handed it over to the branchman on duty to be checked. Then she questioned him to make sure he got every item she had handed in the previous day. Then she travelled the twenty-two miles back again secure in the knowledge that he was at least being well nourished.

After the second week the Special Branch began to question him persistently. It was nothing heavy but O'D got the distinct impression that they were under orders to draw him out. Every branchman who came on duty began talking about the IRA. O'D usually led the line of conversation towards a general discussion of the Northern situation. But the Branch wanted to talk about IRA activities. These conversations often ended up with patient and guard shouting obscenities at each other to the alarm of the hospital staff.

By the third week the branchmen were removed to the corridor and O'D had the room to himself, except at visiting times when the duty guard would enter behind his visitors and stand sullenly at the door taking notes of the conversation. In the middle of the week O'D got a surprise. On a fresh summer afternoon he was daydreaming with his eyes closed. A gentle breeze scented by the Letterkenny countryside blew through his open window. He felt the pressure of someone sitting on his bed and opened his eyes: two feet away he saw the beaming face of Brenda McGlinchey smiling down at him. His first thought was that she was a perfect personification of summer and it almost overwhelmed him. His second thought was a realisation that she looked infinitely more beautiful than Dympna.

'Hello, shithead,' she smiled, bringing him back to earth with a bump.

'Yes, beautiful,' he answered, 'has the BBC come to a grinding halt?'

'I managed to find someone to run it in my absence,' she answered perkily.

'Good, I would hate to see the old institution closing down because of me.'

'What are you doing getting yourself shot? And who beat your face, good-looking?'

He smiled at her, unable to answer for a minute. He wanted to reach up and take her into his arms, but he felt unsure of himself. As a substitute for a full embrace, he placed his hand on her left thigh and squeezed. It was a good substitute.

'Well, you know how it is,' he said, 'they're shooting anything that moves up there now. And the face was an accident.'

'So I've heard,' she said meaningfully.

When he said, 'How is everybody, by the way?' she did not miss his meaning.

'Oh, they are all fine. They told me to tell you that they are taking it easy and living a quiet life, and they send their regards, of course.'

'That's what I thought,' he said disgustedly, 'lazy shower of bastards.'

The branchman made a shuffling noise with his feet. O'D looked at him and raised his eyebrows enquiringly, but before he could speak Brenda put her hand on his and squeezed it.

'Mick wants to know if he can come and visit you,' she said quickly.

'Of course he can,' he answered, raising his voice. 'I'm not in custody or anything, am I? So why shouldn't he come and visit me?'

'If you're not in custody then what's your friend doing here?' Brenda nodded her head backwards towards the branchman.

'He's a fan of mine. As soon as I get discharged he says he's going to take me for a long holiday.'

'That's nice of him.'

'He's a very nice chap.'

Brenda injected a new note. 'Charlie almost came to see

you last week.'

He caught her meaning instantly and hoped that the guard missed the change which seemed to flip into the atmosphere. He could see the bulk of his imposing figure over her right shoulder.

He tried to sound light-hearted. 'Ah, Charlie, he cheers me up tremendously. What happened to him?'

'Mick wouldn't loan him the car.'

'Maybe it's just as well, Charlie would have me laughing so much that it would probably open my stitches.'

Brenda squeezed his hand and asked, 'How is it now anyway?'

He squeezed her thigh and answered, 'It's still sore yet, but it should be okay by next week.'

She nodded her head. The branchman was straining so hard to listen to the words that he missed the movement.

'Are you in pain?' she asked.

'No, it's more of a stiff soreness really, another few days and I should be able to attempt a quick trip around the ward.'

'Chasing the nurses, no doubt.'

'No doubt. Now tell me what you've been doing to the BBC.'

Brenda told him of the job in England. As she spoke he felt for the first time a sense of defeat cross his mind. The thought was quickly pushed aside by an overwhelming urge to take her in his arms and say, 'You're right, I'm not going to achieve anything in this mad nightmare, I'll give it up and we'll take the kid and get as far away from it as possible.' But it only lasted a second and it was gone, leaving him with a sense of the raw reality of a struggle which had to be fought to its conclusion. What that would be he did not know, but an inner certainty sustained him: he had to live by his own ideas and he had the strength to fight for them no matter what the odds. But it nagged at a corner of his mind that a doubt should challenge his conviction – no matter how fleeting it was.

He was in an excellent mood when Brenda left after the

209

two-hour visit, and not just from seeing her. He knew for certain now that someone was thinking in terms of an escape and he immediately turned his mind to the problem. It would not be difficult: one branchman outside his bedroom door and another below his second-floor window. Charlie would have no difficulty working out an operation, if he had not worked one out already. O'D could picture everyone trying to restrain Charlie from hijacking a car and driving single-handedly to Letterkenny Hospital. He wondered abstractly why he should think of Charlie planning the operation instead of Mick. But he did not dwell on it for there was now one glaring priority: he had to get as fit as possible without letting anyone know.

The daytime routine of the hospital was erratic. There were no set times for visits outside mealtimes, which meant that the door could open at any time. He decided the best time to exercise was between eight and ten at night. He had never been disturbed between these hours. Any time after that was too dangerous as it would be heard in the general silence. During the day he would concentrate on exercising in bed.

After her first visit, Brenda came every day and stopped for an hour. On her third visit he slipped her a note explaining the security situation. The following day she gave him an answer from Mick: she held his hand as they kissed and let him remove the note when he was ready. As soon as the door closed behind her he devoured the message. It was in Mick's small, neat handwriting:

Yes Kid,
We have got the situation sized up and Charlie has everything in hand. All we are waiting for now is word to deliver the goods. Tell B when you want to see Charlie and that will do it.
Mick

At eight o'clock that evening O'D was out of the bed like an excited child on Christmas morning. His left leg was still very stiff and painful when he put pressure on it. He dragged it throbbing and swollen across and back, up and down the length and breadth of the tiny ward, silently cursing his sweating body for its weakness. He continued the abuse for an hour until he collapsed panting onto the bed. The next morning was an agony, etched with satisfaction. At least he knew now that he could keep some sort of momentum going for an hour. He felt doubly compensated when the doctor made his daily examination and declared that the leg seemed to be getting worse instead of better. A gentle prod produced a violent reaction from O'D, which surprised the doctor. He rubbed his jaw and scratched his head, wondered aloud how the leg could be more sensitive than the day before. O'D realised that if he were to take one look at the black soles of his feet he would know instantly what the problem was. Fortunately he did not.

During Brenda's visit that day he told her that he would be writing to Mick in the near future. That night after eight he was on patrol again, like a wounded veteran staunchly defying convalescence. The leg was stiff in the beginning, but it took him much longer to break into a sweat. He silently dragged it around the ward until his head became light. After washing his feet he wrote to Mick:

I'm ready when you are, kid. Send C to get me! And don't forget to bring some clothes as I am naked.
O'D

But the next day his mother came instead of Brenda: he felt like screaming. He had the note in his hand when she came into the ward and for the duration of the visit it tortured him like a handful of thorns. His irritation almost overcame him: he was tempted to press the note into her hand saying something like, 'Will you give Brenda a message for me?' But his mother, he knew, would probably open it and answer, 'God, that's great, Hugh, I'll bring you down some clothes if they're letting you out.' Later he stuffed the note into his pyjama pocket and shuffled around the ward for two angry hours.

211

Brenda came the following day. 'I hear you missed me yesterday, but I don't believe it,' she said, perching herself perkily on the edge of the bed.

'Me, miss you?' he said, passing her the note, 'never. Who told you that?'

'Your mother said you were jumping about on the bed like an agitated rooster and that you could hardly settle to talk to her. She thinks you're madly in love.'

'The trouble with that woman is that she imagines things,' he grumbled.

That night he tramped the ward again. The leg was no longer dragging and his breathing was under control, but he was becoming very bored with it all. He felt he could travel almost indefinitely if he could pace himself, but he could not endure more than two hours at a time in the claustrophobic ward. He lay in bed hoping that Mick would send him some news the next day.

Normally his visitors came at two o'clock in the afternoon, but the following day no one appeared. He spent an anxious hour listening to every sound in the corridor. He thought someone might show up at five o'clock, but no one did. At five-thirty he began to get worried. Perhaps something had gone wrong; an accident or even worse. He was on the verge of calling the nurse and asking her to contact Derry when his thoughts were interrupted by a commotion in the corridor. He thought it was a patient grappling with a nurse, but he heard a voice say, 'Watch the cunt!' and he knew it was Charlie. The next moment there was a sound of someone falling against the door. O'D could contain himself no longer: he leapt from the bed and his feet just touched the ground when the door burst open as Charlie backed in, dragging an unconscious branchman. Following him, with determination moulding their faces, were Con McDaid and Mick Mulhern.

'How's the form?' grunted Charlie, dropping the branchman.

'Great now,' said O'D looking anxiously at the body, 'but don't kill him or we'll never hear the end of it.'

212

'We brought you clothes,' said Mick offering him a plastic carrier bag.

'I'll change along the road,' said O'D. 'Let's get the fuck out of here.'

He threw his arms around Con and Mick and swung along on his good leg. Charlie led, plastic bag in one hand, Magnum in the other. Startled nurses gasped as they passed; the hall porter mumbled something between unmoving teeth. The group went through the front door with O'D swinging like a human pendulum and they were gone.

Outside the hospital gate the car turned north and sped away. 'Where are we going?' asked O'D, struggling out of a pyjama jacket, 'this is the wrong way.'

'You didn't seriously think we'd head for Derry, did you?' asked Charlie who was driving.

'Where else?' said O'D, succeeding with the jacket.

'We have a boat waiting on the Swilly to take us across to the peninsula,' said Con.

'That's what I like,' said O'D leaning back to remove the striped pyjama trousers, 'organisation. Now close your eyes before I corrupt you.'

The car tore along the narrow, winding roads of north Donegal like an animal fleeing from a bush fire. It took them less than thirty minutes to reach their destination, an isolated cove on the western shores of Lough Swilly, where a solitary figure stood. Mick Mulhern whistled and the figure waved at them. O'D felt a surge of energy as he stepped from the car, the fresh breeze from the lough caressing his face. His mind sharpened; his senses tingled at the new dimensions of awareness which freedom had given him. A painful stiffness still hampered his leg, but he ignored it. He felt like leaping off the grass verge and tumbling down the sandy slope which separated him from the figure now running along the beach. But he followed Mick's example and went over the edge on his backside. Con and Charlie shouted hasty farewells and drove off. At the bottom of the sandy slope Pious Doherty demanded: 'What kept you, you fucking cripple? I'm standing here freezing my balls off for the past hour!' He had a wide grin on his face as he helped O'D along the beach. A small dinghy was hastily launched with O'D sitting in the bow and five minutes later they were on board a small trawler heading towards the northern exit of the lough and the isolated seclusion of Lenan Bay.

He was lodged in the house of the trawler skipper, Neil Cassidy. Mick stayed for an hour discussing the lack of activity in the city before driving off with Pious Doherty. When he had gone O'D toyed with the idea of bringing the Staff to Donegal for a special meeting. He hesitated only because the idea ran contrary to some of his long-held beliefs: once he was off the scene he felt he had no right to influence it. Then he heard the news and was glad he had hesitated.

He lay sprawled in an old Victorian armchair, comfortable in the atmosphere of a turf fire in the open hearth. Neil stretched his long sinewy arm to the mantelpiece and switched on an old fluid-battery radio. The machine crackled across the flagstone floor as the announcer's voice shattered the silence: 'Gardai are carrying out an extensive search of the Donegal area tonight following an escape from Letterkenny Hospital in which a Garda Sergeant was killed.'

'Oh, Jesus,' groaned O'D.

'Wisht!' said Neil, reaching for the knob to increase the volume.

The announcer gave details of the escape: the Guard had been struck on the head and was dead by the time the doctors examined him. She ended with a minutely accurate description of O'D and appealed for listeners to get in touch with any Garda station if they knew anything. Neil switched the radio off as soon as the item had finished. He returned to his seat and quietly lit his pipe. O'D felt distinctly uncomfortable; Mrs Cassidy looked upset.

Neil rocked gently in the old rocking chair. 'I'd say,' he said after a long pause in which O'D glanced nervously at Mrs Cassidy, 'you'd be best to stop indoors for a week or two.' Then the pipe belched more smoke as he sucked to keep a

214

glow in it. O'D relaxed, falling back in his chair. After a long sigh he spoke: 'That was an accident, you know. No one knew he was dead.'

'Fuck him,' replied Neil, 'he would have done the same to you quick enough.'

'Do you think they'll raid the peninsula, Neil?' asked his wife.

'Aye, they'll raid everywhere, including Dublin, Cork and Kerry, but they won't raid here.'

It was three weeks before he got any news from Derry. One damp morning Mick Mulhern rattled into the yard in a battered Mini. O'D limped out to meet him and knew instantly that the look on his face meant trouble.

'Yes, Mick. What's the crack?'

'Not so good, Hugh. I'm sorry I couldn't get down before now, but I had to go to Dublin.'

'What's the matter with them?' asked O'D, inviting his companion towards the house.

Mrs Cassidy was in the large kitchen when they entered. O'D introduced her and then, like a woman long used to clandestine routines, she made herself scarce. O'D settled into his usual armchair as Mick lowered himself into the rocker.

'Dublin wants you to get out of the country and they've made me OC.' He rattled the words out like so many unpalatable pills his mouth could no longer hold.

O'D looked at him quietly for a long time before asking, 'How do the Staff feel?'

Mick shifted uncomfortably. 'They don't know what to think at the minute. All of them back you, of course, but they are afraid to go against Dublin, especially as you are not there. I think they feel you won't be able to survive north or south now after this branchman thing. If you were in Derry it would be different – they would declare UDI without a moment's hesitation – but with you down here in isolation it's a case of the indians having no chief and being intimidated by Dublin.'

The picture presented itself all too clearly in O'D's mind:

he had become a liability and he was being discarded like an obsolete piece of machinery. He tried to keep his anger from showing. 'What did Dublin say?' he asked quietly. 'And don't be giving me any bullshit.'

'Well, to put it in a nutshell, they pounded me. Told me that you had made a cock-up. You were out as far as they were concerned and I was in. And I was to do fuck all until they say so.'

'I see,' said O'D, unable to resist a burst of sarcasm, 'big daddy pulling the strings from two hundred miles away.'

Mick gave a confused shrug of his shoulders.

'What about the rifles?' snapped O'D.

'Half of them are going to Belfast tomorrow and the other half have to be put in a deep dump until later.'

'Until they're moved to Belfast as well, I suppose.' There was a pause until he said sharply and decisively, 'That's it, I'm going to Derry.'

'Do you think you should, Hugh?' said Mick. 'The Branch are still raiding like mad for you.'

'Yes, I think I should.' He left his seat abruptly, saying over his shoulder, 'I don't have much option, Mick. You see, I don't think Dublin have an idea what I'm trying to do. What's worse, they don't have an idea of what they are trying to do.'

Mrs Cassidy put up a spirited resistance to his sudden departure, but his mind was made up and he pushed her arguments aside gently. He asked her to give his thanks to Neil when he returned from fishing and, after the compulsory cup of tea, he left for Derry. As Mick drove O'D sat huddled in his frayed seatbelt. On reaching Creggan he went to Frank McGuire's house and left Mick to organise the Staff meeting.

Frank strutted about like a war-hardened general in charge of a detachment of frontline troops. He talked excitedly about the Haslitt operation – and about every other operation which came to mind – and how the town had reacted to them. O'D felt he knew the situation intimately by the time the Staff arrived. His confidence had been shaken by his isolation, but Frank renewed it.

The business of the meeting was delayed by enquiries about his injuries and his escape, but once it did get started O'D very quickly stamped his authority on it. No one opposed him as chairman, which meant in effect OC. Mick Mulhern followed his opening remarks by stating that he had resigned as OC and was now following O'D's leadership. When everyone voiced their agreement O'D interjected: 'Let's make one thing perfectly clear: if you elect me now as OC then what you are doing is defying the leadership in Dublin – in other words, declaring yourself independent – and that gives them every right to move against you. Do you all realise that?'

'There's nothing they can do about it if we elect a new OC,' said Dermot Donnelly indignantly, glancing around to see who agreed with him.

O'D answered for the benefit of the others as much as Dermot. 'Technically, Dermot, they're supposed to do that themselves, and they don't like having their orders disobeyed.'

'Fuck them!' cut in Sean Doherty. 'They can like it or lump it! This is the way we want the situation and that's all about it.'

Con McDaid's opinion was a foregone conclusion, but it had to be heard, and O'D asked him. 'You're our OC and that's all about it,' answered Con.

'Right,' said O'D, 'in that case, let's get down to business.' Everyone sat back in their seats. 'There's only one objective we can have at this stage, and that is total war against the Brits by whatever means we can lay our hands to. We may not have done enough training to put our original plan into operation, but we certainly have enough to give them a bad fright and show them that we mean business. We also have to show Dublin what we can do. The idea is to hit the Brits harder than they have ever been hit before. What do you think?'

Discussion was slow to start, but with further prompting from O'D suggestions began to flow like water from a fountain. An hour later O'D left them still planning, criticizing, formulating and reshaping new ideas. There was a pause and a

217

few words of farewell as Mick showed him to the door, but the conversation had resumed before he left the house.

She was not in the flat so he tried her mother's house. He found the key in the front door and let himself in. Soft sounds of music filtered through the living room door as he stood in the hallway. Vivaldi's concerto in D major. He knew it as her favourite piece which she always played when she needed soothing. His heart beat a little faster as he opened the door.

She was sitting on the sofa with her back to him, reading a book. He tiptoed silently across the room and put his lips close to her ear.

'Who's a shithead?' he said softly.

She leapt violently from the sofa scattering the book along the floor. 'Oh, you bastard, you almost took the heart from me!' Then she was in his arms with her face buried in his shoulder. He held her for a moment and her body began to shake with sobs. Slowly he drew away and looked at the tear-soaked face.

'Do I know what the problem is?' he asked gently.

She nodded, making an attempt to smile away the tears. 'Sorry, I must be getting to be a bore: it's the same problem as always. I'll be all right in a minute.'

He led her to the sofa and she noticed his limp.

'What about your leg?'

'It's getting better. . . What about you?'

'They wouldn't let me see you,' she said, almost breaking into tears again. 'They wouldn't even tell me where you were.'

'Who wouldn't?' he asked, a little angry.

'None of them, Mick especially, he's the one I put the most pressure on. The rest of them just refused to talk to me. I was beginning to get worried, I thought you might have died or something and they weren't telling me. What happened anyway?'

His head swam for a second in a confusion of anger and betrayed loyalty. He had assumed that Brenda knew everything. But he realised why she did not and automatically he defended Mick. 'There was a lot of pressure from Dublin,' he said. 'They wanted me kept in isolation with all the activity over the escape. They obviously intimidated him into not telling anyone. I didn't see anyone myself until today when Mick came down.'

'What's going to happen now?' she asked. 'They're looking for you everywhere.'

'I think the next two weeks are going to be the most important we ever had.'

'What does that mean?'

'It means, I think, that things are going to go the way I want them to go. Either that or they are not going to go at all and I will have to forget everything.'

'What do you mean by everything?' she said, sitting upright on the sofa. But before he could answer there was a knock at the front door which made both of them stiffen. O'D reached automatically to where he normally kept his gun before realising that he had none. He silently cursed his stupidity, then asked Brenda: 'Are you expecting anyone?'

'No, but it can't be the Brits.'

'Why not?'

'Because the key's in the door.'

He opened his hand to reveal the key: he had removed it on his way in. 'Bad habit, I have,' he said rising from the sofa. She also rose as he said, 'If it's the Brits, speak loudly so I can hear you.'

'What are you going to do?' she asked apprehensively.

'Take off out the back door.'

'Don't be stupid, if it is the Brits they're bound to have the back covered.'

'Not necessarily,' was all he had time to say before the door sounded again. She kissed him quickly yet passionately before going to answer it.

He stood behind the living room door with his heart pounding. The distance to the back hallway from where he stood was two yards, then there were a further three yards to the back door. He pictured it in his mind and then his heart sank: the door was always locked, and he didn't know where the key was. All he could do was hope that Brenda kept the Brits talking long enough for him to find it. Then he heard her open the front door.

'It's all right, Hugh,' she called a second later, and he fell against the door with relief, realising in the instant that his leg was throbbing painfully. He had a splitting headache and his stomach felt as if it had been danced on by a ballet company. He would not even have reached the back door never mind got through it.

'You look terrible,' said Mick as O'D held the door open for him.

'Sit down, for heaven's sake,' said Brenda, taking his arm.

'How did you know I was here, Mick?' he asked from the sofa.

'I was on my way to Brenda's flat when I saw the car parked at the door. There's something I should have seen you about before you left.'

'What's that?'

'The rifles. I forgot that they're supposed to go to Belfast tomorrow. The Staff thought I ought to come after you and see about them.'

'See what about them?' said O'D knowing what was coming, resigning himself to the fact that the Staff were incapable of making a decision on their own.

'Well. . . do we send them up or what?' asked Mick.

'No fucking way do we send them up, Mick, are you out of your mind?'

'I just wanted to make sure, Hugh. Dublin is going to be screaming if they don't go.'

'The screaming won't do us any harm as long as we have the guns.'

'What if they try to lift them?'

'Don't tell me they know where they are?'

'I'm afraid so, I had to tell them when I was down.'

'That's an entirely different matter,' said O'D rubbing his

nose. 'We better move them tonight.' He turned to Brenda with a sympathetic shrug: 'Sorry, I thought I was going to be with you for the night.'

'Okay,' she smiled, contenting herself with the fact that he was at least safe for the moment. 'Will you come back later?'

'As soon as I can. Will you find some place for us to sleep in case they raid?'

'Yes, just make sure you come back no matter what time it is. I'll wait here for you.'

The two men climbed into Mick's battered Mini and drove off. The first stop was Frank McGuire's house where they picked up Con. 'Can you find a dump for some weapons tonight?' said O'D once they had him outside.

'Aye, surely,' said Con, delighted at the prospect, 'how many?'

'About two hundred.'

'Holy Jesus!' Con choked. 'You're joking?'

'No joke, Con,' said O'D levelly, 'we have to re-dump two hundred rifles in a hurry. Where can we do it?'

'Two hundred rifles is a lot of rifles,' pondered Con. 'It would be dangerous to dump them all in one place. We would be better to spread them out.'

'We can spread them out later,' said O'D. 'The important thing is to get them dumped tonight.'

Con thought for a second and then said, 'What about the school?'

'Yeah, we used that before,' said Mick. 'There's plenty of buildings in it, but can we drive a van in there at this time of night?'

'No problem,' answered Con, 'I'll get the keys off the caretaker.'

'Are you sure he's sound, Con?' asked O'D, 'this is a lot of stuff he's going to know about.'

'You could bet your life on him, O'D.'

'Okay,' said O'D. 'You get the keys from him and wait at your house for us. With any luck we should be back by midnight.'

221

The next contact was Terry Donaghey, the Bogside OC, who promptly rounded up four volunteers to manhandle the cargo and borrowed a van. No one knew where it came from, but it was obviously a precious source as Terry insisted on driving it himself. While this was happening, Mick went in search of the lorry driver who had originally brought the weapons from London. He had arranged to see him the following day, but that would have to be changed. If he could not be found, they would have to break into the warehouse and search for the weapons – and no one but the driver knew what the containers looked like.

Mick entered the driver's local lacking more than a little confidence. He stood in the open doorway looking over the half-empty bar: he could not see him. But as he turned to go he collided with him.

'What are you doing here, Mick?'

'Looking for you, kid.'

'Ah, Jesus,' said the driver.

'Sorry, kid,' Mick apologised, 'I wouldn't do this if it wasn't absolutely necessary. We have to move the stuff tonight.'

'That's what I thought. Where to?'

'Into the Bog.'

'Is that all?' asked the driver suspiciously.

'That's it, from "A" to "B".'

'Thank Christ for that, I thought you were going to ask me to do a run to Belfast or something.'

O'D was briefing Terry Donaghey and his four volunteers when they arrived. He quickly told them the method of approach before all eight set off in two cars and a van. The actual operation was simple. The driver had the keys to the warehouse and opened the large gates to allow one car and a van to drive inside. The other car remained with Mick as lookout. The well-concealed crates were quickly identified and loaded into the van in less than ten minutes. Fifteen anxious minutes later seven of them were back in the Bogside and the driver was rushing towards his local to catch a last pint before closing time.

The four volunteers were dropped at the Bogside Inn and the other three made their way to Con McDaid's house. Con had just arrived before them.

'Got the keys?' asked O'D as soon as Con opened his front door.

'No problem,' Con said, stepping into the darkened street and closing the door behind him.

'You go in the car with Mick,' said O'D, 'and I'll follow in the van with Terry.'

The school lay four hundred yards away on the edge of the no-go area. They had to leave the Bogside, but the area they were entering was seldom patrolled by the army because of the high incidence of sniper attacks. It was deserted when they arrived.

Con manoeuvred his awkward bulk from the Mini and began fumbling with the bunch of keys. He had been shown the two keys required to open both locks, but had promptly forgotten them. Five keys and twice as many curses later he succeeded in opening the main gates. The lights on both vehicles were doused, no longer necessary as the men crept across the deserted school grounds. A hundred windows with the eyes of a thousand memories stared darkly at them from the primary school all four had attended. In the heavy silence which surrounded them as they stepped from their vehicles they experienced an odd sense of long-forgotten security.

'Do you think the head will slap us for this?' said Mulhern.

O'D tittered at the childish joke as he helped unload the crates. 'One of the problems cracking jokes at a time like this,' he said between giggles; 'the nerves tend to take over and make them seem funnier than they are.'

'There was nothing funny about being slapped by the head,' Con said, and O'D spluttered.

It took Brenda several hours to calm him that night. Long after they went to bed in a neighbour's house, he lay staring at the ceiling wondering whether the strain was beginning to tighten too much.

223

Mick called for him at nine in the morning. They drove to Frank McGuire's house, which was rapidly becoming an unofficial headquarters. They had to avoid the main centres as the army were making regular and heavily armed swoops on them. And the days when O'D could disguise himself were gone. His scarred and twisted face made him as obvious as if he were on crutches. Charlie Coyle was sitting in the living room when he arrived. 'How did you get here?' asked O'D, surprised but delighted to see him.

'I met Sean Doherty last night,' said Charlie in his usual perky way, 'and he told me that someone had gone and declared war on the Brits. So I thought I'd better come up and sort it all out.'

'I see,' said O'D smiling, 'he didn't tell you what the Staff had decided, did he?'

'Aye, he told me that they couldn't decide anything. He said Con was to tell you.'

'Oh, Christ,' said O'D lowering himself awkwardly into an armchair. He turned to Mick who had entered behind him. 'You better phone Dublin and tell them the score. As soon as that's done get all the OCs up here till we see what can be done about these gunmen on our streets.'

'I suppose you wouldn't prefer to phone Dublin yourself?' Mick asked hopefully.

'I think you better phone them first and tell them that the Staff decided unanimously to go back to my original plan. They'll probably send someone up and we can sort it out then.'

'Right,' said Mick without enthusiasm and left.

O'D turned to Charlie. 'Did Sean tell you anything about the problem I left them with?'

'He mumbled something about taking over the city, but he seemed a little confused by the idea.'

O'D shook his head with more than slight annoyance.

'So it's true then?' said Charlie.

'Not yet, unfortunately, but eventually I want to take over all the Brit camps on this side of the Foyle and hold them.'

'Jesus Christ! I didn't think we were capable of that.'

'That's what you were being trained for in Killybegs.'

'So all those simulated attacks had some reason behind them after all?' Charlie offered facetiously.

'Do you think the people who came through Killybegs are capable of attacking a Brit position and holding it? You came through the training so if you don't know no one does.'

'Are you asking me could I do it?'

'Could you?'

Charlie thought for a moment, then said, 'I don't know, I would need a very detailed briefing.'

'That goes without saying. Try this for size. . .' O'D launched into a minutely detailed briefing of an imaginary attack on an army observation post.

Charlie sat expressionless until he had finished, then, after a few points of clarification, said: 'I think it would depend to a large extent on the men I had on the operation. If they were okay, I think I could handle it.'

'What about the other section leaders who came through Killybegs, do you think they could handle it?'

'I think a few of them could, but I wouldn't like to take any chances with the rest of them.'

'How many of them could do it?'

'About three or four.'

'Jesus,' gasped O'D, 'is that all?'

'I think so, but then, mind you, I'm no expert. On the other hand, I do know some of the characters who came through that course and, to tell you the truth, some of them I wouldn't send on a message to the Waterside.'

'What about the evasion training they did? And the map-reading, that must show that they have some initiative?'

'Some, yes,' said Charlie, 'but I don't think it qualifies them to command the sort of operation you just outlined. I think most of them would freeze up.'

'I think I'm sorry I asked you,' said O'D with false cheerfulness.

'Why's that?' asked Charlie.

'I'll tell you: an hour ago I felt confident we could take over the town with one decisive stroke; now I'm not so sure.'

They fell silent for a time and then Charlie spoke slowly, as if his words were forming haltingly with his ideas. 'Why don't you try a dummy run on it first?'

'How do you mean?'

'Well, I'm not exactly sure what you have in mind, but I assume it's a simultaneous attack on all the Brit posts.'

'That's it,' agreed O'D.

'Well, then, why don't you try it out on one post first and use the section leaders, and if that's successful you could hit the rest.'

'I thought of that as an ideal sort of training exercise, but the problem is that it gives the Brits too much of an opportunity to surround us. They would swamp the place with reinforcements and we wouldn't be able to breathe fresh air for a month never mind operate. I think we only get one chance at this operation. It's got to be all or nothing.'

Charlie didn't hesitate with an answer. 'You might be overreacting a bit. If we wipe out an observation post the Brits won't know what happened and they certainly won't know what to do about it. In the first instance, there will be a blind panic. They will fly about like a gaggle of pregnant geese thinking up all sorts of excuses to tell their politicians. There will be conferences, enquiries, press handouts, and the local clergy will be canvassed to turn out condemnations by the ton. Come to think of it, they might even decide to play up the publicity angle for a week or two rather than react immediately on a military level. I don't think they would flood the town with troops. For one thing that would show that we had them at a disadvantage.'

Charlie paused, but O'D was caught up in the excitement of the idea and anxious to hear more. 'Go ahead,' he encouraged, 'don't stop there.'

Charlie leaned forward, elbows on his knees, emphasising with his hands. 'Let's assume that we have our entire battleplan worked out in advance with everything ready to operate within hours, right?'

'Right,' agreed O'D, sitting on the edge of his chair.

'Then we mount this attack on one observation post. If it goes according to plan we pull out of it quickly before the Brits have time to surround us. Then we pick out the obvious leadership material from that attack and assign them an observation post each. And while the Brits are still confused and licking their sores we hit them again, only this time for real, the following day. Can you think what the second attack would do to public opinion in England?'

O'D stared silently at the latest addition to his Staff and wondered how he could have been ignored for so long.

'Charlie, I think you might just have come up with the answer.'

Eleven

CHIEF INSPECTOR WALL was afflicted with a fortnight's depression after O'D's escape. The death of the
three soldiers brought condemnation from the usual
sources and from his superiors. But what fed the depression
was the fact that the murders seemed to be a mystery. None
of the usual informers had been able to report anything. Only
one person had seen anything at all. An old man who had a
caretaker's flat on top of a nearby building had contacted the
police the day after the murders; but it turned out that he had
seen nothing of substance. He had observed a young man in
a leather jacket standing at a corner speaking to one of the
soldiers. A few minutes later he had heard three shots and
ran to the window from which he had seen three bodies lying
on the street.

Wall decided that Policewoman Colhoun would not go back
into the no-go area. She had been close to the incident so
that there was a possibility of her having been seen in Inspector Miller's car. For a day or two he had toyed with the idea
of sending her to Letterkenny to visit O'D. Her flat was kept
under surveillance for a week and then forgotten about.

It was quite by accident a fortnight later that Sergeant Ward
from the traffic division came across a second witness and
informed Inspector Miller. He told Miller that he had been
collecting his car from the bottom of Magazine Street when
he heard the shooting and saw what he took to be a very
frightened pedestrian coming charging through the gate and

NO TIME FOR LOVE

disappear up the hill. The man had certainly been alone and not carrying a gun. In his mid-twenties with dark, curly hair, he was wearing dark-coloured trousers and a leather jacket.

'Are you sure it was a leather jacket?' asked Miller.

'Yes, positive, a black leather one.'

When he took the information back to Inspector Wall, Policewoman Colhoun was in the office.

'Oh, God,' said Dympna before he had finished, 'that's Charlie.'

'Charlie?' asked both men in unison.

'Why didn't you come out with this before?' asked Wall.

'Because I didn't connect the leather jacket – but now that I hear the description. . .'

'And he was following you,' said Wall, feeling a surge of elation. A picture was beginning to emerge after weeks of darkness.

'Do you think he saw her getting into the car?' asked Miller.

'Not a doubt about it, I would say,' said Wall. 'That's what he was there for and that's why the army missed O'Donnell when they raided.'

'And he recognised me, of course,' said Miller dejectedly.

'Well, the very least he did was get your car number. What were you driving?'

'My own Opel.'

'Which is known by every IRA man from here to Cork!'

'What about the soldiers then?' said Miller.

'What do you think?' asked Wall, turning to Dympna, 'is your Charlie capable of killing three soldiers at close quarters?'

'He's a ruthless little character, sir, and he looks quite capable, but I don't see how he could have managed that himself.'

'We don't have any alternatives,' said Miller.

'You're right,' said Wall, 'which means that you are going to take a look at some photos, Policewoman Colhoun. That is unless you have a second name for your Charlie.'

She did not have a second name and Charlie did not appear among the Charlie mug shots. He did not appear among any of the other police records either. But the following afternoon

229

while she was listlessly ploughing through one of the many files of riot photographs he did appear. He was standing casually with a brace of petrol bombs cradled in his arm and he was, quite unknown to himself, smiling straight into the eye of the camera. A beautiful photograph, Miller thought, by any standards. Still they had no second name, but within twenty-four hours every foot patrol on the streets of Derry had a copy of the photograph. Special police patrols were set up to comb the area; informers were contacted urgently. Charlie was a wanted man.

At the same time as Chief Inspector Wall was concentrating his forces in the no-go area, O'D and Charlie were organising theirs outside. They spent most of the day talking over Charlie's plan, trying to shape it into some sort of tangible operation. By the time O'D returned to Brenda that night he knew exactly what he wanted to do. After gulping some food he sat down and committed everything to paper. He rose at three the following morning, drained, but with the finished plan in his hand. Over the next days O'D continually briefed the local OCs on patrolling their own areas. The army and the police came under increasingly heavy attack and were forced to cut their mobile patrols to a minimum and their foot patrols completely.

Chief Inspector Wall increased undercover surveillance patrols, but they were largely ineffective under the conditions. Patrols could run into spot checks mounted by civilians at any time; and if they had strange accents, strange faces or even strange clothes they were immediately suspect. The army could not enter the area during daylight hours without attracting a deafening clamour: women beat their bin lids with sticks, stones, and broom-handles: some beat them on their bins, others beat them on the ground, and all would have beaten them on soldiers or police if presented with the opportunity. After this came the gunfire, which the army came to expect at every corner they turned. In between the corners were youths of the area, armed with stones, bottles and sticks who roamed the streets in gangs. One of the favourite haunts of the gangs was the junction of Westland Street and Lone Moore Road. The army had to pass this junction at least once a day to relieve the one entrenched outpost which still existed between the Bogside and Creggan. This post came under attack from sniper fire, machine-guns, nail bombs, mortars, petrol bombs and stones, and from the mouths of the factory girls who worked beside it.

In approaching this beleaguered post, the presence of which allowed the government to insist that no-go areas did not exist, British army officers were inclined to displays of bravado. Commanders of the armoured personnel carriers stood in their open turrets to defy and taunt the rioters. Stones and bottles bounced and crashed off their bullet-proof, perspex canopies but they barely flinched, like royalty on a whistle-stop tour. The people who had to bear the brunt of the rioters' fury were the ordinary soldiers in the back of the APCs, who were forced to sit with the rear doors open, shouting appropriate obscenities at their pursuers.

A Saracen had reached the junction and turned up the incline of the New Road towards the Essex factory only to discover a small barricade blocking its way. The driver braked and swerved onto the footpath. The soldier sitting beside the rear door saw the trouble coming as the rioters caught up. An off-duty docker with a hurley was bearing down on him. The soldier tried to raise his rifle but it jammed awkwardly under the seat; as he tugged frantically to release it the docker grabbed him by the throat and pulled him from the Saracen. With a short, sharp swing of the hurley he broke the soldier's jaw. Rioters swarmed past the docker, over the soldiers to clamber inside the Saracen which quickly became a violent chaos of writhing, screaming bodies. Only when reinforcements arrived, firing live rounds into the crowd, could the Saracen move on with its battered cargo.

O'D had issued volunteers with shortarms and ordered them to mix with the rioters. At the Lone Moore junction a hole had been dug across the road and camouflaged with cardboard and clay. As the Saracen rumbled across the road, its driver's

231

attention was on the throng of two hundred youths standing at the corner. The Saracen's massive front wheels disappeared through the cardboard into the hole and it lay prostrate in the road like a great iron beast stooping to drink from a stream. Bodies swarmed from everywhere to clamber over it. Hurley sticks, hammers, crowbars and scaffolding poles were rapidly brought to bear on the beast. The noise resounded up to half-a-mile away as the crowd pounded on the iron shell. Marooned and disorientated by the shuddering wave of sound, one of the soldiers opened a spy-hole on the side of the Saracen. Immediately a two-inch scaffolding pole penetrated the gap and smashed into the face of the soldier. Swung like an erratic pendulum, the pole connected with other soldiers inside. The driver was trying in vain to reverse out of the hole. With four of his soldiers unconscious and bleeding, the commander opened another hatch, SLR in hand. When the muzzle of the gun appeared the crowd stared at it for a moment in disbelief before it fired and a man went down clutching his shoulder. From the top of the Saracen a volunteer thrust the barrel of his .45 revolver through the opening and emptied it. With that, the crowd scattered in all available directions. The Saracen lay silent in the hole with the pole like a great hollow spear hanging from its hip. Inside three soldiers lay dead, six injured, and a young officer's tears mingled with the blood that flowed from his forehead.

For days the pattern persisted of volunteers assisting and encouraging rioters in attacks against all things military in the area. The army responded by stepping up activities outside the area and reducing its presence inside. This gave O'D the breathing space he wanted and by the end of the following week his units were operating openly in armed patrol cars.

One of these cars drove slowly along the Lecky Road area of Brandywell early one morning and pulled in behind a lemonade lorry which was delivering to a shop. Charlie Coyle, accompanied by three men, got out of the car and approached the driver and his mate. 'We need your lorry,' said Charlie casually.

'What for?' said the driver, sizing him up.

'IRA business,' said Charlie.

The driver glanced at the four men. 'How do I know you're IRA?' he asked belligerently.

'There's my ID,' said Charlie, lifting his jumper to reveal the butt of a Magnum, 'do you want me to produce it?'

'Don't bother,' said the driver, resigning himself to his fate. 'What do you want me to do?'

'Just go along with these two in the car and they'll keep you happy until your lorry is returned.'

The driver and his mate went quietly with the two men who took them to the Bogside Inn and bought them drinks. The lorry was driven to a garage where the contents of twelve dozen lemonade bottles were exchanged for petrol. One hour later it again sat on the Lecky Road. When the exposed petrol had evaporated two men climbed into the lorry and drove off: Mick Mulhern took the wheel and Charlie sat beside him. They drove straight to the army checkpoint at Bishop's Gate, the entrance to the old walled city. Two handguns were carefully concealed in the cab as they came to a halt beside the soldier on duty.

'Where you for, mate?' asked the soldier.

'Masonic Hall and then a few bars around the town,' said Mick pointing to the Masonic building only a few yards from where they had stopped.

'Where you just come from then?'

'Waterside,' said Mick, remembering the instructions O'D had given him, 'and one delivery in Bishop Street.'

The soldier was satisfied that the two men were workers who made the trip regularly. He did not walk across the road to consult the book of snapshots of suspect terrorists which all checkpoints possessed; nor did he look at the special photograph in his breast pocket, the one issued to every soldier the day before. But he proceeded with the routine search. 'Pull over to the side there.' He pointed to where a civilian searcher stood.

Mick pulled the lorry to the side of the road, parked, and

jumped from the cab to meet the searcher. 'Lovely day,' he said brightly to the searcher.

'Yeah,' said the man. 'Got your driving licence?'

Mick handed him the false driving licence containing his own photograph. The searcher scrutinised it and then asked the same questions the soldier had asked, to which he got the same replies.

'Is it all soft drinks you have?' he asked, climbing onto the back of the lorry.

'That's right,' confirmed Mick, climbing along with him and making sure he stood on the spot containing the petrol bombs.

'Take a couple of them with you,' Mick offered encouragingly.

'Are you sure?' asked the searcher, lifting a second bottle.

'Yes, certain,' said Mick, 'it won't break us.'

'That's great,' said the searcher making his way off the wagon with the free bottles, 'thanks.'

'Don't mention it,' said Mick, swinging into the cab, 'it's a pleasure.'

The searcher waved his unoccupied hand, clutching his lemonade with the other, as Mick started the lorry and drove the short twenty yards to the Masonic Hall. He parked opposite the caretaker's door.

'Now comes the tricky part,' said Charlie removing the concealed weapons. He handed Mick a snub-nosed .38 and kept the favoured Magnum for himself. They climbed from the cab and walked to the caretaker's house which was attached to the Masonic Hall. Mick stood on the high front step with a millboard under his arm and rang the doorbell. Charlie stood eight inches lower on the pavement with his hands in his coat pockets trying to disguise the massive bulk of the Magnum. The door was opened at last. A small stocky man in shirt-sleeves and waistcoat glared at them. He looked like a very strong retired wrestler. Charlie's heart sank.

'Mr Stoneycroft?' said Mick with a smile.

'Yes?' grunted the man.

'We have twelve cases of soft drinks for you with the compliments of McIvor's.'

'What?'

'Would you mind signing for them?' said Mick, stepping into the front hall and handing him the millboard.

'Yes, of course,' said the old man cordially, 'but what's it all about?'

'It's a sales promotion, goodwill gift,' said Mick with authority as he patted his pockets. He turned to Charlie, saying, 'I've left my bloody biro in McLaughlin's, have you got one?'

'I haven't even got a pencil,' said Charlie as he stepped into the hall behind Mick.

'It's all right,' said the old man, 'I've got one in the kitchen. Just a sec. . .' He turned to move towards the kitchen. Before he had gone two yards Charlie stepped into the hall and closed the door. With the abrupt departure of light, the old man turned and looked at Charlie, a questioning frown on his face; but before he could speak Mick produced the .38 revolver and pointed it at his head.

'Don't move or you're a dead man.'

'Why you!' said the old man, instantly leaping at Mick who had no time to react. The gun was knocked from his hand and he was pinned against the wall by the throat. The old man started shouting: 'Martha, get the army!'

He had the sentence out before Charlie brought the Magnum crashing onto the back of his skull. As he crumpled to the floor, almost taking Mick's windpipe with him, Charlie ran along the hallway in search of Martha. He turned right at the end of the entrance hall and sprinted along a narrow corridor which contained the living quarters. She was standing at the kitchen door trying to conceal herself: she was clearly petrified as Charlie approached her, but her plump, five-foot figure stood its ground bravely.

'Where's your daughter?' said Charlie, menace in his voice.

'She's at work,' said Martha, reluctantly taking a step backwards.

Charlie took a step closer, putting the gun in front of her

face: 'Don't lie to me old woman or I'll blow your fucking head off! Now, where is she?'

She collapsed at his feet in a sudden, soft slump. He stepped over her and glanced quickly around the kitchen: it was empty. He stepped back to the hall and listened intently. The normal sounds of daily activity filtered through the brickwork and glass of the musty building. A minute later Martha began to recover and he assisted her back along the hall.

Mick was standing in the middle of the entrance hall massaging his throat. 'Well,' he croaked weakly.

'She seems to be the only one,' said Charlie, nodding at Martha, who looked as if she was about to faint again at the sight of her husband sprawled on the floor. 'Get that bastard away from the door before he comes around again,' continued Charlie, and then to Martha by way of explanation; 'Don't worry missus, he's not dead, we just put him to sleep for a wee while.'

'What now?' asked Mick.

Charlie glanced at him and smiled sardonically. 'We follow the plan, what else?'

'Do you think the army heard the shout?'

'They would have been here by now if they had,' answered Charlie flatly.

'Yeah, I suppose they would.'

'Let's get these two tied up and gagged then.'

A window-less store-room to the right of the hall proved ideal for the task. Martha did not speak as her husband was dragged into the store, tied and gagged. She did not protest even when the same fate befell her. Charlie did the tying and gagging, saying to Mick, 'You better get out to the lorry and make like a worker before the Brits think we have left them a bomb.'

'Right,' said Mick.

Charlie joined him as the last crate was stacked in the front hall. 'That's it, kid,' said Mick when they had finished, 'I'll get the lorry back and be up again in half an hour.'

'Good enough,' said Charlie.

They stood staring at each other for a few seconds as if neither of them knew what to say next, as if theirs was a parting of lovers.

'Right,' Mick said without moving, 'I'll go then.'

Charlie was the one who moved, turning abruptly and walking to the door, holding it ajar. 'Right, on your way, and don't forget to ring four shorts and one long when you come back.' As soon as the door closed, Charlie took himself on a tour of the house checking windows, door and closets, making sure to keep out of sight of the army who were camped in the garden of the large Victorian mansion.

While he was doing this and Mick was returning the lorry O'D was touring the local OCs to pick up twelve men who were earmarked for the operation, all section leaders who had been through the Killybegs course and had shown potential. That night the twelve men made their ways to two pick-up points before being conveyed to a rendezvous inside the area. The meeting house was large by Derry standards but the twelve diminished its space to cramped proportions. None of them knew exactly why they were there as they relaxed in the well-furnished living room.

O'D began by giving a brief outline of the operation. Then he broke the men up into three groups – two attacking and one supporting. He continued with a detailed plan of the attack and a blow-by-blow account of how it should proceed. He finished with a free-for-all in which everyone had his say. In the end each man knew in the smallest detail what he had to do.

O'D handed over to Dermot Donnelly and left for Con McDaid's house; they climbed into the battered old van which Con was using and drove to the school. After Con had gone through the fumbling ritual with the keys they removed twelve SLRs and four Sterling SMGs from the dump. In less than ten minutes the van was loaded, the guns stashed in a box with its lid firmly nailed down. Before they had travelled thirty yards a soldier stepped out of a side entry, closely followed by two more, and called them to a halt.

'Oh, Christ,' moaned Con, 'a set-up! Don't stop, O'D.'

'Don't be stupid, Con, we'd be dead before we got into second gear. Just keep your head and say you're only here for the ride.'

O'D rolled the driver's window down and stopped beside the soldier.

'Where are you coming from, mate?'

'The school there,' said O'D, nodding his head sideways.

'What you been doing there then?'

'I work there,' said O'D, glaring indignantly.

'You a teacher or something?'

'Not at all, I'm the caretaker,' said O'D, casual to the point of carelessness.

'Got any ID?'

'Surely,' said O'D handing him a forged driving licence.

'What's your date of birth?'

O'D quoted the one on the licence. The soldier walked to the front of the van and began to speak into the radio. Another soldier approached Con's window and put him through the same procedure, and when he asked Con about the contents of the box in the back, O'D cut in: 'It's spare parts for the boiler that just arrived from England.'

'What's it doing lying in 'ere then?'

'You want to feel the weight of it,' said O'D brazenly. 'I had to pick it up from the station this afternoon, and I can tell you there's no way I am going to lift it myself. It takes at least six men to manhandle it about the place.'

'I see.' But he looked only half-convinced. 'What were you doing in the school at this time of night?'

'Checking the classrooms. We've been broken into three times in the last six months.'

The first soldier completed his radio conversation and was returning to the van. O'D held breath.

'Okay, mate, you can go,' said the soldier returning the driving licence.

'Thanks,' said O'D, starting the van, putting it in gear, releasing the handbrake and driving off before he even had the licence in his pocket.

'Funny thing,' said the soldier who had questioned Con.

'What is?' said his mate.

'If that box in the back is so heavy how come it's not depressing the back suspension all that much?'

'What? You think there's something fishy?'

'Right now,' said the soldier, 'with only two weeks left to do in this dump I couldn't give a shit if they were carrying enough to blow the whole fucking town apart.'

Before the operation could begin the weapons had to be got into the Masonic Hall. Dermot Donnelly took the van from O'D and drove to a double lock-up garage in the Bogside. A volunteer helped him transfer the weapons to a coffin, which they placed in the back of a borrowed hearse. In a dusty corner of the garage they changed into black suits, white shirts and black ties. Fifteen minutes later they drove the hearse into Guildhall Square and pulled up at the checkpoint that stood between them and the Masonic Hall. The soldier on duty left the job to the civilian searcher.

'Is it full or empty?' said the man, sticking his head through the driver's window and giving a nod at the silent coffin.

'Full,' said Dermot, 'but I hope you don't want a look at it.'

'Bad, is it?' asked the searcher with morbid curiosity.

'Bloody awful,' said Dermot screwing up his face. 'Worst car accident I ever saw: half the face gone.'

'Jesus,' said the man with a shudder, 'I don't envy you your job. Go ahead.'

Two minutes later the hearse parked in front of the Masonic Hall to the distraction of the soldiers nearby, who exchanged remarks about the hazards of their job. Dermot climbed cautiously out of the hearse and approached the door. It opened before he reached it. Mick greeted him with a solemn expression.

'You look just like a mourner,' said Dermot, running his eye over Mick's dark blue suit and black tie.

'That's how I'm supposed to look,' said Mick, missing the joke. 'Get the back door opened.'

As soon as the coffin was ready, Mick and Charlie appeared from the house, both wearing suits, and the four men carried it inside. Charlie kicked the front door shut and the box was rushed along the hallway and deposited in the first available bedroom. After a few snatched words of conversation Dermot and the volunteer left. 'Tell O'D we've got the daughter as well,' said Mick, as he saw them to the door.

'Any problem with her?' asked Dermot.

'None. She was working late at school so we put her in the closet with her school books and there hasn't been a peep out of her since.'

The six attack-group volunteers arrived over the next two hours and were taken on a tour of the house. After familiarisation each was shown his position; the main escape route was pointed out, and two alternative routes. Then they settled down to wait.

Back at the house Dermot briefly amused the rest of the nine-man support group with the story of how the coffin had been delivered. But soon the night stretched taut and silent. At two-thirty they changed into British army uniforms in an atmosphere as still as the dark night outside.

'Okay,' said O'D making a last check of their uniforms. 'Just keep one thought in your heads: our job is to make sure that no Brits get out of the place alive and that none of our men are trapped inside.' He paused for a few seconds and then said, 'That's all we have to do, so let's go to war.'

In four cars they drove to Bishop Street where they left Con McDaid on guard. From there they cautiously made their way on foot through the Fountain area of the city, a Protestant area with a light army presence. To an observer they would have been indistinguishable from a large army foot patrol.

The forbidding walls surrounding the city bore fading symbols of homely pride where patches of whitewash were all that remained of demolished terrace houses which had once backed onto the walls. The corporation had employed several men to give the entire wall a facelift and scaffolding had crept slowly around the walls leaving a glowing patch of workmanship in its wake. It now stood beside a bastion which was just out of sight of the army observation post on top of Bishop's Gate – the post which covered the Masonic Hall and most of Bishop Street. At exactly three forty-five that morning eight uniformed figures climbed the scaffolding and dropped lightly onto the walls.

In the caretaker's house Mick Mulhern and Charlie Coyle had occupied the floors with three volunteers each; they waited in tense silence. Shortly before four Charlie mumbled a barely distinguishable command to two of his men, who rose silently and moved to the large windows in the west of the room. These were their only sources of light and the two figures were thrown into startling silhouettes as they quietly lowered the windows as far as they would go.

In the room below, Mick and his volunteers were doing the same. As the hour approached the eight men stood beside the open windows, their arms filled with petrol bombs. Beneath them, the camp was as silent as a deserted ship. Charlie stared at his watch and spoke in a quiet, even voice. 'Aim for the farthest huts first.' He stretched and threw an unlit petrol bomb the full length of the small camp. It crashed against the perimeter wall and smashed with a night-shattering sound which startled even the men who were prepared for it. Instantly, it was followed by a hail of bottles which flew in quick succession, smashing against wood, tarmac and corrugated tin to fill the camp with a stench of petrol.

Almost twenty unlit bottles had smashed before a muffled scatter of feet was heard and a lone voice, more in annoyance than anger, shouted: 'I say, guard, what the bloody hell's going on out there?'

'Someone's throwing bottles, sir,' came the reply from a distant guard.

A few figures in various stages of undress began to appear and a bottle smashed close to one, who yelled in alarm: 'That's petrol they're throwing! Watch out!'

241

'Right, light up,' said Charlie.

Four lit petrol bombs flew through the air and their impact on the night took even Charlie by surprise. A blinding explosion of flame engulfed the entire camp immediately setting more than half the huts on fire. Even as they threw more petrol bombs, the eight men in the house felt the searing heat.

Screams could be heard now: officers shouting orders, guards roaring in confusion, men yelling in panic and in pain; it was as if the silence had never existed. Soldiers were fighting to get out of their burning huts; petrol burned fiercely on the tarmac; the camp was a furnace.

Then the shooting started.

One of the volunteers beside Charlie Coyle was thrown suddenly backwards across the room. The attack stopped momentarily, but resumed as Charlie shouted: 'Keep back from the windows!'

The single shot from the sentry in the observation post on the wall started a barrage of fire. It was the signal for most people with weapons to use them, both inside and outside the Masonic camp. Mick had to scream at his three volunteers to make himself heard above the noise. 'Start picking them off with your weapons.'

Four rifles fired together.

Noise and confusion filled the room. The camp was ablaze and everything in it. Three human torches ran in blind circles, flapping their arms in their attempt to beat the flames engulfing them. Two soldiers approached the perimeter of a fiercely burning hut with fire extinguishers in a heroic attempt to save some of their comrades. But in a moment both of them lay dead on a small patch of unlit tarmac beside the two trickling extinguishers.

As the two bodies lay in the madly flickering light, the soldier who had fired on the attackers prepared to leap from his observation post on the perimeter wall to escape the heat. Mick saw him step to the wall, saw him poised for the jump, but before Mick had time to level his rifle there was a muffled burst of automatic fire and the man dropped backwards into the flames. O'D had arrived at the other side of the camp.

The first crashing bottle had been O'D's cue to move his men into position. He led them silently along the wall to the twin observation post on top of Bishop's Gate. One side of the post looked inside the walls to the only entrance to the camp and the other looked outside and south along Bishop Street. O'D and his men could hear the soldiers speculating about the noise and reporting their opinions on the radio. When the petrol exploded and the shooting started, O'D moved.

He kicked in the door. The two young soldiers did not have a chance, turning only to stare wide-eyed as he shot both of them dead. Dermot and one volunteer were left in the post to cover the front gate of the camp. O'D took the other five to capture the last observation post, which was impossible to approach without being seen, perched on the edge of a large bastion with fifteen yards of open space to its entrance. In their uniforms, O'D and two volunteers trotted across the open ground at a casual lope while the other three stayed out of sight. The guards opened the door for what they assumed was an approaching officer. O'D entered and emptied the contents of his weapon at them. The post was evacuated and the small group made its way to the rear of the camp, O'D replenishing his magazine as he ran.

As they reached the wall surrounding the camp they saw the silhouetted figure of the sentry making an attempt to leap to safety. O'D waited a minute after killing the man before sending three volunteers to fetch Con and the cars.

The attack continued for a few minutes before halting abruptly. As soon as Charlie threw his last petrol bomb, he shouted at his men: 'That's it, let's get out of here!' No one was going to escape from the furnace they were leaving behind. He did not have to repeat the order.

'What about his weapon?' said one of the volunteers, pointing to his dead comrade on the floor.

'Leave it,' said Charlie, 'it will only hinder us.'

Mick was waiting for them in the hallway. 'You're a man

short?' he said.

'Yeah, he's dead,' said Charlie.

Mick called his men from their firing positions and followed Charlie to the front door. The street was empty but blindingly bright in the fierce light of the fire. Charlie stepped half-way out of the door and looked up at the observation post, half expecting a hail of bullets; instead he was greeted by O'D's anxious face twenty yards away. The men were quickly called from the twin posts and the back of the camp. The group of twelve, five of them in army uniform, emerged from Bishop's Gate as Con and the volunteers arrived in four cars. They jumped in and sped off into the cool, dark, anonymous safety of the Bogside.

Chief Inspector Wall was having a restless night thanks to the Chief Constable when his phone rang.

'Sir,' said a young female voice, 'I've been asked to tell you to come straight in.'

Thirty minutes later he was sitting in his office listening to Major Barry Down lamenting the lack of intelligence work in the city. He was about to object when the phone rang.

'Yes!' he snapped into the receiver. The Major fell silent at the violence of the exclamation. 'Thanks, Tony,' said Wall eventually and replaced the receiver. He sat silently contemplating a pencil rolling hypnotically between his thumb and index finger until the Major spoke.

'Was that anything relevant?'

'Yes,' said Wall, very deliberately, still watching the rocking pencil, allowing the Major to suffer in his ignorance. 'Saor Eire.'

The Major's body arched forward from the waist. 'I say, how do you know?'

'There's a body and a rifle at the scene,' said Wall with apparent calmness. 'A Saor Eire volunteer for definite, and the rifle is no doubt a German SLR.'

'I see,' said the Major, 'so it's this chap O'Donnell again.'

Wall seemed to emerge reluctantly from a pensive confrontation with himself. 'Major, how many men can you give me today; right now, in fact?'

'In connection with this business I'll give you every damn soldier in the city, including the Brigadier if you want him.'

'When can they be ready?'

'Four hours, I should say,' said the Major.

'Could you make it two?'

'That's cutting it a bit fine!'

'Maybe,' said Wall with a determined thrust of his chin, 'but I'm willing to bet that most of the bastards have gone straight to their beds without washing themselves. If we can pick up the right ones and smear test them, we will have them: we'll get forensic on the clothes at least.'

Wall had the phone to his ear before the Major left at a half-trot. He had little time to consider the wider implications of the attack on the Masonic Hall, but even as he conveyed his orders in a series of phone calls he knew that the security forces had been dealt an unprecedented blow which would have serious political repercussions. What the government in London made of it was their business. He had already heard that the Prime Minister was likely to return to Whitehall, cutting short a visit to the United States, where Irish-American supporters of the republican cause would undoubtedly be in a high state of jubilation. Politics was for others, but the Chief Inspector knew only too well that the reaction in Whitehall could easily rebound on him; the attack had taken place under his nose, and it wasn't as if there had been no signs of impending disaster in the city. It was imperative that he get results, and that he get them quickly.

The sun was bright at seven-thirty that morning but a grey mist still clung persistently to the ground. It was a heavy mist which seemed to push in from the sea and hang like a penance over the city, and it shrouded the activities of more than a thousand soldiers who moved like ghosts through a graveyard.

They knocked on the door of every Saor Eire activist and sympathiser and most of them they arrested without ceremony. Of all the men sought by Chief Inspector Wall, only two escaped the net: Charlie Coyle and Hugh O'Donnell. Shortly before noon Charlie was making his way along Central Drive in search of O'D when he was brought to a halt by an English voice.

Charlie froze, then turned, heart thumping, to face a soldier walking towards him with a rifle cradled casually in the crook of his arm. Two other soldiers remained stiffly and separately in the background, obviously nervous and ready for trouble. 'What's your name, mate?' asked the soldier with neither warmth nor aggression.

'Eric Higgins.'

'Where do you live?'

'On the Limavady Road. I'm on my way to visit one of my father's employees who is sick.'

'How did you get here?'

'By car.'

'Where is it now?' asked the soldier, looking around.

Charlie's mind was on the verge of panic. 'Actually the chauffeur has it,' he said quickly with a strained smile. 'You see, I can't drive.'

'That so?' said the soldier. 'Where's this chauffeur now then?'

'He's gone off to see some relatives of his close by. He's to pick me up again in an hour.'

'I see,' said the soldier. 'Just a minute.'

Then one of the soldiers began to speak on the radio. Charlie realised he would have to act. He reached under his coat and pulled the Magnum clear of his jeans in one continuous movement. The three soldiers saw it instantly, but the one with the photograph did not stand a chance as Charlie's first shot hit him in the side of the head before he could react. The next bullet sent the second soldier tumbling backwards over the body of his companion.

He had deliberately left the radio operator to last, but as

he swung on the young soldier he realised in the pit of his stomach that he was too late. The rifle was levelled at the centre of his chest. Charlie tried to side-step. But as he did so flame spat from the barrel and his body crashed against the pebbledashed wall splattering it with blood. The soldier fired two more rounds but Charlie was already dead.

Wall heard of Charlie Coyle's death ten minutes later in the canteen. Tony Miller came rushing through the door, coat flapping, hair dishevelled. 'You're never going to believe this. . .'

'What?' Wall sat his cup back on the table with a bang.

'Two more soldiers have been shot. . .'

'Oh, no!'

'With a shortarm, on foot patrol. We think it's the same man who shot the last three.'

'You mean he's done it again.'

'Looks like it, but we got him this time. One of the soldiers shot him.'

'Thank God for that. Who identified him?'

'The soldier did from the photograph and some of the neighbours have identified him as Charlie Coyle.'

'Good. Is there any sign of the other one yet?'

'Not yet. He seems to be the only one who has escaped the net.'

'He damn well hasn't escaped it yet. And he better not escape it.'

'He could have run by now, Mervin.'

'O'Donnell won't run. He'll stop till the bitter end. And, by God, I hope it's bitter for him. If I have anything to do with it, it will be.'

Major Barry Down was co-ordinating army activities from Ebrington Barracks. Wall burst into his office.

'Ah, Chief Inspector,' he said, flustered at Wall's sudden intrusion. 'I'm glad to see you. This is an awful show about these two chaps. Both of them came from the same small village in Somerset, you know. Lots of people are going to be awfully upset over this.'

247

'You're damn right,' said Wall, throwing himself into one of the Major's armchairs, 'and I'm going to upset a lot of them.'

'Ah, yes, quite,' said the Major uncertainly. 'Do you have something in mind, old chap?'

'Yes, I have,' said Wall, pulling a cigarette from a pocket and jamming it into his mouth. 'I want to block every exit from Creggan and the Bogside and begin a house to house search for O'Donnell.'

'I say,' said Down, springing upright in his swivel chair, 'that's a tall order.'

'I know that, Major, but it will have to be done. I'll have every available policeman out as well. But I would prefer if we blocked the roads and you did the searches.'

The Major was reluctant to overstretch his men, but the Chief Inspector was listening to no arguments. It was just after midday when the army began the search of Creggan and Bogside. Army landrovers toured the area telling the population through loud hailers to remain indoors unless they could prove they were on essential business; it was an unwritten form of martial law.

O'D had taken care of his own security by sleeping in a house he had never used before. Only Brenda and Mick Mulhern knew where he was. As soon as he heard Mick Mulhern had been lifted, O'D changed his billet again and he was in a pensioner's cottage in High Park when Brenda reached him with news of Charlie's death. The thought crossed his mind that Charlie had been executed and that the army would shoot him on sight.

For two hours Brenda kept him informed on the progress of the search. They had started at the lower end of Creggan and were working towards the top. Each street was cordoned off as they searched it; a solid wall of soldiers advancing in front of the search party interrogated anyone trying to enter or escape the net.

'What are you going to do?' Brenda asked as the progress

of the search grew near.

'Get off-side is the only thing I can do, I suppose, until the heat dies down.'

'How are you going to do that with the place surrounded? They even have soldiers up on the back hill to make sure no one escapes across the fields.'

'I'm sure we'll think of some way.' After minutes he said slowly, 'The safest way of all would be across the Letterkenny checkpoint.'

Brenda reacted as if she had been slapped. 'Are you mad? That's the biggest checkpoint in the town. There are dozens of soldiers there.'

'I know, but it's the last place they'll expect me to cross.'

'It's the first place they'll expect you to cross – that's why they have dozens of soldiers there.'

O'D shook his head philosophically. 'Not under these circumstances. They'll expect me to take to the fields or get out of town on a lorry, or something like that. The last thing they'll expect me to do is drive across their biggest checkpoint in a family saloon. Another thing they won't expect. . . Is Jim Carlin still working in the Post Office?'

'I think so. He lives close by here, doesn't he?'

Half an hour later O'D was walking through Creggan dressed as a postman, cap, bag and all. Twice in two minutes he saw foot patrols enter the street he was in. Each time he dodged into the driveway of the nearest house and made a hurried exit across back gardens to the next street. Soldiers were everywhere. He hardly turned a corner without seeing them. A foot patrol in Cromore Gardens made him hurry towards Inniscarn Road. He wanted to avoid this direction because it was close to home, but he had no option. Just before he turned the corner, his mother opened the front door and stepped onto the street. He was only fifty yards away and she couldn't help but see him – and she would certainly recognise him even with the postman's uniform. He felt certain the place was staked out, but he could see no one.

"Old on, mate!'

The soldier's voice made him start. He swung around to see a khaki-clad figure emerging from a high-hedged garden.

'You're a postman then?'

'Yes.' His voice sounded so unnatural he almost wept.

'Got your ID then, mate?'

'Sorry, I don't.' The quaver in his voice seemed to him as obvious as falling masonry.

The soldier pulled a small walkie-talkie from his pocket. 'Got a postman here with no ID.'

There was a pause before a static-distorted voice answered.

O'D could not decipher what it said, but the soldier answered. 'Yeah, sure he's a postman. He's got all the gear, ain't he? A great big bag and cap. It's all there.' The voice crackled again, and the soldier spoke to O'D: 'Okay, mate, you're clear to go.'

'Thanks.' He staggered forward unsteadily, expecting a challenge at every step. Out of the side of his eye he could see his mother standing at the front door, one hand pressed against her chest, staring intently at him.

He had almost reached the bottom of Inniscarn Road before he saw the next landrover. It came from the roundabout at the bottom of the road and sped towards him. He walked steadily clasping his mailbag. As the landrover passed the officer in charge reacted: his hand shot up in a warning for O'D to wait as he shouted and the landrover braked hard to a halt.

O'D knew he had been recognised. He turned into the first pathway between houses. As he did so the first shout rang out.

'Halt.'

He kept walking towards the alcove.

'Halt.'

He walked on, hoping his knees would hold out. The land-rover had stopped now, doors were flung open, boots began pounding on the street.

'Halt or I'll fire.'

That was enough. O'D dropped the bag, ducked into a run and dashed the last few steps towards the alcove. A shot rang out. He felt the bullet pass behind the back of his head. He dashed on to the chorus of rising shouts and crashed through the garden gate.

An open garden with a shed at the bottom leaning against the high cemetery wall. He ran at it, leapt like an athlete, one foot on the neighbour's fence, one on the shed, and he was on the wall before the first soldier was in the alcove. He cleared the wall without looking where he was going, dived off it in full flight and landed on the trot, too fast, tumbled, rolled and rose again all in one motion and continued sprinting down the graveyard as if he had hardly broken his step. He didn't look to see where the soldiers were but he could still hear them shouting as he pounded towards the first gravestones.

Only when he reached the maze of high headstones did he chance a glance back. The first soldier's head was just appearing above the wall, but it was only a small black dot of a beret over a hundred yards away. O'D bent double until he was concealed by a headstone and ran then in an awkward crouch as fast as his lungs would let him. He reached the bottom of the graveyard a quarter of a mile away without being challenged and lay against the perimeter wall, heart pounding, chest heaving.

He slid down against the wall and half-crouched, half-lay facing towards the graveyard and wondered what to do. He couldn't reach Brenda without going through the army again so he would have to scrap that idea. His Bogside options were also narrowed drastically because of the army's presence. They were everywhere, which meant that he couldn't move without being spotted. It took him five minutes to recover enough to think of Mrs McDaid. He knew Con had been lifted that morning, but his mother would still help, and it was the nearest house he could think of. Three minutes later he was standing panting on Mrs McDaid's doorstep when she opened the door.

'Good God!' she gasped, 'am I glad to see you. They're all over the place looking for you. Come in.'

'How do you know?' he asked, squeezing past her in the porch.

'The whole town knows,' was her quick reply. 'Aren't they asking for you all over the place. I think they got everyone else even before they shot wee Charlie.'

O'D didn't want to think about that. 'What about Con, have you heard any word on him?'

Mrs McDaid dismissed the question with a wave of her hand. 'Oh, he'll be all right. He's big and ugly enough to look after himself. You're the one they missed so it's you we have to think about. Are you going to get out?'

'I think so.'

'I think so too, son,' she said with great sympathy. 'Don't let them catch you whatever you do.'

'Well, for a start, has Sheila got an old trouser suit I can borrow?'

'I'm sure she has, but what it'll look like I don't know.'

Wall heard about the sighting of O'D on the army radio frequency. For the first few seconds he thought they had him cornered but when one minute of silence passed, and then another, he realised that O'D must have somehow fooled the soldiers. He snatched the phone off its cradle and angrily demanded to be put in contact with Major Barry Down. Two minutes later the cultured accent crooned softly into his ear. 'Hello, old chap. Have you heard the news?'

'You're damn right I have and it's dreadful.'

'I say. . . what?'

Wall didn't give the Major time to continue. 'Is this some kind of farce or did your men really lose O'Donnell in Creggan?'

'I wouldn't say we lost him, old boy. We know where he is, it's just a matter of wheedling him out.'

'Major, you're talking a load of cock.'

252

'I beg your pardon.'

'Cock, I said. It's a bloody cock-up and that crowd of zombies you have working for you are responsible. . .'

'I say, hold on there, that's a bit heavy.'

'It's a fuck-up, that's what it is!'

'There's no necessity. . .'

'Do you know where O'Donnell is now?'

'Roughly speaking, yes.'

'You do in your arse, Major. He's in the Bogside.'

'If you're going to be offensive, Chief Inspector. . .'

'Don't give me that, Major. You let him slip through the net. I suggest what you do now is move all your men to the Bogside so that he doesn't get out the Letterkenny Road.'

'I think it would be better if we searched the immediate vicinity first. I'm not sure he has escaped.'

Wall had to fight hard to control his anger. 'Major, if you do that you'll lose him permanently.'

'I don't think so. My men are not as imbecilic as you make out.'

Wall began to think that the situation was slipping out of his control. 'Major,' he said, 'for God's sake, can't you be reasonable. Don't you realise that if O'Donnell was still there you would have flushed him out by now. He has obviously gone over the cemetery wall.'

'That's the one thing he hasn't done. I spoke to the officer in charge and he assures me O'Donnell didn't have time to get over the wall. And furthermore, the officer is not an idiot; he put a man on top of the wall as soon as he got into the yard.'

'Major,' he said slowly and firmly, 'I still think he is in the Bogside. And if he is there without being chased, he will have plenty of time to think, and he might just work out how much of a cornered rat he really is and decide to run for it.'

'You're not seriously suggesting that he would attempt to cross the Letterkenny Road checkpoint. . .?'

'That's exactly what I'm suggesting and I want you to do something about it.'

'But my dear fellow,' the Major said, 'don't you have your

253

chappies there to stop him? Or do you need us for protection?'

Wall took the insult like a slap across the face. 'Damn you, Major. . .'

'Goodbye.'

The phone went dead before Wall could slam it back on the receiver. 'Good God,' he said to an empty office, 'what a time for relations to break down!' He rose from the desk and stormed out of the room.

Ten minutes later, after telling Tony Miller his plan, he was on his way to the Letterkenny Road checkpoint in an unmarked car. It was swarming with policemen when he arrived. There seemed to be landrovers everywhere. A line of civilian cars snaked back along the road for over fifty yards. Wall passed them on the wrong side and parked behind a land-rover. 'What's happening, Sergeant Roberts?' he asked the RUC man in charge.

'Nothing much, sir. Lots of tourists going to Donegal, but no terrorists. Not that I can see anyway.'

'I have a feeling there's going to be one, so keep a sharp lookout.'

'Aye, sir.'

Wall glanced along the line of cars. An assortment of faces stared blankly ahead; some old, some middle aged and very few of them young. Those that were young were all respectable looking. But something odd struck Wall before his eye had reached the end of the line. There was something incongruous about the situation. What was it? Yes, that was it: one old lady walking her dog having to leave the footpath to get by. There were almost as many police landrovers as there were civilian cars.

'Sergeant Roberts?'

'Yes, sir.'

'Sergeant, I want you to get some of these men out of here and utilise them better. I think O'Donnell is in the Bogside so we might try flushing him out. Are the men in the land-rovers?'

'Yes, sir, checking the cars as they pass.'

'You can do that from here. Follow me.' Wall strode off, Sergeant Roberts marched behind. They spoke to the drivers one at a time, telling them what they had to do, and one by one the landrovers pulled out of position, manoeuvred through the line of cars waiting at the checkpoint and drove back towards the city. They were to block off the Bogside and begin a random house search on most of the streets.

O'D had been sitting in the line of cars at the checkpoint when Wall drove past on the wrong side of the road. O'D recognised him instantly and started. Mrs McDaid, behind the driving wheel, noticed the movement.

'What's the matter?'

'That was a branchman just drove past.'

Mrs McDaid was the essence of cheerfulness. 'Don't worry, he has no chance of recognising you in that disguise.'

O'D was dressed as a blind woman in a trouser suit with a large plaster covering his nose. But he still sweated. He saw Wall scrutinising the cars; there was nothing he could do if Wall recognised him. And Wall was sure to recognise him, O'D thought – even with the dark glasses. The plaster would only act as an invitation. When Wall spoke to the Sergeant and walked towards one of the landrovers O'D felt certain it was a trap. The car he was in was almost level with the last landrover, and the driver was beginning to give him a hard stare. O'D kept his head pointing rigidly ahead, but he watched the driver closely out of the side of his eye, and the man was definitely suspicious. Then the landrovers began pulling out of line and heading towards town. O'D was confused: they seemed to be evacuating the checkpoint. His heart raced excitedly. Maybe they were calling the operation off and his escape route would be clear.

But Wall and the Sergeant stayed behind and his spirits sank again. Mrs McDaid continued to inch the car towards the checkpoint without showing any emotion. O'D's feelings were soaring wildly from one extreme to another.

'Will he recognise you?' Mrs McDaid said quietly.

'Would you?'

255

She glanced at him for a second. 'I don't know.'

'I do.'

'That means he will.'

'He will. So would you if you were looking for me.'

'Do you want me to turn the car around?'

He gave a short, compulsive burst of laughter, almost like a cough. 'You'll get us both shot if you do that, Mrs McDaid.'

'Well, I don't want to get you shot, Hugh, so we'll keep driving.'

The car inched forward and O'D kept his eyes focused straight ahead. There was only one car between him and the checkpoint when someone approached Wall and spoke to him.

Wall closely scrutinised the occupants of every car as it approached. He spoke to anyone who remotely resembled O'D. One thing he was convinced of: if O'D made a run for the border that day, he would do it via the Letterkenny Road. All other routes were too difficult and too dangerous. A blue Cortina pulled up in front of him with a middle-aged man behind the wheel and what looked like his daughter in the passenger seat. No way either of them could be O'D: the man was too fat, the girl too pretty, and both had perfect noses.

But the car behind was interesting. The person in the passenger seat appeared to be blind and there was a large plaster across her nose. The shape was wrong for O'D: she was too thin and her hair was too long. . . Still, it would be a good disguise. Wall decided to speak to the blind lady when her car stopped. She was next in line.

Just as he decided to approach the car a young soldier spoke into his ear. 'Major Down's on the phone, sir. Wants to speak to you.'

Wall's heart leapt. There was only one thing Down would ring him about and that was O'Donnell's capture. Wall pictured his man lying captive in the back of an army landrover and turned to rush towards the phone inside the checkpoint. Mrs McDaid pulled up at the checkpoint as Wall disappeared through the door. O'D sat staring ahead. A soldier approached.

'Where are you going to?'

'Just out,' said Mrs McDaid in a calm, natural voice, 'to visit relatives.'

'Across the border?' asked the soldier suspiciously.

'No, this side of the border.'

'Okay, go ahead.'

From the side of his dark glasses O'D could see a figure emerging from the army post. He knew it was Wall without turning his head. 'For Christ's sake, hurry up,' he said tensely to Mrs McDaid.

'That's the last thing I'll do,' she said calmly.

Major Down had been apologetic on the phone. 'I'm frightfully sorry old chap, but it appears you were right about this bounder. He does appear to have got through the net.'

'I'm glad you realise it at last,' Wall said impatiently. He went on to tell the Major to deploy his men in the Brandywell and then slammed down the phone to rush back to the line of cars. The car with the blind woman was just moving off. 'Hey, hold on!' Wall called, raising his hand.

'It's okay, Chief,' the checkpoint soldier said to Wall, 'I checked her out – she's okay.'

The car was still within stopping distance as Wall answered him. 'What about the blind woman, did you speak to her?'

'Yeah,' lied the soldier, 'she's okay too.'

Wall watched the car receding towards the border. It was too late to stop now. Then he thought of Major Down tearing the Brandywell apart. It would be a long wait, but they would get the bastard sooner or later.

Epilogue

'SOONER RATHER THAN later,' said Brenda, they're going to get you.'

She sat facing O'D across the formica-topped kitchen table of a house like thousands of others in the Dublin suburb of Tallaght. Her body was tense, she shifted nervously, and her face was a mask of determination.

O'D sat silently, his eyes seeming to be focused on his hands clasped in front of him on the table.

'You don't need me to tell you about the Brits and all their technology for getting information. You don't need me to tell you about all the forces on their side, including the government down here. And we've been through enough arguments already for me to know I can't tell you about Saor Eire's chances in Derry now.' She looked up from the point on the table on which her eyes had been fixed, but O'D had not lifted his head.

'What I can tell you and what I must tell you is about me and about you and me. I've lost my job; I don't blame you for that, it was my choice. But I have to face the fact that I have to think about our child, about Philip. Now, you may be able to live on the run from day to day; you probably could, even if you have got the best known ugly mug on the whole bloody island. And maybe once I could have gone along with that, seeing you now and then. But that won't work for Philip and it won't work for me. That was why I went to London, and just because I've thrown up that job and come back for the moment doesn't mean that the same reasons aren't still there. Philip needs what every child needs: enough protection and security and stability in his life for him to be able to grow.'

O'D stood up, his eyes still avoiding hers, and he moved over to the window through which he could see the Dublin mountains darkening as light thickened in the dusk.

'For his sake and, yes, for mine as well, I have to get another job, and a place for us to live, where he can make friends and go to the one school for several years. And either he will have a real father who is there, and who he knows will be there, or he will have no father. You just can't mess him around, you can't play with a child's life like that.'

O'D did not stir from his stance at the window and his words were addressed as if to the distant, dark horizon.

'You're right, of course. I've had plenty of time to think over the last weeks. A few months ago I thought we could get victory in a year or two. I know now we can't.'

Brenda looked up at him, but he still had his back to her.

'But there is more than one way to fight our struggle. Our organisation may be smashed in Derry for now, but while the same conditions exist we will always be able to rebuild our organisation. The Masonic attack may have been a disaster for us in some ways, but we've taught the Brits a lesson they'll not forget in a hurry. We may not have won a short, sharp victory, but in the long run our resistance will prove stronger than the Brits.'

'But where does that place you?' Brenda's voice rose with a note of irritation. 'You can't go back to Derry.'

'Maybe not. But there's more ways than one to skin a goat.' He turned now from the window to face her. 'I'm sorry, Brenda: my role isn't over yet in this. . . struggle, this revolution. If I gave up on it now, if I committed myself to you and Philip and we went and lived somewhere out of the way and safe. . . If I gave up now I think you'd very soon find you had a bitter and frustrated man on your hands. And what good would that be to you? What good would it be to either of us, or to our son?'

There was a change in Brenda, almost a reaction of relief, as her shoulders relaxed and her tension dissipated. There was a calm and measured sadness in her voice. 'You know, don't you, what I have to do: that I won't be writing to you, that you won't know where I am, where Philip is. That we will never see each other again.'

'Yes, Brenda, I know. If we had got married before Philip was born – and I know you weren't ready then, and there's no blame on either of us for that – we could have had a life together.'

'And if it wasn't for this murderous war,' she added, 'which you call the revolution. . . but we'll not get into that. In fact I don't think we should say any more. I don't think it would be a good idea for you to say goodbye to Philip. I'll do my best to explain to him. . .'

'Let him hate me if he has to, but let him know that it's not his fault. I know it can be difficult for a young lad to understand that his father is less than perfect. . .'

'Enough, Hugh, enough.' Brenda moved swiftly to him and hugged him close to her for a moment before turning and walking out of the kitchen. A moment later O'D heard the front door bang shut.